THE FLOWER FARM

RACHAEL LUCAS

ABOUT THE AUTHOR

Rachael lives on a beautiful stretch of coastline in the north west of England with her family and two very enthusiastic spaniels. When she's not writing at the kitchen table with a cup of coffee by her side, she's out walking the dogs on the beach or in the nearby pinewoods. She's never far from her Kindle - her ten year old self would have been over the moon to be able to carry a whole library around in her pocket - and a lover of sweet, funny, romantic, small town stories, which is exactly what she likes to write. She's a big Hallmark movie fan, wanted to be Anne of Green Gables when she was growing up, and Jo March was her literary heroine. (She still is.)

PRAISE FOR RACHAEL LUCAS

Absolutely delightful - The Winter Cottage is ROMANTIC and FUN and like a big, squishy hug.

— MARIAN KEYES

Rachael Lucas has created an irresistible world to disappear into once again

— LOUISE O'NEILL

A gift to anyone in need of comfort, calm, and a deep breath of Scottish fresh air. Charming, tender and funny. (Also: nice dogs, hot men, and big houses!)

— ELLA RISBRIDGER

The most deliciously wintry, sizzlingly romantic hug of a book - the perfect Christmas comfort read

— CRESSIDA MCLAUGHLIN

Published by Rachael Lucas in 2022

ISBN (Mass Market Paperback) 978-1-7398040-1-5

Cover design by Diane Meacham

For Rory,
with all my love.

CHAPTER ONE

SPRING ALWAYS SEEMED to sneak up on the little Highland village of Applemore. The sun rose over the distant pine-covered hills and stole through the windows of the cottages that looked over the bay, illuminating rooms which had lurked in gloom for the winter months, showing up long-hidden dust. You could mark the end of winter, Beth Fraser thought, by the sudden bustle of activity as windows were washed clean and rugs hung out to air over washing lines. Even though it was only nine in the morning, the village was a hive of activity.

For Beth, however, spring started with seed catalogues and bulb planting and plans – so many plans – back in the early autumn of the year before. She glanced over her shoulder, looking at the back seat of her car. Between twin car seats lay the usual detritus of parenthood – battered plastic beakers, tired picture books, discarded raisin boxes. But there was also a box of pale, unbleached tissue paper, and behind that the boot was stuffed with bunches of narcissi and hyacinths she'd grown in the greenhouse, which were headed for the Applemore Farm Shop. In an ideal world, she'd have delivered them in her little white van, which was kitted out with racks and shelving. In an ideal world, her ex-husband Simon wouldn't have come down with a stomach bug meaning he couldn't do his share of the childcare at the beginning of a week which was shaping up to be the busiest she'd had in a while.

It had been eighteen months since they'd split up, and they'd reached a reasonably amicable sort of truce. He lived with Morag, his bank manager girlfriend, in a new-build house in a town eight miles away. Beth pulled the car into a passing place to allow a tractor to come the opposite way, waving to Jimmy, the elderly farmer who she'd known since childhood. He touched his forehead with a finger in greeting, and the tractor rumbled past.

She headed up the winding road that followed the line of the coast towards the grounds of Applemore House, the crumbling stately home where she'd grown up. Ploughed fields were warming in the sunshine, hazed with green where the shoots of early barley were beginning to show through. It had been a particularly cold winter, and everything was taking longer to come to life as a result. The hedgerows, too, were showing the faintest hint of the pale, acid green that would soon paint the whole landscape. But it was enough to fill her with hope for days when she'd be working outside in a jumper and jeans, her fingers bending freely and not frozen solid as she got everything organised on the acre of walled garden where she ran her flower farming business. Soon Applemore would be full of tourists making their way down the coast, stopping off to take photographs of the pretty little village and spend lots of money – she hoped – in her sister Polly's farm shop.

She turned off the road at the newly-painted sign. In

neat lettering, it announced *Applemore House Wild Camping and Farm Shop*. In the eighteen months that had passed since she and Simon had split, a lot had changed – not only becoming a single parent to toddler twins, but her family pulling together for the first time in what felt like forever. Her brother Lachlan had moved back from Edinburgh and set up home in the big house with his girlfriend, Rilla, and together they'd set about diversifying in order to make the place pay. Where the driveway had been potholed and overhung with shaggy rhododendron bushes, the two of them had worked tirelessly to clear and tidy it up so now the grass was neatly trimmed and visitors could make their way up to the campsite without being savaged by overgrown foliage. Soon the campers would return.

Last summer had been Lachlan and Rilla's first season and they'd been surprised by how successful it had been. Rather than making it into a traditional campsite, they'd used clearings in the woodland that surrounded the house, which provided campers with a place where they could escape and be embraced by nature, albeit with the luxury of several compost loos (Beth smiled at this as she passed one of the little wooden sheds which held one, thinking that by no stretch of the imagination would she consider a compost loo a luxury, but she was very definitely not a camping fan). There was even a wooden shed they'd built, which held two gas-powered showers. And that was only one of the ways they'd diversified, along with many of the residents in this part of the world. Getting together with Rilla, who'd been a childhood friend, had been the making of her brother. It was lovely to see them together – still clearly as besotted with each other after a year and a half or so as they'd been when they first reconnected.

'Morning.' Polly, her younger sister, was standing outside the farm shop when she pulled up into the yard.

'Flower delivery for you. I might come to life after eighteen gallons of coffee, if there's any going?'

'Do you need to ask?' Polly opened the boot and lifted out the black plastic buckets, each one stuffed with closely-tied bunches of narcissus, buttery yellow petals just peeking through the papery buds. 'Oh I love these. They're like sunshine in a vase, aren't they?'

Inside the old outbuilding, which Polly had converted into the farm shop, the air was – as always – scented with the delicious smell of freshly brewed coffee, as well as the warm and welcoming scent of the newly baked bread delivered by a local artisan bakery. When Polly had first opened the shop, it had been one room with a hastily-knocked-together wall of rough wooden shelves. As the months had passed, she'd brought in a joiner who'd created a far more aesthetically pleasing set of fittings; the wall into the adjoining outbuilding had been knocked through, and a little kitchen and coffee shop had been created. A broad slab of wood edged with bark acted as a table, where metal chairs were already populated with people from the village. Beth smiled hello to Jenny, one of the mums she recognised from the nursery run, and her mother Dolina, who was holding court about something.

'…and when I heard,' she was saying, her mouth pursed in disapproval, 'I said to Helen that it's not the sort of thing we want in our little village. I mean it's bad enough we've got all these tourists coming in all over the place every summer and it's getting worse.'

'Flat white?' Tom, who ran the little coffee shop, lifted an eyebrow in Beth's direction. He'd started preparing it even before she'd nodded acknowledgement. He flicked her a brief glance, which spoke volumes.

'If we didn't have *all these tourists*,' he said lightly, tamping down the coffee and flicking the machine handles as he did so, 'This place wouldn't be making any money and I wouldn't have a job.'

'Aye,' said Dolina, her mouth still downturned, 'Fair enough, but you know as well as I do you can't get parked on the main street from April to September, and it's getting worse. We don't have the infrastructure for tourism. There's one public toilet, for one thing.'

'Kirsty at the book shop says if it wasn't for the summer trade she'd have closed down. She sells countless guidebooks and maps and all the rest of it every day.' Tom swirled the milk, pouring it into the cup and making a pretty design before sliding it across the counter to Beth.

'And I sell loads of flowers,' Beth said, tearing open a packet of sugar and tipping it into her cup, feeling guilty for desecrating Tom's design.

'Really? I'm surprised at that,' said Jenny, sounding like her mother. 'I mean what are people on a holiday going to do with flowers?'

Beth laughed. 'I haven't a clue. Decorate their camper vans? Take them home the next day? Put them in their granny's caravan in Ullapool? Whatever it is, I'm glad they are.'

'Well maybe it's just those of us who are inconvenienced by it and aren't making a profit who don't appreciate it,' said Dolina, her mouth looking ever more like a cat's bum.

Beth took a very slow breath in, not rising to it. 'Perhaps.'

'What's up?' Polly, who'd been arranging the flowers on the little wooden stand by the door, came up to join them, wiping her hands on her jeans. 'Am I missing hot village gossip?'

She tucked her long blonde hair behind her ears, and reached across, helping herself to one of the chocolate brownies that lay on a plate on the counter. 'I'll owe you for this,' she said to Tom, her mouth already full.

'Have you not heard?' Dolina sat up slightly in her chair, bristling with self-importance at being the one to convey the news. 'All those comings and goings at the old Mackay place?'

Beth exchanged a glance of complicity with her sister. She wasn't about to admit to Dolina, the gossip queen of Applemore village, that yes, they'd been talking about it on the phone the other night. She didn't let on that they'd had a good look at the plans on the council website, either. 'It's an outdoor adventures place. White water rafting, orienteering, that sort of thing.'

'Not just adventure holidays,' said Dolina, looking at them over the top of her cup, lips pursed. 'It's some sort of holiday centre for delinquents.'

'Delinquents?' Tom gave a snort of amusement. 'What kind of delinquent?'

'I don't think they call them that nowadays, mother,' said Jenny. She fiddled with a sugar packet, looking down at the table.

'Well, I'm sure there's some modern word for it that's more politically correct but the truth is they're going to be shipping up a load of teenagers from goodness knows where, who'll be stealing our cars and going joy-riding and all the rest.' Dolina folded her arms over an ample bolster of bust.

Tom shook his head. 'I think it's more likely they'll be here learning stuff that'll make their lives better.' He lifted up a pristine tea-towel, using it to polish the front of his coffee machine, which was his pride and joy. 'And to be honest, Dolina, as someone who's spent the whole of his life dealing with other people's disapproval, I can tell you that I'll be welcoming whoever it is with open arms.'

Dolina had the decency to look a little bit shame-faced. Tom had grown up in Applemore, and moved away to college in Glasgow as a teenager. When he'd returned with his partner Gavin, he'd confessed to Beth – with whom he'd gone to primary school – that he'd half-expected the village to be horrified that a gay couple were going to run the coffee shop. He'd been surprised, he admitted, but pleasantly so, that on the whole the little village had been fairly accepting. Even now, he'd explained, homophobia was something they experienced every day. Beth had told him the story of her dad, who'd been in a secret relationship with Rilla's father for years, and he'd nodded sagely. 'It's funny, isn't it? People think that the world's moved on, but it really hasn't. Not in lots of ways.'

Dolina was still chuntering away. Polly had noticed a couple of customers looking for something and disappeared off to deal with them. Jenny was breaking a wooden sugar-stirrer into tiny pieces, half-listening to her mother who was grumbling about the sort of terrible miscreant teenagers who'd be roaming all over the place doing goodness knows what else, running amok over people's gardens.

Beth felt a tiny wave of shame at her own thoughts. She cast her eyes down, looking at the contents of her mug, wondering what sort of person she was that the first thing she'd thought was that she hoped her flower farm wasn't going to be invaded by rampaging teenagers who'd set her greenhouse on fire or behead all her dahlias in some sort of spree of destruction. But really – she'd worked so hard on the place, taking it from completely overgrown jungle and turning it into a – finally – profitable business.

'I'm sure whoever it is will have all the right safety stuff in place,' she said, finally. 'You've got to have all sorts of safeguarding things, don't you?'

'Let's hope so,' said Dolina, darkly. 'Time will tell. At the end of the day, they're going to be your neighbours, so you're the one who'll feel the brunt of it, Beth. I'd string some barbed wire along the top of your wall if I was you.'

Beth laughed at this. 'I think that might be a bit extreme.'

She finished her coffee, and said a quick goodbye to Polly, glancing at her watch as she did so. She had so much to do, and nursery pick-up time would come around before she knew it. Whatever was going on with this new adventure holiday place, she had more than enough on her plate to deal with. Running the flower farm wasn't merely a job, it was a way of life. It took up every hour she had and several others, besides. If it hadn't been for Simon having the children half of the time, she really would struggle. Thank God that they'd agreed right at the beginning that while they hadn't worked out, he was determined to make sure that the children were still part of his life. After the initial humiliation of his affair had passed, Beth had admitted to herself that their relationship had dwindled away over years, becoming more of a friendship than anything else for a long time before they'd split, which made it easier.

Beth drove past Applemore House, for once taking a moment to look up as she did so. The soft sandstone glowed warmly in the spring light. The house had been built in the Scottish Baronial style – all crenellations and tall, pointed turrets. Lachlan and Rilla's camping guests were inevitably taken with it, and their Instagram accounts were filled with images of the beautiful building. Over the last year and a half – helped by a windfall when Lachlan's brewery had been sold – they'd invested money in the repairs which had been decades overdue, and now the house stood tall and proud, as if it could feel the love and dedication that had been poured into it to safeguard it for the Fraser family for years to come. Lachlan had made a decision that – as he'd been the one to inherit, as eldest son – he'd plough the majority of the money he'd made into a trust, which would ensure that Applemore would be passed on, and would never again be left to crumble away.

She glanced in the rear mirror briefly as she passed, seeing the tall trees that surrounded the house she'd grown up in. Even now, with the place renovated and re-decorated, there was no part of her that hankered to live there. Growing up in a place like that had seemed exotic and exciting to her friends at school, but the reality – she shivered, remembering – was that they'd been property-rich but cash-poor. The house had always been freezing, apart from the kitchen, which had been warmed by a huge Aga that was on all year round. Jack Frost decorated the inside of her bedroom turret window with ornate fern frond patterns each winter, and the temperamental central heating had done little to make a dent in the arctic temperatures of the place, so she'd grown up getting dressed under the bedcovers and dreaming of one day living in a tiny little house like her schoolfriend Claire's place, which was deliciously warm, stuffed full of her mum's china ornaments and smelled of furniture polish and things baking in the oven for after-school snacks.

It was no wonder, she thought, bringing the car to a stop by the little painted door in the wall which marked the entrance to her walled garden, that she loved her tiny, cosy, and most importantly *warm* little farmhouse a couple of miles down the road. She had her house, her two cats, the twins, and her business. She didn't need anything else.

Beth took pleasure in the routine little habits that she used to mark out her working day. She put her phone down on the table which stood at the entrance to her pride and joy, the brand new polytunnel, making sure the volume was turned up in case the nursery called. One blessing at least was that in the last year a new mobile phone mast had been installed on a nearby hill (to the horror of the more eco-conscious members of the community who were convinced that the population would suddenly become radioactive or something equally terrible) and so now Applemore, which had been a mobile reception black hole for years, had entered the modern world. She put her hands in her back pockets and surveyed the greenhouse.

'Bloody hell, it's so cold out there,' said a voice a moment later. 'Aren't you freezing?'

She spun round, to see Miranda, who worked for her three days a week, standing in the doorway.

'Miraculously, no.'

'That'll be because you're sensible enough to be potting on sweet peas in the polytunnel and not preparing a flower bed for your slavedriver employer.' Miranda tugged off her gardening gloves and scratched her nose.

'Slavedriver?' Beth grinned. 'Have you thought about reporting me to the National Farmers' Union or whatever they're called?'

'I bloody well will,' said Miranda, hitching herself onto the table and puffing out a breath, 'if you don't get that heater cranked up.'

'The heater's for the benefit of the early sweet peas, not you,' laughed Beth.

'I need it more than they do. *Work on a flower farm*, they said, *it'll be romantic, they said…*'

'Just think of the endorphins.' Beth made a face, which made Miranda laugh.

'I think my endorphins have frozen to death.'

It was a standing joke between them whenever they were covered in mud and frozen to the bone. When Miranda applied for the job as part-time worker, she'd been quite open about the fact that she wanted a job working outside because it was the best thing for her mental health. Each winter she fought seasonal depression, but being outside in the thin winter sunlight and working with nature helped to stave off the worst of it. Beth admired her determination to keep going even on the days when it was clear that she wasn't feeling her best. Miranda's dry sense of humour about her mental health struggles had helped this winter when Beth had struggled to cope with life as a sleep-deprived single parent. Together, Beth thought, watching as Miranda checked her phone, they made a pretty good team.

She cut another handful of paperwhite narcissus, plunging them immediately into neck-deep water. It was the end of March – this was the first year she'd managed to grow them this early, and she'd been amazed what a difference it had made having the polytunnel. It had been a bit of an experiment – most successes were, she'd discovered, when she chatted to other flower farmers online – but it meant that she'd been able to start ramping up sales far earlier this year than previously.

'Dear God,' Miranda held out her phone, waggling it in Beth's direction. 'Look at that.'

Beth put the bucket down carefully, not wanting to damage the delicate budding stems. She cocked her head sideways. 'Is that…?'

'It is.' Miranda snorted.

'Online dating going well then?'

'If by well you mean am I being sent a selection of slightly unsavoury photographs on a daily basis, then yes.'

'Seriously, I don't know how you do it.'

'I keep thinking there has to be a rose among the thorns, or something like that.'

'That doesn't look much like a rose.' Beth scrunched up her face in horror. 'Or a thorn for that matter.'

'You could sign up, y'know. It'd give you something to do in the evenings.'

'I've got two small children who're about to turn three, and a business to run. I don't have evenings.'

'All work and no play, and all that.' Miranda said, teasingly.

'I'm quite happy being a dull girl. I've done the whole marriage thing. I happen to think I'm very good at being divorced.'

Miranda wriggled down from the table, hitching up her jeans and tucking her t-shirt in before pulling down her purple fleece. Her long brunette hair fell halfway down her back, and her face was scattered with freckles all year round – partly from working outside with Beth, but also because she loved nothing more than to spend time outside with her dogs, who'd taken over as the loves of her lives once her teenage son Joe had headed down to university in St Andrews. She was forty-three, looked about ten years younger, and had a wicked sense of humour.

'Give it time,' Miranda said, sagely. 'I was on my own for years after Tully left. Turns out there's such a thing as too much space in the bed.'

'Not in mine. It's full of cats and babies.'

Miranda shot her a look. 'We'll see.'

'We will not.' Beth was firm. 'Anyway, changing the subject, have you heard about what's going on across the wall?'

'You make it sound like we're in *Game of Thrones*,' Miranda laughed.

'Well if Dolina Allen is right, we're going to have a whole horde of wildlings rampaging around. Apparently, the log cabin they've been building is going to be hosting some sort of activity centre for – I quote Dolina – *delinquent teenagers.*'

'I gather she's taking it with her usual zen calm,' said Miranda, drily.

'I suspect there'll be an Extraordinary General Meeting of the village improvement society announced any day soon.' Beth wiped the plant scissors with the cleaning mixture she kept in a tub, scrupulously careful as always to avoid any risk of contamination.

Miranda put her phone back in her jeans pocket and gathered some twine and wooden pegs, ready to mark out one of the beds. 'I think it'll be a good thing. Nice to have something to shake this place up a bit.'

'Mmm,' said Beth, who was still feeling slightly off about the whole thing. 'As long as they don't set my greenhouse on fire or something, I'll be fine with it all. Plus we've got Phoebe. We don't need any more shaking up.'

'Talking of which,' Miranda said, pulling on her gloves and flexing her fingers, 'When is she in next?'

'She's in college today and tomorrow. Back on Wednesday morning.'

'Let's hope she doesn't accidentally chuck any more dahlia tubers on the compost heap.'

Beth shook her head. 'Don't even go there.'

Phoebe was her newest recruit – an apprentice, who

spent two days a week in college and three working on the flower farm learning the practical side of the business. She was nineteen, utterly lovely, and a complete liability. But she made them both laugh, and she was learning – slowly.

With impeccable timing, there was a dull metallic clanging in the distance. The silence they'd taken for granted all this time was being broken on an all-too-regular basis by whatever was going on as lorries trundled up and down the road delivering construction supplies.

'Anyway, don't you go making judgements about this holiday adventure place until you know more about it,' Miranda said, tipping her head in the direction of the distant rumbling as she headed back to work, 'or you'll end up like Dolina if you're not careful.'

Beth widened her eyes in mock horror. 'I will not.'

She turned back to her work as Miranda headed off. Despite everything, the prospect of her peace being invaded made her feel faintly green with horror. Whatever was happening, she resolved to be as friendly and welcoming as she could, no matter what. Even if – she took a deep breath and tried to quash her apprehension – she didn't have a particularly good feeling about any of it.

CHAPTER TWO

JACK McDONALD WATCHED the water of the River Clyde pass underneath them as they left Glasgow and headed north. Traffic was light – they'd missed the rush hour, and at this time of the year the flood of tourists that made their way up towards the Highlands hadn't yet started in earnest. Beside him, head lolling against the window, mouth hanging open as he slept the untroubled slumber of youth, Danny gave a snort, almost waking himself up. Jack turned briefly to check on Archie, his scruffy brindle terrier. He was sitting on the back seat, wearing his travel harness and an expression of outrage at being deposed from his usual position in the passenger seat.

He had thought that the final time he drove over the Erskine Bridge and headed up towards Loch Lomond might feel heavy with significance. He had Radio 1 playing – a hangover from the school run with his daughter Anna sitting beside him, latte in hand, staring out of the window humming along to whatever identikit song was top of the charts that week. He grinned at himself – it wasn't that long since he'd been a music-mad teenager, so when did he become so out of touch? A lorry pulled out in front of him and he stood on the brakes, dislodging a precarious pile of wetsuits which he'd thrown on the back seat next to Archie before he left. He'd been flat out for the last couple of weeks, getting everything organised for the final adventure of the winter season.

Right now, over on the Loch, the minibus would be decanting a motley collection of teenagers who'd never experienced anything like stand-up paddle-boarding or kayaking in the pouring rain, and who arrived with their own baggage... but theirs was emotional rather than physical. Working with children from disadvantaged backgrounds mattered to him. The challenge of trying to get through the layers of disinterest or bravado they'd built up over the years as a defence mechanism made every day different, and as interesting as the first day he'd started working for Wildcat Adventures fifteen years before. Of course, back then he'd been a very different person – not that different to the kids he worked with, not that he'd ever let that show.

He thought back to his final day on the loch. As it turned out, the day had been uncharacteristically uneventful. Yes, one of the lads he was in charge of had paddled his kayak in the opposite direction, crashing into an unsuspecting elderly couple who were clad in matching yellow waterproof suits, paddling along sedately in their twin canoe. And admittedly he'd had to deal with a fight that flared up out of nowhere, where two of the girls had squared up to each other, eyes heavy with black liner and false lashes glaring, long hair tangling around their necks as it blew in the wind. He hadn't managed to find out what the scrap was about – they'd clammed up as soon as he'd asked, mirroring each other with folded arms and closed expressions. It was all fairly standard stuff – and it made sense to him. Most of the teenagers he worked with had very little in the way of material possessions – their lives were chaotic and unregulated, their parents absent either physically or emotionally. He felt for them, knowing how it felt to get home from school and have nobody to talk to about what had happened in class, or to make a warm drink on a rainy evening.

All of that – well, that was why he was where he was. He'd taken a final look at the centre, switching off the lights of the log cabin where they started and ended each day, checking as he always did that the kettle and cooler were switched off, the wetsuits and life vests hanging on the racks near the radiator to dry overnight. The next time he did these checks he'd be somewhere entirely different – somewhere that didn't echo with memories. He hauled in a deep breath, pulling himself together. This was all for the best. Right now it hurt like hell, but if there was one thing he'd learned, it was that the human spirit could overcome pretty much anything, given time. He locked the door, putting the key back in the metal safe and punching in the security code. It was done.

As he'd driven through the city earlier that morning, he'd known he'd made the right choice. Everywhere he looked the architecture of Charles Rennie Mackintosh reminded him of what he'd lost. There was no way he could have stayed here alone, with every building he turned to a sharp reminder of what had been. He'd paused at a junction and checked his phone, hoping there might be a reply to the WhatsApp message he'd sent. It remained unread. The lights changed and he'd thrown his phone back down on the passenger seat, checking the sat nav to make sure he was heading in the right direction.

Twenty minutes later he was driving through a maze of tiny streets in an estate of identical houses pebbled with tiny white stones.

"You have reached your destination."

"Jack!"

Danny's excited voice entered the pick-up a moment before he hauled the door open. Ruddy faced with sandy-gold hair, he looked the epitome of a Scottish highlander. He'd fit in at least, thought Jack, wryly.

"You organised?" He looked at the pile of bags Danny had dumped at his feet. "Never heard of packing light?"

"I don't want to get all the way up there and discover I've forgotten something."

"They do have shops in the Highlands, you know."

"Aye but they might not sell my favourite flavour of pot noodle. That bag —" he indicated a massive grey hold-all, which he picked up and threw over his shoulder, heading for the boot, "is full of sweet and sour king size ones. And chocolate."

"You are joking."

"I am not." There was a tell-tale rattle of plastic pots as Danny shook the bag slightly.

Jack found himself laughing despite his gloom of earlier. "This is going to be some adventure. Get in, and let's get going. We've a long drive ahead of us."

It was late March, but as they drove north it was clear that spring had yet to make a mark on the west coast of Scotland. The trees stood tall, black sentinel around the lochs and rivers as the pick-up wound its way along the narrow roads. Danny zipped up his fleece, complaining that the car was freezing cold.

"I've got the heating on."

"I know. I'm not acclimatised to living in the frozen north." Danny rubbed the sides of his arms and faked chattering his teeth.

"You're going to have to work out how to acclimatise pretty bloody quickly. There's snow forecast for next week." Jack adjusted the heating to a level that felt uncomfortably warm. Danny looked slightly less like a human icicle after a few moments.

"You excited about moving up there?"

Jack nodded briefly. "Not sure excited is the word I'd use, but I'm looking forward to the challenge."

"Me too." Danny looked at his phone again. "Why can't I get any service? I've been trying to send a message for ages."

"Welcome to the Highlands," Jack said, lifting an eyebrow. "I did tell you the other day you'd struggle to get your fix of TikTok or whatever it is you're obsessed with."

"Yeah." Danny held his mobile up to the windscreen with a hopeful expression, "but I didn't think you meant no service when you said no service."

Jack burst out laughing. "You're just going to have to talk to me instead."

Danny groaned, but was smiling as he did so.

"Okay go on then. Tell me a bit more about this place. You've been up there, you know what it's like."

"Pass me a bag of crisps then," Jack said, balancing the steering wheel with his knees as he opened them. "What d'you want to know?"

As a perennial overthinker, Jack admired Danny's total lack of guile. He'd been working for Wildcat Adventures for a couple of years, making himself invaluable as Jack's right hand man. Where Jack was cautious and tended to hold back, judging before he jumped into anything, Danny was the opposite – he made his decisions on instinct and leapt without thinking, not worrying whether the end result would be a raging success or a total failure. As someone who'd always calculated every move as if life was a game of chess, Jack sneakingly admired Danny's chutzpah.

Even so, Jack had been surprised that he'd grabbed the opportunity to move location. While he was a big outdoor lover, Danny was a city boy at heart. He loved his big nights out with the lads, his trips to the cinema on a Sunday, shopping for expensive designer gear festooned with labels, and his hungover brunches on the weekends. The charity they worked for had been given a huge injection of funds from a National Lottery grant, which enabled them to buy a piece of woodland which edged into a Loch near the tiny West Highland village of Applemore – it had come at the perfect time for Jack. His heart had been aching with loss, and every street seemed to carry echoes of the life he'd given up. Danny's sunny, cheerful "when do we start, mate?" had meant more to him than he'd ever let on. And now here they were, two months later, heading to a new life – the most unlikely pair you'd ever see. Jack smiled at the thought.

"What's the village like?" Danny broke into his thoughts.

"Looks like a postcard." Jack paused for a moment, realising that Danny was only twenty-three and probably had no concept of what a postcard was. "Looks like you'd imagine a little Highland village should. White houses in a row looking over a pretty little bay. There are a few fishing boats in the harbour, and the hotel looks decent – I thought we might have dinner there tonight, instead of cooking when we get to the cottage."

"And the cottage?"

"Looks like a wee kid drew it. White painted, red door, windows in either side."

"Has it got Wi-Fi?" Danny put his hands together, petitioning the gods of internet.

Jack chuckled. "Apparently, aye. I suspect it might be a bit temperamental. The walls in these old places are really thick."

"Go on. So you've been up there… what are the people like?"

Jack thought for a moment then puffed out a breath of air, choosing his words carefully.

"The guy who owns the hotel seems sound. Harry? Harvey? Something like that. I stayed there both times. He's got some decent beers."

"You and your weird ales. Does he have decent vodka? Any chance of a lads' night out?"

Jack snorted. "I'm not matching you shot for shot."

"We could call it professional bonding." Danny reached around, passing a crisp to Archie, who'd been loudly objecting to the lack of food for poor starved terriers.

"You can call it what you like, I have no desire to get completely plastered and roll home singing rugby songs."

"Fine," said Danny, grinning. "Let's see how you feel after our first week."

Jack felt an overwhelming sense of relief that he'd managed to dodge the question. He carried on talking, quickly, hoping Danny wouldn't notice he was papering over cracks.

"Anyway, the place that adjoins us is some posh country estate owned by a Lord or something. I can't imagine we'll have much to do with them, somehow – you can imagine what they're like." He shook his head derisively. He had no time for people like that, who'd been born with a silver spoon in their mouth and never had to work a day of their lives.

Thanks to a crash on the A9, the drive took over six hours. By the time they arrived in Applemore the little village was in darkness and the cottage chilly and bare. They dumped their bags, and fiddled with the heating thermostat so they'd hopefully get home to a slightly warmer welcome when they returned later to unpack.

'You weren't kidding when you said this place was small.' Danny scratched his head in bemusement as they walked along the single street of shops, past the vet, and on towards the Applemore Hotel.

'Did you think I was exaggerating?'

'I looked at it on Google Maps,' Danny admitted, 'But I sort of didn't quite compute that it was literally *one street* of shops and stuff.'

'I hope you're not having second thoughts,' said Jack, drily, as he opened the door into the hotel bar. 'I don't want any barking from you, either,' he said, fixing Archie with a warning stare.

'I told you, I'm up for the challenge,' Danny said as they walked in, his Glasgow accent echoing around an almost empty bar.

Danny looked at Jack, an eyebrow raising almost imperceptibly. Jack shot back a look that said *just don't go there.* An old man sat on one of the barstools and stared at them with undisguised interest. At a table by a roaring log fire, two women – one older, with short, brightly coloured plum hair, the other about his age, with a pale strawberry blonde ponytail, wearing a checked shirt with her sleeves rolled up – looked up at them. Jack nodded a hello.

'You're not from round here,' Danny said, under his breath in a terrible attempt at an American accent. 'Bloody hell, are we gonna have pistols at dawn?'

'Handbags, more like,' Jack said, equally quietly. 'I guess they don't get much passing trade out of season.'

'Well hello there.' It was Harry, the barman he'd chatted to last time he'd been up and staying in the hotel.

'General Kenobi,' said Jack, almost without thinking.

'You get one on the house for that.' Harry grinned, glancing up at a signed photo of Harrison Ford as Han Solo which took pride of place above the bar. 'Nice to see you back.'

'Am I missing something?' Danny looked at them both in confusion. Harry and Jack exchanged a look of amusement.

'You had to be there.'

'Oh God,' realisation dawned on Danny's face. 'Is this some *Star Wars* geek thing?'

'Something like that.' Harry pulled two pints and passed them across the bar. 'You looking for some dinner as well?'

'Please.' Jack took a sip. It was a relief that after such a long journey there was at least a decent drink at the end of it. He liked Harry, who'd chatted to him last time he'd come to the village. He seemed genuinely interested, where the other locals he'd encountered previously had seemed somewhat wary – whether that was Highland reserve, or something else, he wasn't sure.

Harry pulled a couple of printed menus from a pile at the side of the bar and slid them across. Danny – who'd demolished several packs of crisps and a bag of sweets on the latter part of the journey – snatched it up and started scrutinising it as if he hadn't eaten in days. 'This looks good. I'll have the steak pie, please. And extra chips.' He went to put down the menu, then picked it up again, looking at it thoughtfully. 'Can I have some of the onion rings as well?'

'Course.' Harry took a note of his order, then scribbled down Jack's request for fish and chips.

'So,' Harry said, stacking glasses on the shelf above their heads. 'Word on the street is that your place is pretty much ready to go. Is this you up here for good now?'

The old man sitting at the bar sat up slightly, making no attempt to disguise the fact that he was listening intently to their conversation.

'Yep. We've got to get the inside sorted, get the place ready for the first group, that sort of thing.'

'And will it just be the two of you running it?'

Jack shook his head, aware that the way forward was to be as open as possible. It wasn't hard to work out that the village had some reservations about the project, and he could understand why. 'No, we've got a couple of other team members who'll be starting in the next day or two. They've been working on a winter offshoot project we had near Inverness, but that's coming to an end now, so they'll be staying in Applemore as well.'

He knew perfectly well that one of the objections the locals were likely to have was that they were bussing in their own workers rather than trying to create job opportunities for locals. They'd be recruiting for other members of staff very quickly, but for now they needed to get things moving as soon as possible in order to be up and running for the beginning of the season – and that meant sticking to the team they already had in place, who'd all been safety-checked and were registered with the authorities. Working with young people meant a lot of box-ticking and form filling – something Jack had accepted as a necessary evil. Paperwork was not his strong suit, being dyslexic, but he got there in the end.

'Have you worked here long?' Danny asked Harry, who nodded his head and laughed.

'I was born here – literally. I took over when my parents retired. I'm trying to drag the hotel into the twenty-first century, but it's taking a while. People in Applemore are quite set in their ways.'

Jack grimaced, watching as the old man – who still hadn't spoken – folded up the newspaper he'd been reading and picked up a flat cap, placing it carefully on his head.

'I'd say more circumspect than set in our ways, if you want my opinion,' said the man, in a soft Highland accent. He adjusted the collar of his coat and looked at them steadily, a twinkle in his dark blue eyes.

'Call it what you want, Murdo,' Harry said, laughing, 'But you know as well as I do that the rumour mill went into overdrive when I put in for planning permission to knock through the back wall in the ladies' toilet. I've still not recovered.'

The old man surprised Jack by breaking into a rumbling chuckle. 'Aye, well. We just do things slowly, that's all.' He fastened the zip on his coat. 'Good evening to you,' he said, nodding to Jack and Danny. He bent to give Archie a scratch under his bristly chin

'I'll take that as a win,' Jack said, as the door closed behind him.

'I would.' Harry agreed. 'Murdo's wife Greta is chair of the village improvement society, so if he's given you the nod, you might just be considered acceptable.' He put down the cloth he'd been wiping the bar with, and headed off towards the kitchens, leaving Danny looking nonplussed.

'Is he serious?'

'Half, I suspect.' Jack slid off the bar stool. 'These small villages are a bit of a law unto themselves. Shall we get a table?'

They headed across the room towards the tables, passing through a little stone archway hung with black and white photographs of the village from the olden days. Despite the fact that spring was supposed to be on the way, it was still cold in the evenings and the flames of the log fire looked warm and inviting. Jack had hovered by the bar with a purpose, noticing the two women had been putting on coats and preparing to leave. The older of the two had disappeared – to the scandal-beset loos, he assumed. The other one was looking at them as if she wanted to say something.

'D'you want this table by the fire?' She looked at Jack, a proprietorial hand gripping the back of her chair. He nodded. She was tall, with very good posture, and the tanned complexion of a person who spends a lot of time outdoors all year round. A fan of fine lines at the corner of each eye suggested that she laughed a lot more than her currently not particularly welcoming face would indicate. But she stepped away, motioning to the table with an open palm.

'Thanks.'

'I hope you don't mind me asking,' she said, looking at him from beneath the woolly hat she'd pulled on over her ponytail, 'But I couldn't help overhearing. I assume you're the people from the new outdoor activity centre?'

Danny nodded. 'We are.'

She looked at him thoughtfully, not saying anything for a moment. In the meantime, the other woman returned, hitching her bag over her shoulder. She looked at her friend quizzically.

'I told you they were,' the first woman said. 'You definitely look the type.'

Jack shot Danny a sideways look.

'Outdoorsy,' she said, indicating their clothes. 'Anyway, it's good to put a face to a name. Your place adjoins our land. I'm Charlotte Fraser.'

'Jack McDonald. And this is Danny.' Jack looked at the tall woman with new eyes. So this was one of the Fraser family – she looked remarkably normal and approachable, considering she was one of the landed gentry. He suppressed a smile at the thought that popped unbidden into his head that he was probably supposed to bow or something. Well, she could forget that idea.

'And I'm Joan.' The plum-haired woman offered a genuine smile, and held out her hand in welcome. She seemed friendly enough, Jack thought – she had more of a pronounced Highland accent than Charlotte, who sounded as if she could have come from somewhere in England. I bet she went to some posh boarding school, he thought to himself as they shook hands.

'I'm sure we'll bump into each other again soon enough.' Charlotte picked up her purse, which she'd left sitting on the table, and they set off to leave. Danny was just sitting down as Joan's curiosity got the better of her.

'So what exactly is it you're going to be doing?' She turned back to look at them. Charlotte widened her eyes almost imperceptibly, as if to tell her to be quiet, but Joan carried on regardless. 'You've certainly put the cat amongst the pigeons up here, I'll tell you that much.' She gave a chuckle, as if the idea of village gossip amused her more than anything.

Jack took a breath and launched into his well-rehearsed spiel. 'We work for a charity that provides funded adventure breaks for teenagers who've had a bit of a rough start. We've been working at Loch Lomond for years, but when the woodland came up for sale here, we thought this place was perfect for a wilderness adventure.'

She looked interested. 'What kind of rough start?'

He could see Danny beginning to bristle, almost reflexively. Working for the project meant they'd heard pretty much every preconceived judgement under the sun when it came to the work they did. Sometimes they played bingo, checking off the standard responses one by one as they met and overcame the challenges that came as part of the deal with a job like this. Jack gave him a warning look and he started fiddling with a beer mat, flipping it between his fingers.

'We try and focus on their futures, not their pasts,' Jack began, pausing for a moment, gauging their reaction. Harry appeared from the kitchen, as if sensing a disturbance. Charlotte was looking at him shrewdly.

'Alright? Do you two want another drink? Your meals won't be long.'

'That sounds great.' Jack exhaled carefully.

'It sounds interesting,' said Charlotte, not altogether convincingly.

'I think it's a good thing,' said Joan, giving Jack a warm smile. 'You can't go judging people on what they've done in the past, can you? We all make mistakes.'

Jack gave her a brief nod of gratitude. There was a person who'd seen more than she was letting on, he thought. It took a certain level of wisdom to be able to take people for what they were and not make snap judgements. The two women made to leave, Charlotte giving Harry a brief kiss on the cheek as she did so.

'I'll see you soon,' she said, as they headed outside into the chill of the evening.

'Nice catch,' said Danny, as he watched them pass the window, deep in conversation. Jack grinned.

'If it's any consolation,' Harry said, returning with a couple of frothing pints of beer a moment later, 'not everyone in the village has their hackles up at the thought of what you're doing.'

'It just feels like it.' Danny took a sip of beer then wiped the foam from his upper lip. 'You forgot to mention the fact that we were about as welcome as Ebola,' he said pointedly to Jack.

Harry snorted with amusement. 'It must take some juggling though, keeping a load of kids on the straight and narrow.'

'You'd actually be surprised.' Jack sat back in the chair, stretching his feet out underneath the table. It had been a long drive, and it felt good to unfold his limbs. 'When they've got a focus, they transform. Most of the kids we work with haven't ever had anyone listen to them. They've been forced to grow up too quickly, or they've had to make their way on their own. Having to work together makes a huge difference. They learn a lot.'

'I'd love to come and see it in action.' Harry noticed someone coming in the door, the little bell tinkling as they did so. 'I better go and earn my keep.'

'Any time,' said Jack.

'I'll take you up on that.'

They headed home an hour later, replete after a delicious dinner, which had been served to them before the unexpected rush for tables had begun. Contrary to Danny's assertion that the place was like a ghost town, it had been interesting to watch the hotel restaurant come alive as the clock struck seven, and the place began to buzz with chatter as people greeted friends and ordered drinks at the bar. They'd been aware that they were the subject of several curious glances, and the decision to drink up and head back to the cottage had been a silent but mutual one.

'On a plus note, maybe it's not that dead here after all.' Danny looked cheered at the prospect as they opened the door to the cottage. Thank goodness it had warmed up a bit, and when they flicked the lights on it looked pretty and welcoming. The owner had left a basket on the kitchen table with a loaf of crusty bread and a pack of shortbread as well as a bottle of red wine, and there was milk, butter and cheese in the fridge.

'That's breakfast sorted.'

'Never mind that,' Danny said, on his knees in the sitting room. 'I've found the router. Here, I'll share the Wi-Fi password with you.'

Jack laughed. 'Essentials, eh?'

'You're no' joking.' Danny sounded very Glaswegian all of a sudden. 'I've got Netflix to catch up on, for one thing.'

'I'm going to grab a shower then unpack.' Jack headed for the door, intending to bring in his things and try and get a bit organised before the morning.

'Cool.' Danny stood for a moment at the bottom of the stairs. 'Do you want the bedroom up there or the one down here on the ground floor?'

'I'll take downstairs,' said Jack, 'That way when I get up first thing in the morning I won't disturb your beauty sleep.'

'Watch it, old man,' Danny laughed. 'I'm not the one pushing forty.'

'Thirty-five is hardly pushing forty.'

'Just as well I'm taking the upstairs room,' said Danny,

ducking as Jack swiped him, laughing, 'Those old knees won't be up to the stairs.'

'Sod off,' said Jack, laughing. 'I'll see you in the morning. Let's see who's the weakling when we're sorting out this treehouse.'

'Challenge accepted.'

CHAPTER THREE

'HELLOOO?'

Beth paused for a moment, her hand on the hot tap, and sighed. It was lovely having her sisters living on her doorstep most of the time, but sometimes – generally at the end of a long day when she was feeling frazzled from work and touched-out from being with the twins – she secretly longed to live somewhere where she could close the door and not have one of them drop in with the latest village gossip. The bathroom was already full of steam, and the half-full bath was frothing with scented foam, which was calling out for her to climb in and close her eyes and switch off from everything.

She straightened up, giving the bath a longing look, and headed downstairs.

Her elder sister Charlotte was standing in the hall, a woolly hat covering her long dark blonde hair. Beth could hear her Land Rover engine running outside, so she clearly wasn't planning to make it a long visit.

'Sorry,' Charlotte said, with a rueful expression, 'have I interrupted?'

'Yeah, I was about to get in the shower with Jason Momoa.' Beth said, drily.

Charlotte snorted with laughter.

'Right. Nothing that can't wait, then.'

'What's up?' Beth tightened the dressing gown cord around her waist and nodded to the sitting room door, so Charlotte followed her in, explaining.

'I was on my way back from a drink and a catch-up with Joan and I thought you'd want to hear this, so…'

'Go on?' Beth sat down on the arm of the sofa, picking up a small pink sweatshirt and folding it, absent-mindedly. Sometimes she felt like if she wasn't careful she might disappear under a tsunami of miniature clothes, shoes, wellie boots and socks.

Charlotte disappeared outside for a moment, and returned with the car keys in her hand. 'I've turned the engine off. So. Your new neighbour. Well, our new neighbour, I suppose, if you're talking about Applemore as a whole.'

'What about him?'

'I met him this evening.' Charlotte lifted both eyebrows and looked at Beth.

'And?'

'He seems very nice.'

'Right.' Beth widened her eyes at her sister in an expression of mild exasperation. 'I love you very much, but it's my weekday night off from the babies, I'm about to have a bath, I'm frozen to the bone and I'm knackered and you've popped by to tell me he's very nice.'

'Touchy,' said Charlotte, teasingly, but she sat down on

the coffee table in front of Beth and looked at her directly. 'Seriously though. You okay?'

'I'm like a human icicle. You know it always makes me really grumpy when I'm cold,' Beth apologised, feeling guilty.

'I didn't mean in this moment, I meant more... globally. How's it going? I know you like to do the whole *I can cope with everything* thing, but a year of single parenting is hard work.'

Beth sat back against the sofa, exhaling. She'd always got on well with Charlotte, her calm, practical sister. Charlotte had a habit of observing more than she spoke, so she tended to notice things that Lachlan – wrapped up in his new relationship with Rilla and with running the house and little estate – and Polly, who was bouncily exuberant and never stopped, often missed. When she'd admitted that she and Simon had split eighteen months ago it had been Charlotte who'd been the most practical help. She glanced out of the window at the Land Rover, the lights illuminating the gravel drive outside the little farmhouse.

'D'you want to switch that off and have a glass of wine with me before you go home?'

Charlotte made a thoughtful face for about half a second then caved. 'Go on then. I'll give you the full rundown.' She stood up. 'You get the wine.'

Beth took a couple of glasses from the cupboard and unscrewed the bottle of red she'd opened the other evening. Drinking alone didn't hold any appeal for her, which was just as well, really, or she'd be knocking it back every night after the twins went to bed. Back in the years before she and Simon had split they'd often shared a midweek bottle. She poured their drinks and was unloading the dishwasher when Charlotte returned.

'Leave that,' Charlotte said, sitting down at the table. 'In fact, you sit down, I'll do it.'

Beth went to carry on, but Charlotte took her by the shoulders and gently pushed her down to sit on the wooden bench at the kitchen table, took a sip of wine, then quickly and efficiently unloaded the jumble of melamine plates and sippy cups and Tupperware.

'There, that's done. And now – and I'm not hanging around because your bath's going to go cold and I need to get back and feed the dogs – I'll give you the latest in Applemore goss.'

'So you've met the new neighbour.'

'Neighbours. There's Jack, who is the guy in charge, and a younger lad in his early twenties. And more to come, I gather, once they get up and running. But he's the one running it – he's like a survival expert or something, Harry was telling me.'

'Excellent. He can teach us how to cope when the power goes off.'

'I think it's more how to forage for the right kind of mushroom and not kill yourself and less how to survive in a castle when the electricity goes on the blink.'

Beth – who was eternally grateful for the work she and Simon had put in to finish the farmhouse before the twins were born – groaned at the thought of the dodgy wiring at the big house.

'I'm going to have to look out for him.'

'I think they're up here permanently now, so I don't imagine it'll be long before you bump into them. Murdo was telling me that they've finished building the cabin where they'll be sleeping, and all the rest of the equipment was delivered on a lorry the other day. I'm surprised you didn't notice, given you're outside all hours.'

'Outside but slaving over a hot flowerbed,' Beth smiled.

'You've done bloody brilliantly, you know,' Charlotte looked at her steadily. 'I know it's been hard work, but you've made a go of it, and you've juggled the twins as well as managing to have a civil relationship with Simon. You're like the poster girl for single motherhood.'

Beth snorted. 'I'd hardly say that. I'm permanently knackered.'

'But you're doing it. And you're happy.' Charlotte glanced at her. 'Aren't you?'

Beth narrowed her eyes and surveyed her sister over the top of her wine glass, pausing for a minute. She nodded. 'I am. You know what? I am. I know it's not very British to blow your own trumpet but actually, I'm doing okay. And I'm happy. Life is basically pretty good.'

Charlotte drained her glass. 'Well I'd call that a win. Here's to life on an even keel, as Dad would've said.'

'I'll drink to that. D'you want a bit more?'

Charlotte shook her head. 'Nope, I'd be over the limit, and anyway you've got a bath waiting and I need to get going. Let me know if you spot Jack and tell me what you think. I think you might be pleasantly surprised…'

'I hope so. I feel really awful for even admitting it, but I have more than a few reservations about having a load of disruptive teenagers creating havoc on the other side of the walled garden.' She cringed as she said it, knowing how privileged it made her sound. 'I'm sure it'll be fine.'

'I'm sure it will.' Charlotte picked up the car keys. 'I can understand your reservations. You've had enough to deal with, and now life's actually going okay.'

She was making for the door when Beth's phone rang. Mouthing a goodbye, she picked it up, and seeing it was

Simon, answered. Charlotte gave a brief wave and headed home.

'You okay?' Simon said, which put her on edge. She'd spent enough of her life married to him to know that what he meant by that was 'I'm not'. He had always had a habit of talking in questions, instead of offering straightforward answers.

'Yeah, fine,' she said, straightening the edges of a pile of books that lay on the coffee table.

'Good, good,' said Simon, heartily.

'Are Edward and Lucy okay?' Beth looked out of the window as Charlotte climbed into her Land Rover. At the far edge of the sky, the final streaks of dark pink hung over the tall poplar trees that stood sentry outside Applemore House.

'Yep, yep, fine.'

Was he going to repeat everything twice? Beth took the final sip of her wine and watched as a small blue flame licked around the edge of a log in the grate, which hissed and spat for a moment.

'So...'

'Alright. Look. No point beating about the bush. Morag's pregnant.'

'Oh.' She put her glass down. 'Well. That's a bit – sudden?' Then she gathered herself. 'I mean congratulations, of course.'

He gave an excessively hearty laugh. 'All change around here,' he continued. She could hear him swallowing in that way he always had when he was uncomfortable. Beth felt a fluttering of anxiety in the pit of her stomach.

'In what way?' Beth enunciated each word very clearly.

Even as she was saying it there was a feeling in the air that something was about to change. She had an overwhelming urge to end the call and pretend that the line had gone dead.

That moment she heard the sound of something being clonked in the background on the other end of the call – a mug on a table, or something like that.

'Have you got me on speaker?'

'Don't be ridiculous,' said Simon, in exactly the same tone he would use if he had her on speakerphone.

'Okay,' Beth said, pursing her lips and inhaling deeply to try and gather herself, 'Go on.' There was clearly more coming. She knew him well enough for that.

'Well. Right. The thing is we've decided what would work well is if I stay at home and be house-husband, and Morag goes back to work after the baby is born. Or babies,' he added, as an afterthought.

'House-husband?' She couldn't help snorting. Simon had shot back to the office virtually while they were still sewing her up post-childbirth. 'So you're going to stay at home and look after the children and not...' It struck her in an instant what he was saying. '...and not work. Not work?' Her voice went up about three octaves.

'I'll be working,' he said quickly. 'I'm planning a start-up.'

'Is this start-up going to make enough money for you to pay child maintenance for the twins?'

'Well it will do... in time,' said Simon, and she could picture his face so well that she felt her hand clenching into a fist, as she imagined walloping him hard on the nose. She flexed her fingers and took a deep calming breath.

'Excellent. And in the meantime while you're being start-up house-husband, I'm supposed to do what exactly?'

'You said yourself the flower farm was going great guns.'

Beth closed her eyes and sank back against the cushions of the sofa where only a few moments before she'd gaily told her sister that everything was going pretty well, thank you very much.

'Simon, I'm going to go now before I say something I regret. We will speak about this tomorrow.'

CHAPTER FOUR

'Oh, hell.'

Jack stepped back, dry twigs crackling underfoot. A crow shot into the air, squawking disapproval, and then the air was still. Bloody Danny and his impetuous nature.

They'd set off for the perimeter wall of their land early that morning, planning to tidy up the huge oak which was going to be home for the treehouse they'd designed. If there was one thing he'd learned in his years working with youths of all ages it was that everyone loved a treehouse, especially one decorated with twinkling lights and shaggy sheepskin rugs. Over at the log cabin that would be the centre base the kayaks and paddle boards were stacked neatly, and the waterproofs and wetsuits hung up on their pegs. Everything was pretty much falling into place – after years of doing everything on a shoestring it was a bloody miracle to have the injection of cash from the grant which meant that decent equipment was ready to go. All they had to do was sort the treehouse, wait for the overnight staff who were heading up later that day, and it would be all systems go. It had been going alarmingly smoothly.

That was, he thought, head in hands as he surveyed the scene in front of him, until now. The number one rule of cutting was that you had to factor in what was around you, not just what was directly underneath. And it turned out that the wall of the Applemore garden definitely counted as an obstruction. One moment he'd been striding across the woodland, having held back to take a call from Sarah in the charity head office down in Glasgow, and the next he'd heard the familiar creak of splitting wood and then a crash, and quite a lot of swearing. He'd broken into a run and discovered Danny standing by the eight-foot-high stone wall with a pole-saw in hand, and an expression of wide-eyed horror.

'What the hell?'

'I thought I'd just take that branch down,' Danny motioned to an empty space. 'It wasn't that big and I figured it'd land on the ground in front of me but it hit another branch and sort of veered off and the next thing I knew…' he motioned to the wall.

Jack balanced the ladder against the wall and climbed up to survey the damage with a sense of impending doom. In the millions of Health and Safety directives that dictated their every movement there weren't any explicit rules about knocking down oak branches onto polytunnels and bursting through the plastic, but Jack was intelligent enough to recognise that doing so was hardly going to endear him to his new neighbour. The plastic bore a huge, ragged scar where the branch had landed. Inside he could see wooden shelves and the floor covered with scattered earth and mangled-looking plant seedlings. Well, that wasn't exactly an ideal situation. The only positive – he scanned the walled garden, seeing neatly trimmed paths between well-maintained beds – was that whoever owned this place was clearly not short of a bob or two. Hopefully that would also mean they were loaded enough not to sue him when he'd only just got to work, before any kids had even turned up in the village.

'I'm sorry,' Danny said, grimacing as Jack climbed back down the ladder.

'Mistakes were made,' Jack said, shaking his head in disbelief. 'We'll sort it. Somehow. But for God's sake, man, please don't knock down any more trees before I get back.'

'Where are you going?' Danny was shaken out of his habitual cool.

'Damage limitation.' Jack groaned. 'Don't bloody move. I'll be back shortly.'

There had to be a gate, somewhere. He walked around the perimeter of the garden, wondering why it was that some people had everything and others had nothing. When he'd been growing up in Glasgow he hadn't even realised places like Applemore existed. Now here he was with neighbours who were probably on first name terms with royalty. Life was pretty weird, sometimes. He kept on walking and eventually reached a wooden gate painted a dusty pale green, pausing for a moment before pushing it open. It gave a creak of disapproval.

From the ground it was even clearer that the neatly planted flower beds – some metres long, others short and square – had been scrupulously well maintained, presumably by a fleet of gardeners. The grass paths between the beds were neatly trimmed, and there wasn't a weed to be seen. Serried rows of vibrant green shoots were edged with neatly trimmed lavender bushes, which were showing the first signs of spring growth. In another month this place would be unrecognisable. But right now there was the slight detail of the polytunnel which stood in the far corner, and which was sagging very noticeably where a surprisingly hefty oak branch was pinning it down. There wasn't any sign of anyone around. Hopefully he could haul the branch off, and somehow repair the worst of the damage. He made his way across the gardens, keeping a cautious eye out.

But as he approached the polytunnel he noticed a pair of blue and white spotted wellington boots standing outside, and a grey sweatshirt inside out and lying in a heap. Oh God, was there someone in there?

'Hello?' He stepped into a sub-tropical atmosphere and almost immediately stepped back as he was blasted by an explosion.

'What the *hell?*' said a woman's voice.

'Shit.' He took in the scene. The subtropical polytunnel thing was stuffed full of plants and neatly dug out trenches, and standing in the middle of them, with the sagging and very definitely torn back end behind her, was a very pretty woman with a blonde ponytail, a blue and white striped t-shirt and an expression of righteous fury.

'I don't suppose you're responsible for –' she waved an arm in the direction of the chaos, eyes snapping in temper '-this?'

'Shit,' he said again. 'I'm so sorry.'

She raised a supercilious eyebrow, and folded her arms. 'I should bloody well think so.' She had a neutral accent, with only the faintest hint of a Highland twang. Definitely posh.

'I'll sort it.' He took a step forward but stopped when she widened her stance as if she was challenging him. Bloody hell, this woman wasn't just posh, she was tough. He shifted his approach slightly, trying to work out how to deal with her.

'Look, I've messed up. I'm sorry. If you give me a sec, I can work out how to fix it – even if it's temporary. But I'll make it good, I promise.'

Her eyebrows dropped down to their regular level and she unfolded her arms. Her expression still indicated that he was about as welcome as an infestation of slugs.

'There's no need.'

She didn't move – standing protectively beside the wheelbarrow as if she was worried he was going to drop another branch of the oak tree on them, too. He moved past her carefully, noticing freckles dotting her nose and cheeks. She clearly spent a lot of time outside. He looked up at ragged tear in the plastic.

'I'm so sorry. I'll get it sorted.'

'I doubt you'd know where to start,' she said crisply. 'I'll sort it, you can pay for the bloody damages.'

'Deal.' He put out a hand to shake hers, suppressing a wry smile. He liked her already, despite himself.

'Right.' She shook his hand. 'That's that sorted.'

'Excellent.' He gave a nod of agreement. 'I'm Jack, by the way. This isn't really the best way to introduce myself.'

'Jack?'

'Your new neighbour. Well, I'm not actually living next door, I'm in the village itself, but we've bought the wood and the ten-acre field that runs alongside it.'

She still hadn't said anything more. She cocked her head slightly, looking at him with a strange expression. 'I wasn't expecting you to be so…'

'…good at lopping off branches and wrecking your polytunnel?' He gave a wry grin. 'I mean I could admit at this point it wasn't actually my doing, but a man doesn't drop his mates in it, so –'

'That's not what I was going to say,' she said, after a moment's thought, 'but no. I have to admit that when I heard what you were going to be doing, I didn't think a tree landing on my polytunnel was going to be my major concern.'

'Well,' he said, trying to be conciliatory, 'I guess it's good to be unpredictable?'

'Mmm.' She looked at him for a moment, a thoughtful expression on her face, then glanced down at her wheelbarrow full of cut flower stems, the buds still closed but glimpses of pastel colour showing through. Anemones, he thought – they'd been his mum's favourites. 'I need to get on, I'm sorry.' She cleared her throat.

'Oh of course,' he said, stepping out of the way so she could wheel the barrow down the middle of the tunnel. 'At least let me clear some of this up?'

The floor was strewn with seed trays and carpeted with black compost. He bent to pick a couple up, putting them down alongside several others on the metal shelf that ran at hip height along one side.

She gave a brief laugh, which threw him. 'Much as I'd like to take you up on that, I have to admit that this mess is all my own doing. I've been meaning to sort it.'

'But the –' He waved an arm in the direction of the torn plastic.

'You've mangled the roof of my tunnel, but the chaos is all my own fault.'

'I'll get it sorted.' He looked up, frowning. 'I'll order a new cover, and we can get it fitted. Danny – he works with me – can help.'

'Honestly,' she paused, putting down the wheelbarrow

and turning to face him, pushing a long strand of hair out of her face with the back of her arm, 'It's as easy for me to patch it – if we start replacing the whole plastic cover thing I've got to dig out the trench and – well, loads of technical stuff that I'm fairly sure you're not actually interested in. It's just one of those things.'

'I don't want all your flowers dying of cold overnight.' He looked at all the tiny seedlings, vivid green against the dark compost. She picked up a tray. He glanced down at her fingers, noticing they were mud-stained and the nails grubby, and she noticed him noticing and curled them out of sight, then turned away and started walking out of the polytunnel.

He followed her out and was surprised that she paused for a moment, as if good manners had overcome her previous temper. She extended a hand.

'Forgive me for being so rude. I'm Beth, by the way. Beth Fraser.'

'Jack MacDonald.'

'Convention states that at this point I say *pleased to meet you*,' Beth said, but there was a hint of humour beneath the crisp tone, 'however, I might hold back judgement on that, considering. At least until I've fixed my tunnel.'

'Fair enough.' He felt himself smiling at her despite himself. He got the distinct impression that under different circumstances, she might be quite charming and funny, and he liked her dry sense of humour.

'I'll see you later, Jack MacDonald.'

And with that, she strode off across the walled garden, heading to the far corner where a woman in a blue woolly hat was rotavating a bed, oblivious to what had been going on.

'How did it go?'

Danny looked up with a sheepish expression. To be fair, Jack thought to himself, he'd done a decent job in the interim – he'd cleared the path that led to the oak tree and the base for the treehouse was ready to be hoisted up and fixed into place.

'I think I've managed to smooth things over. If you can avoid trashing anything else before we get started though, that would be helpful.'

Danny grinned. 'I'll make sure I don't.'

By the end of the afternoon they'd assembled the treehouse and hung it with battery operated fairy lights, stashing away the sheepskin rugs and blankets in a waterproof box inside. Heading back, Jack felt a sense of relief that they were finally getting there.

By the next evening, though, he felt that he'd cursed himself by feeling pleased with their progress. Everything that could have gone wrong had. A delivery they were expecting hadn't turned up, but Nathan, the charity boss had – unexpectedly. He'd been determined to have everything organised when that happened, but instead he was caught on the back foot and felt irritable and out of sorts that he'd not been ready, although Nathan had professed to be delighted with how everything was looking. He'd wanted to pop over and see if there was anything he could do to make up for damaging Beth Fraser's polytunnel and hadn't had time, and by the time he had, the walled garden had been deserted. And then Melanie, who would oversee the running of the bunkhouse as well as teaching outdoor skills, had called to say that she'd been held up because of a family emergency and wouldn't be arriving until the end of the week. The only positive he could find in all of it was that tomorrow had to be better...

His bad morning had started first thing with a call from

Rebecca, his ex. As soon as her number had flashed up on the phone he'd felt a lurch of fury remembering their last bitter exchange. They'd split by mutual agreement after Anna was born – it had been for the best. Only twenty, he'd been nearly ten years younger than her – his friends had teased him and said he was her bit of rough. She was an up and coming architect in a city firm, determined to make a name for herself. But he'd stayed close by, renting a place in the same part of Glasgow, commuting across the city to the project he was working on at the time, determined to be a part of Anna's day-to-day life. As his career had grown – with everything that meant, given his past – he'd done everything he could to make sure he was there for her in the morning to take her to school a few days a week, pick her up afterwards when he could, turn up to every ballet performance and make an idiot of himself at sports day… he did everything he could.

But then Rebecca had been offered the dream job, right at the point where they were facing a situation neither of them wanted to contemplate. He'd known that they had no choice. If they'd been together, he could have travelled over there and they could have been a family – safely installed in Paris, far away from everything in the past. But they weren't, and Brexit had put paid to that. He'd told Anna that it was the opportunity of a lifetime, promised her he'd come over for holidays and weekends, with a smile pasted on his face while inside he felt like he was having his heart ripped out. Being a good father meant everything to him, and that meant making a sacrifice so she could have the best of everything… if only she'd seen it that way. Anna had taken the news as badly as possible – for the last couple of months she'd been terse and monosyllabic. His visit to Paris in February had been a complete disaster. And now here he was sitting in a tiny hotel bar in a village that was so small you could walk from one end to the other in ten minutes, looking out over a sea and a pale evening sky that stretched out beyond the harbour and over the hills of the islands out to sea. He looked down at his pint, realising he'd been lost in thought for so long that it had gone completely flat. He shook his head, told himself to get a grip, and decided to go for a walk.

The village was completely silent. A string of fairy lights twinkled gently on the trees, giving the place a magical air. Gulls whirled overhead, beady eyes focused on the fishing boat that was heading back into harbour. On the pavement ahead he saw a woman pushing a toddler bike with a long handle, and he stepped aside to let them past, nodding a greeting. The toddler waved cheerfully. He paused, looking down the road at the little main street. There was a heap of building equipment outside what looked like an old shop – sacks of cement on wooden pallets, a couple of pots of paint balanced on top. It made him smile to see them – back where he'd lived in Glasgow, if that had been left overnight the next morning the owners would have returned to find the paint daubed everywhere and the contents of the sacks emptied all over the pavement. This was going to take some getting used to.

He strolled across the road, where a metal rail divided the pavement from the little path down to the tiny harbour. As one fishing boat returned, another was heading out for the night catch, and he stood watching it as it disappeared slowly out of view. Maybe he ought to start fishing by night to stave off the insomnia that was haunting him. As it was, night time and the prospect of bed held no pleasure for him. He hitched the laptop under his arm and turned for the cottage.

Belach Cottage was a white painted cottage which – as he'd told Danny when they were driving up from Glasgow – looked exactly as if it had been drawn by a child. Low and wide, it had two little windows on either side of a brightly painted red door, and on either side of the step, two squat little pots of cheerful yellow daffodils, the broad leaves of tulips jostling for space alongside them. Inside, however, it was sparse. It had been owned by a couple who'd recently moved into a retirement home in the nearby town, and their children had clearly decided to rent it out without making any attempts to modernise it. He went into the kitchen, which must have been at least forty years old, and flipped on the kettle to make a cup of tea. There was no sign of Danny, who was probably upstairs with headphones on watching something on Netflix. If he was going to be awake half the night, he might as well get some work done. He moved the bottle of whisky he'd been given as a parting gift from the kitchen worktop, putting it on the windowsill. He'd had a pint in the pub – or rather, he'd ordered one then forgotten to drink it – but he had one rule about drinking, which was that he never did it at home alone. That way madness lay, he told himself. He'd seen for himself the effect that alcohol could have on people and he didn't ever want to go down that road. He made a cuppa and headed into the sitting room, where the papers he'd been reading earlier on were strewn across a coffee table tiled with hideous olive green tiles.

He picked up his phone, checking out of habit in case Anna had replied to his message. It remained unread, as did the one before that from the other day when he'd driven up, the car loaded with everything he could fit, and sent a picture so she could see where he was going. He tossed the phone down again.

Right. He opened the laptop. There was no point in spending the whole bloody night feeling sorry for himself. The first group of teenagers would be there before he knew it, and he needed to get the activity programme drawn up.

～

He headed up to the wood first thing the next morning, rising from a fitful sleep at six when the first pale fingers of light were reaching across the sky. Winding up the road up towards Applemore Wood, he stopped the car for a few minutes to allow a farmer to chivvy a herd of black and white cows across the road, their puffs of breath white in the still-chilly spring air. The silence was broken with the sounds of shuffling hooves and mournful mooing, and then a cheerful 'alright, thanks for that' from a young farmer with sandy blonde hair and a dark blue boiler suit who rapped a thank you on the bonnet of his car and gave a wave.

The road forked right away from the entrance which was marked 'Applemore House' and he drove on, wondering about Beth Fraser. She'd looked exhausted and completely frazzled – as if his trashing the polytunnel was the final straw on a day when she'd already had enough. If he'd been her sort of person, he'd probably have bought her a box of chocolates as an apology, but he'd always found that sort of thing a bit awkward. Practical stuff – yeah. He could do that. He parked the car at the side of the wood and headed for the walled garden. If he could have a proper look, maybe he could get it sorted properly for her. It would be one less thing for her to think about.

The big wall was about eight feet high. He dropped the chainsaw over with a rope, pulled the ladder up, climbed up and vaulted over, landing on the other side carefully, like a cat. There was nobody around. He glanced around, making sure, then fired up the chainsaw. First things first – he'd get the errant branch chopped up and lobbed back over the other side of the wall before she got back, and then he'd see if there was a way to repair the polythene cover…

'Hello?'

He'd just stopped the chainsaw and turned, still wielding it. The motor gave a final apologetic splutter and died in his hands.

Beth looked from him to the chainsaw and down to the stack of wood at his feet.

'How the hell did you get in here?'

He looked across the garden. The gate was wide open, as it had been when he'd vaulted over the wall, but something told him that a smart-arsed answer was definitely not the way forward at this point. He could virtually see smoke coming out of her ears and suppressed a grin.

'I thought I'd nip over and get this branch out of the way. I'm waiting for the electrician to turn up first thing anyway, and I didn't want you worrying about having to deal with it, and…'

She was still standing there with her arms folded, an expression of absolute fury on her very pretty face. He thought it might be a good idea to stop talking, given the way she was looking at him.

'You're trespassing. Again.'

'I know,' he began.

'Ah –' she looked pleased with herself. 'So you're admitting it. I could have you done for criminal damage as well, come to think of it.'

'Bloody hell.' He picked up a couple of hefty chunks of oak branch and lobbed them over the wall. 'I said I'd pay for the repairs. I'm sorry, I didn't mean to land a branch on your polytunnel.'

'It's my livelihood,' she said, crossly. A gust of wind blew a long strand of hair across her face and she tucked it behind her ear with an irritable expression. Jack wanted to tell her to sit down and chill out before she blew her top completely, but was circumspect enough to realise that telling her to calm down was liable to send her into a whole new level of fury. His training over the years of working with angry adolescents had taught him more than enough about how to de-escalate difficult situations. He took a step back, and put the chainsaw on the ground, raising both hands in a vague impression of someone putting their hands up in a shoot-out.

'Okay,' he said, taking another step back. 'I think we got off on the wrong foot. I shouldn't have climbed over – I thought I was doing you a favour.'

'You'd have been doing me a favour if you hadn't dropped a bloody great oak branch on my polytunnel in the first place.'

'Well yes,' he said, rubbing his chin, 'that's obvious. But now I have, there has to be some sort of way for me to make it up to you.'

She didn't seem to be softening. Her arms were still crossed, her whole body language suggesting what she'd like to do is sock him one. She seemed a lot crosser about the situation today than she had been when it happened. He lifted an eyebrow, hopefully.

'If you tell me what it is you need I'll order it and it'll be here tomorrow. I can get it sorted asap.'

She looked at him with a wryly amused expression and shook her head. 'We live in the Northern Highlands. We don't get overnight deliveries. They come in their own sweet time. Meanwhile, my baby plants are going to freeze to death.'

'Shit,' he said, feeling terrible. 'I'm really sorry. What can I do to make it better short term?'

'Nothing,' she said, crisply.

'What if I –'

For a moment he looked at her and thought she was about to burst into tears as she sagged slightly. Then she seemed to gather herself.

'Look, I need to get on. I've got a mountain of daffodils to pick and they need to be processed first thing.'

'Do you want me to –' he inclined his head towards the pile of logs. She shook her head.

'No, thank you.'

She glanced from him to the wall and back again. 'I'd suggest you use the gate this time, rather than scaling the wall. That might be how you do things in Glasgow but it's not really done up here.'

He lifted an eyebrow as he looked at her steadily. Cross, he could deal with. Patronising and stuck up, not so much. He'd felt sorry for her a moment ago, but the implication that he was somehow up to no good rubbed him up the wrong way, because – well, it was a bit close to the bone, given everything. The last thing he wanted was to be reminded of the past. He hitched the chainsaw up and strode back across the garden towards the little green gate, aware of her eyes on him the whole time.

CHAPTER FIVE

BUGGER, thought Beth, watching as Jack disappeared out of the gate. She'd always been the Fraser sibling with a temper, and when she was under pressure it was harder to keep it under control. She'd barely slept the night before, mulling over Simon's bombshell about the child maintenance, and when she'd finally passed out some time after five in the morning she'd been woken what felt like seconds later by Edward climbing into her bed, hair mussed up with sleep, and asking for breakfast. A moment later Lucy had appeared, trailing Bluey, her faded now-grey stuffed rabbit, thumb in mouth.

'Can we watch *Sarah and Duck* please?' The words were muffled and Beth's heart had melted despite the ridiculously early hour.

'Of course you can, baby,' she said, rolling out of bed and staggering downstairs, lifting them one by one over the safety gate at the top of the stairs. The cats wove their way between her legs as she heated up milk in the microwave, demanding breakfast despite the early hour. Only once she'd done the whole television, breakfast, tantrums over getting dressed (them, not her) and getting-everyone-in-the-car-to-go-to-the-childminder routine did she have a chance to remember once again with a lurch of dread that she'd somehow got to make the flower farm pay this year in a way it hadn't before. She slammed the boot of the car shut unnecessarily hard, swearing under her breath as she did so. Bloody Simon. Bloody stubborn pride.

She'd dropped the twins at the childminder for eight, heading straight to the garden to get the daffodils cut and conditioned first thing. By the time she'd arrived, she was so cross about the whole situation that it wasn't surprising that she'd given Jack MacDonald short shrift, even if he was trying to help. She looked again at the gate which was still swinging slightly in a light breeze. It didn't help that he was – she screwed up her face and shook her head, as if to eradicate the picture of him from her mind – tall, dark, and ridiculously easy on the eye.

An hour later she headed down to the farm shop for a coffee and to drop off another batch of tied bunches of daffodils wrapped in brown paper. Gavin was outside tipping coffee grounds into the compost bin by the side of the old lodge cottage when she pulled up. He bashed the metal container on the edge of the bin and looked up with a welcoming smile.

'Ah, you shouldn't have,' he said in his lilting accent. 'All those for me? And daffs as well. You know the way to a Welshman's heart, cariad.'

Beth grinned. As always, a bout of hard work had cured her of her mood and she was back to her usual cheerful self.

'You can have the lot, if you'll play childminder this week. Deal?'

'No bloody way,' snorted Gavin. 'Your two are very

sweet but I'm steering well clear of small children. I've got my fur babies and that's as much as I want.'

She laughed, pulling open the back of the van and sliding out the first tray of flowers.

Gavin and Tom owned two sweet sausage dogs called Will and Fred, who were pampered beyond belief and had a better wardrobe than she did. Every time she saw them they were dressed in impeccable matching little coats, with collars which never seemed to have a speck of dirt on them. They were so far removed from the scruffy, perpetually muddy spaniels that Beth had grown up with it was almost hard to believe they were the same species.

She headed inside. Polly had worked hard overnight, hanging up a display to advertise the gifts and cards she had on sale for Mothering Sunday, which was coming up. The wooden shelves which held a succession of seasonal delights were laid out with handmade gifts from local artisans, boxes of the delicious chocolates that Anna from the village made in her little seaside cottage, and cards and paintings from several of the artists who lived in the surrounding area. On the bottom shelf were three aluminium buckets waiting for her posies of daffodils. She placed the first batch in carefully, arranging them so their stems were in water but the brown paper which wrapped them stayed dry. Then she brought in the little posies of anemones, hellebore and daphne. Only when she was happy with the way they looked did she straighten up, dusting off her knees. She'd need to stop faffing around if she was going to make some serious money this year, and twiddling around making the flowers look pretty was probably not the best use of her time. Polly, who had emerged from the storeroom and was chatting on the phone to a supplier, gave her a smile of greeting and pointed towards the coffee shop with a 'shall we?' motion.

Beth nodded, heading to the car. She could afford a quick catch up before she delivered the rest of the blooms to the other shops on her rounds.

'I don't know what you want me to do,' a now-familiar Glaswegian voice could be heard saying as she headed for the car. There was a crunch of footsteps on gravel, and she saw that Jack MacDonald was pacing back and forth on the path beside the farm shop, the door of his beaten-up truck still ajar.

'I just want – look, I've sent I-can't-tell-you-how-many messages. Not one reply. You've got to back me up, Rebecca. I need you on side.'

Beth tried her best to busy herself with the flowers, trying not to overhear. She pulled out the tray but a couple of posies toppled over and she had to reach inside to get them. He was still talking, and clearly not happy with whoever it was he was talking to.

'I'm beginning to think I need to come over again and spend some time –' he said. At that moment he looked up, seeing Beth. He lifted an eyebrow in greeting and she gave a brief apologetic smile, feeling bad for how off she'd been with him earlier.

She'd finished arranging the second batch of daffodils – briefly this time – when he came inside.

'Hello again,' he said, pretending to duck as if he was expecting her to throw a punch. 'Am I safe, or shall I come back when you're not here?'

'Sorry I was off with you earlier,' she said, joining him as they headed towards the counter of the coffee bar. The shop was quiet, unusually – normally at this time of the morning there was a rush of post-school run parents who dropped in for coffee and cake and to get first dibs on the delicious fresh-baked bread. The loaves were stacked neatly in their baskets, filling the air with a scent that made Beth's stomach rumble. The twins had been up so early that breakfast felt a long time ago.

He shrugged. 'I'm the one who made the big entrance by trashing your place. I'm sure if you'd come over and set fire to the log cabin I'd have been as pissed off as you were.'

'Hardly the same,' said Beth, feeling conciliatory.

'Maybe not.' He grinned. 'Anyway, what d'you recommend?' He motioned to the blackboard, which was neatly chalked with the day's specials.

'Gav makes a killer flat white,' Beth said, as Gavin turned, hearing his name, 'And if you're in need of a sugar hit, the brownies are amazing.'

'That sounds pretty much perfect,' said Jack.

'Same for you?' Gavin said, giving Beth a very old-fashioned look. 'And maybe an introduction?'

'Sorry,' Beth said, looking from Jack to Gavin. 'This is Jack, who's running the new outdoor activity centre. Gavin and his husband Tom run the coffee shop.'

'Tom's not here, the dirty stop-out,' explained Gavin. 'He's gone to the wholesaler in Inverness to pick up some supplies. He'll be sorry he's missed you.'

'I'm sure he will,' said a voice over Beth's shoulder. 'I'm Polly, Beth's sister.' She put out a hand in greeting, saying hello to Jack and giving her sister an almost identical look to the one that had passed between Beth and Gavin. 'Nice to put a name to a face.'

'I'll get these,' said Jack, as Beth went to get her phone from her pocket to pay at the little contactless machine. 'Least I can do.'

'Are you sure?'

'Of course.'

Beth passed over the reusable coffee cup which she'd

59

brought in, tucked under her arm, from the car. It remained a standing joke between her and Miranda that she was never more than five metres from her coffee. They watched in silence as Gavin got to work, the machine grinding fresh beans and his hands working deftly as he whirled the milk into ornate patterns, then when Jack nodded to 'Are you taking these away?' wrapping the brownies in brown paper. Beth, who'd hoped for a chance to apologise properly for being so snarky earlier, felt a little pang of regret.

'I'll pop round later, see what I can do to sort out those logs. And repair the damage, of course.' Jack gathered his things. 'If that's okay?'

Beth nodded. 'Of course.'

'Nice to meet you, albeit fleetingly,' said Gavin, as he nodded a farewell.

'And you.'

'Well that was short and sweet,' said Polly, a moment later. They'd all three watched as Jack strode across the shop, the silence not broken until the door closed with a gentle thud.

'Disappointingly so,' said Gavin, making a little *moue* of dismay. 'I was hoping we'd have a bit of hot Glaswegian eye-candy for a bit longer than two minutes.'

Polly gave a giggle, and looked at Beth for a reaction. She pulled her long hair over her shoulder, twirling her ponytail thoughtfully, crooking one eyebrow with a knowing expression.

'Don't look at me,' protested Beth. She shook the packet of sugar and made careful work of tearing off the top, not looking at her sister for a moment, but she felt Polly's eyes boring into the side of her head.

'I'm sorry,' said Polly, shaking her head slowly, with a

tone Beth knew all too well. 'Don't tell me you hadn't noticed Jack MacDonald isn't exactly hard on the eye.'

'I don't know what you're talking about.' Beth, who'd never been any good at hiding her emotions, felt her cheeks going pink. She tipped the sugar into her coffee and stirred before looking up to see two pairs of eyes looking at her.

'You're blushing.' Gavin looked delighted. He crossed his arms and leaned back slightly.

'He's cute,' Polly said, firmly. 'Thanks, darling.' She took the coffee that Gavin had prepared for her, and then looked at Beth over the top of her cup.

'Hadn't noticed.' Beth tried to sound casual.

'Bullshit,' said both Gavin and Polly, in unison.

'I need to get on,' said Beth, putting a lid on her coffee. If she didn't make an escape now, she was in for a dual-pronged attack and the next thing she'd be being quizzed again on why she hadn't signed up for online dating... it was as bad as getting it in the ear from Miranda, who wasn't around today. That meant that she could head off, do her deliveries, and get back to the farm to do some of the million and one things that were outstanding. If she had 24 hours straight a day to work in spring, it still wouldn't be enough.

'I thought you had time for a chat.'

'I wish.' Beth made an exaggerated motion of looking at the clock on the wall of the farm shop. 'But look at the time. I must get off. Flowers to pick, business to run, that sort of thing...'

She picked up her phone and shoved it in her pocket, checking before she did – as always – in case there was a message from the nursery. Her heart squeezed at the sight of the cute photo of the twins which was her screensaver. It was the weirdest thing, being a parent – simultaneously desperate for time and space to herself, then missing them like mad every moment they were out of her hands.

'You can't outrun me forever, Fraser,' said her sister, teasingly. 'I'll be coming round later to see the babies and I expect all the gossip. I saw the way you two were with each other.'

'Definite chemistry,' agreed Gavin.

'You see?' Polly sounded triumphant.

'Will you two *please* shut up?'

Beth hid a smile as she left the farm shop. It was undeniable that Jack MacDonald – with his broad shoulders, scruff of spiky dark hair, and dark eyes, not to mention his athletic body – was extremely hot indeed. She might have sworn off men but the moment she'd set eyes on him it was pretty bloody difficult to ignore the basic fact. But she wasn't going to let on to herself, let alone to her sister or her partner in gossip. Not for one second.

'Beth!'

She was climbing into the car when Rilla, her brother's girlfriend, appeared at the door of the old dairy on the other side of the courtyard. Her long dark curls were tied back from her hair in a ponytail, and she was wearing a black apron over a striped shirt and jeans.

'You okay?' Beth climbed back out of the car, her pleasure at seeing Rilla overriding her desire to get on with work.

'I need some herbs. I've had a –' she pulled a face that made Beth laugh '– slight technical hitch with this batch of gin.'

Beth closed the door and headed across, giving Rilla a kiss hello. She smelled rather strongly of juniper berries and rosemary – a sprig of which was tangled in her hair. Beth removed it with a smile. 'How was the van trip?'

'Amazing.' Rilla tucked a long dark curl that had loosened back behind her ear, beaming from ear to ear, her freckled nose wrinkling with pleasure in memory.

She and Lachlan had been away on a month-long trip in the campervan she'd built to the south of England, taking advantage of the quiet period before the tourist season began and their campsite started filling up. They'd messaged the family group chat to say they were home the night before but clearly weren't hanging around, getting straight back to work distilling the gin that they'd created and which was making a name for itself locally. Lachlan had owned a brewery with his friend Gus when he'd lived down in Edinburgh, but when he'd returned to the Highlands and got together with Rilla, he'd switched track and together they'd added Applemore Gin to their portfolio of businesses designed to keep the little estate going.

'Have I missed much?'

'Not a lot.' Beth looked around the converted dairy where they made the gin. There was a tangled heap of woody herbs sitting on the granite worktop, and in the corner of the room the copper stills they used to make the gin glowed gently in the early morning light that shone in through the window. 'Well, apart from the fact that Simon's girlfriend is pregnant, he's giving up work and becoming a house-husband and I'm having a minor panic about how to make up the shortfall moneywise.' She grimaced as she spoke. Saying it out loud sent a horrible cold feeling down her spine.

'Pregnant?' Rilla looked up quickly, an odd expression on her face. 'He can't do that, can he?'

'He can. Well, he is.' She noticed that she sounded remarkably laid-back for someone who'd been awake fuming about it half the night.

'Surely you can stop him?' Rilla lifted the lid of the copper still, sniffed and made a face. 'That does not smell right,' she said, half to herself. 'It smells disgusting, in fact.'

'It's up to him. If he wants to, I'll just have to get on with it.' Beth lifted her chin slightly. 'At the end of the day, I haven't got much choice.' She leaned over. 'It smells fine to me?'

Rilla grimaced, putting a hand to her mouth as if she was going to throw up. Through her fingers, she continued. 'We've got the money from the brewery. D'you want me to have a chat to Lachlan? I'm sure he'd –'

'No,' said Beth, firmly. She shook her head.

'I'm sure we could sort something,' continued Rilla, hopefully.

'Honestly, no.' Beth put a hand down on the cold granite surface, feeling it chilling her fingertips. She shivered. 'My mess, I'll sort it.'

'Any other news?' Rilla took a cloth and started wiping the pile of herbs into a plastic tub. 'Ooh,' she said, before Beth had a chance to speak 'I have some. Not great for us, and definitely not for Polly. I haven't spoken to her about it yet. Have you heard they're talking about turning the old village store into a mini supermarket?'

'Shit.' Beth frowned. 'Seriously?'

'Apparently so. There's rumours that they've put in a planning application, or something. I heard last night at the garage when we were filling up the van on the way home.'

The village shop had closed eighteen months ago, and Polly's farm shop had taken over to a certain extent – although lots of the older villagers caught the bus into the town eight miles away for their shopping, and Beth suspected that a mini-supermarket would be a big hit, and it would have a major impact on Polly's finances. The financial blows seemed to be coming thick and fast.

'I bags not being the one to tell her.' Poor Poll, Beth thought, imagining the look on her irrepressible younger sister's face when she heard the news. She'd worked seven days a week on the farm shop over the last year and a half, turning it from a disused farm building into a thriving hub of the community. But a shop in the middle of the village was going to be far easier for locals than having to jump in the car and drive the three miles to Applemore every time they wanted something. It looked like it wouldn't only be her trying to find new ways to make money…

Having instructed Rilla on where to find the rosemary and mint she needed in the re-organised greenhouse, Beth headed into town. There she found that once again she bumped into Jack MacDonald.

'This is beginning to be a bit of a habit,' he said, grinning. He was standing outside the cottage he was renting, a ladder propped up against the wall, with Mrs Birnie from the little harbour cottage next door standing beside him beaming happily. Mrs Birnie had been Beth's primary school teacher years before and she'd been elderly then. At eighty, she was still spry and full of energy, but Beth was relieved that she'd at least conceded that maybe climbing a ladder was beyond her.

'Ah, Beth, lovely to see you,' she said, her wrinkled cheeks lifting in a smile that lit up her face. 'I see you've met my hero.'

Beth looked at Jack with a dubious expression. 'Your hero?'

'He's an angel, this laddie. He's unblocked the gutters.

We've got a storm forecast, you know, and I've been on at my son Robert to sort them for months now, and along comes Jack and – hey presto.'

Jack shifted from one foot to the other, looking slightly uncomfortable.

'Well I hope he's better with gutters than he is with poly-tunnels,' said Beth, archly.

'What's that?' Mrs Birnie looked from Beth to Jack. Her hearing wasn't what it had been, and she had a habit of shouting, which drove Robert mad. He'd taken her shopping for a top-of-the-range hearing aid but she didn't like to wear it ('I don't want to wear it out,' she'd explained to Beth the last time they'd met in the street).

Jack shook his head, smiling despite her teasing. 'Let's say we got off on the wrong foot,' he explained, tying the top of the garden refuse sack and pulling the ladder down so it telescoped back to normal size. 'I'll take this back round to the garden for you.'

'Well I think he's going to be a right boon here in the village, no matter what other people might say,' said Mrs Birnie, to his retreating back. If he heard, which Beth suspected he did, he didn't let on. She carried on as he disappeared out of sight. 'I suppose you've heard that everyone's up in arms about the place being overrun with tearaway teenagers.'

Beth nodded, feeling slightly guilty that she'd had the same thought. Now she'd met Jack, she could see that he seemed the sort of steady, level-headed person who'd be able to deal with troubled teens without getting stressed about it. 'I had, yes. I suspect once everyone sees that they're no trouble they'll realise it's not a big deal. When are they arriving?'

'A couple of days, I think,' said Mrs Birnie. She looked

thoughtful. 'I'd have liked to do something like that myself, you know. It's a bit late for all that now.'

'Never too late,' smiled Beth. 'Maybe you could get out for a spot of kayaking, or doing some mountain climbing.'

'Maybe indeed,' chuckled Mrs Birnie, pulling her cardigan around her shoulders.

Beth delivered more flowers to Harry at the Applemore Inn, and headed back to the car where she was parked along the road from the row of cottages. Jack was standing outside talking to a woman in a grey polo-necked jumper, her slim legs clad in black jeans and expensive-looking boots. Beth reflexively brushed at the front of her fleece, which was covered in stray bits of compost from grubbing around in the greenhouse earlier.

'I was just talking about you,' Jack said, beckoning her over.

'You were?' She jingled the car keys in her hand, feeling suddenly very scruffy and un-chic compared to the woman who was now looking at her with a curious expression.

'You're right,' she said, turning to Jack, 'She'd be perfect.'

'I would?' Beth realised slightly too late that she was sounding like a complete idiot.

'I'm Gina Lewis from Green Lion Productions. We're an independent company making a show for the BBC about life up here in the Highlands. Unfortunately a couple of our potential subjects have had to pull out at short notice due to, er, family issues, and we're looking for someone who'd be happy to take part.'

Beth shook her head, eyes widening. 'I'm definitely not television material.'

'I think you'd be great,' said Jack, looking at her with his direct, dark-eyed gaze.

'Really not,' said Beth. 'Why don't you do it?'

A fleeting look of something she couldn't quite name passed across Jack's face. His eyes darted to the side and he gave a slightly too hearty laugh. 'It's not really my thing. I'm more outdoors and just getting on with it.'

'As am I,' said Beth, firmly.

'Just think of all the polytunnel repairs you could pay for if you did it.'

'I wouldn't need any polytunnel repairs done if *someone* didn't keep dropping trees on it.'

'If you will insist on leaving your polytunnel parked right underneath my treehouse,' Jack said, laughing, 'this wouldn't be a problem.'

'I think you'd *both* be great, actually,' said Gina, looking delighted. 'You'd work really well together on camera.'

'Together?' Beth and Jack said, in unison.

'Jack said your flower farm place adjoins his?'

'It does,' admitted Beth, 'But…'

'I don't think it's exactly my thing,' said Jack, taking a physical step backwards as if to underline his reluctance. At the same moment, a lightbulb went off in Beth's head.

'Do we get paid?'

'Of course,' said Gina, brightly, naming a sum that would make up for at least six months of Simon's soon-to-be-disappearing child maintenance. 'And of course there's the publicity, which is invaluable.'

'I'll do it if you will,' Beth blurted out, suddenly brave. God, she had to do something, and this seemed like the perfect opportunity landing straight in her lap. Maybe the publicity would lead to loads of new business. And at least she didn't have any skeletons in the closet waiting to tumble out. Her life had been spectacularly dull until now.

'I…' Jack rubbed at his hair, so the dark spikes stood up

on end untidily. He frowned, and for a moment Beth was convinced he was going to say no. She could see the conflict playing out on his face as his brow furrowed in thought.

'Oh go on,' said Gina, warmly. 'It's only a few hours filming, and it would be utterly fab publicity for your place.' She rubbed her hands together. 'Hopefully it might warm up a bit soon, too. Gosh, your Highland springs are chilly, aren't they?'

'Might help people up here see that you're doing a good thing,' Beth said, without thinking. Jack shot her a look as soon as she spoke, but Gina's journalistic instincts were on it immediately.

'Oh, we love a bit of controversy,' she said, cheerfully. 'Have you put the cat among the pigeons, then?'

Jack shook his head vehemently. 'Not at all. We're just an unknown quantity, that's all. And you know what small towns are like.'

'Oh yes I do,' said Gina, cosily. She put a hand on his arm. 'I think you'd be perfect, as I said.'

'Go on,' urged Beth. 'I'm game if you are. You're supposed to be the one who likes challenges.'

Jack groaned. 'Fine. But if this all goes wrong, you owe me one.'

'If it all goes wrong,' Beth reminded him, archly, 'You can call it quits for the polytunnel vandalism.'

He gave a rueful grin. 'You've got me there.'

CHAPTER SIX

A WEEK LATER, Jack leaned back against the log cabin that was the activity centre headquarters and gave a sigh of relief. The first group of teenagers from a specialist school near Glasgow had just left, and they'd managed an entire programme of outdoor activities without incident.

'That went well,' said Danny, watching as the minibus bumped down the single-track road away from the centre.

'It's a blooming miracle,' said Jack, turning to look at the jumble of wetsuits that lay on the veranda waiting to be sorted. There had been a couple of slightly hairy moments on the first day when two of the lads had – egging each other on – started messing around with the equipment and he'd had to separate them, sending one on a fictional mission to help chop down a tree which had made him feel like top dog, and the other helping him with something. But keeping busy had meant he hadn't had a moment to think about what he'd signed up for, and despite bumping into Beth continually the week before, he hadn't seen her once.

He'd finally met Lachlan, her older brother, when he'd

been out walking his dogs in the woods with his girlfriend. Archie had been delighted to romp with the three spaniels and they'd stood and chatted for a while. Once again, he'd been surprised by how normal and down to earth he'd seemed – they both had – despite living in an actual castle, complete with turrets. He shook his head. It still blew his mind to think of people living in a place like that.

The good news was that the next set of visitors was a group who were using the bunkhouse for a team-building activity, so they'd be sorting themselves out and all he had to do was facilitate the activities alongside Danny and the other team members. That, and work out how he was going to deal with the fact he'd agreed to a TV show – partly because he'd seen it as a chance to get to know Beth better – when there was absolutely no way he could do that sort of thing. It wasn't worth the risk. He'd have to get Danny on board – he'd probably love the chance for his fifteen minutes of fame on television.

He went into the cabin to make a coffee before he got to work clearing up. Wiping up the kitchen, waiting for the kettle to boil, he wondered how Beth was getting on. He'd been into the farm shop a couple of times, picking up bread and some bits and pieces, but he hadn't bumped into her again. He'd had an email from Gina at the TV production company with some forms to sign – disclaimers and suchlike – which he'd forwarded on to head office down in Glasgow, half-hoping that someone would flag it up as unsuitable, but they'd been utterly delighted at the prospect of free public- ity. The only person with misgivings, it seemed, was him. Realistically speaking – he looked around at the cabin, which was still pristine and welcoming, with a half-circle of chairs set around the log burner from an end-of-session chat earlier – this was the perfect time to show off what they did, and the difference their work made. It was just – well. If someone saw his face and put two and two together…

He shook himself. The chances were minimal. Maybe it was time to start living life and forget about the shadows of the past?

An hour later, having hung up the wetsuits to dry off and banked up the log burner, he headed out, wandering round the perimeter of the grounds to check that nothing had been left lying around. At least that's what he told himself he was doing – the reality was he was half-hoping that he might bump into Beth on his travels, and have a chance for a chat. The villagers he'd bumped into in town so far had been slightly wary, in the main – it was clear that they were still expecting the outdoor centre to be a non-stop supply of freshly delivered trouble-makers from the inner cities, and he was being eyed with suspicion as a result. There was a village meeting coming up, and he'd told Danny that the two of them were going to go and be as charming and open as possible in an attempt to assuage the fears that people seemed to have. Hopefully the fact that the first set of residential guests had come and gone without incident would go in their favour.

He wandered through the wooded path, inhaling the scent of the pine trees and listening to the gentle crackle of twigs underfoot. Spring was on the way – the late afternoon air was filled with the sound of birds, and everywhere he looked trees and bushes were on the verge of coming to life, leaf buds bursting out everywhere. Through the trees, he could see the sea in the distance, and beyond that the purple outlines of the islands. As if drawn there inexplicably, he turned, heading down the path that led down to the tiny beach that belonged to Applemore House. There was an ancient wooden sign on the wooden stile that marked the path as private, but he decided he'd take the risk. It wove between two fields, hedgerows on either side hazed green with the beginnings of leaf growth, looking like they'd been caught half-dressed. He stepped over a muddy puddle, noticing fresh footprints on the ground. Probably one of the Frasers out walking their dogs. He'd met all four siblings now – it was surprising to him as an only child how different each of them was. Lachlan was friendly and approachable, laid back in his manner, and didn't seem at all grand despite owning the big house which lent its name to the village. Charlotte, who he'd met first, he'd bumped into at the shop the other day. She was brisk and always on the go, very different to her youngest sister Polly, who kept the farm shop going with her cheerful, outgoing manner. And then there was Beth, who was – he paused, putting a hand up to shade his eyes – was there someone on the beach? He thought he saw something at the top of the dunes, then shook his head, looking again. He'd come this far now, he'd just have to risk it.

He strode across the ploughed field and onto the bright grass of the *machair* – exclusive to the Highlands, and one of the rarest habitats on earth. It fascinated him – the idea that this stretch of seemingly innocuous-looking grassland along the edge of the Atlantic could produce a wildflower display which was out of this world, thanks to the fragments of seashells that blew up from the dunes and fertilised the sandy soil. He stopped for a moment to listen to the two-note call of the tiny ringed plovers, with half an ear out for the distinctive sound of the corncrake – the rare birds which returned to the Highlands and islands each spring from their winter in Africa. No sign yet – it was probably a bit early, but he knew that later in the season the coastline would be populated by patiently waiting birders, who'd stand with their scopes for hours waiting for a sighting.

There was a dip in the dunes where a track led him down to the white sand of the beach, which stretched out towards an impossibly blue sea. And – he hadn't been seeing things – there by the water was Beth, bent over a tiny toddler in bright red wellie boots, and a few metres away from her was another, wielding a huge piece of driftwood almost as big as the child itself. As if aware of his eyes on her, she turned around.

'Hi.' She waved as he walked towards the trio.

'Sorry,' he said with an open-handed gesture. 'I saw the sign. I know it's private, but I –'

Beth laughed. The wind had whipped long strands of blonde hair free from her ponytail and she tried in vain to push it back from her face. 'Oh God, that sign is from about fifty years ago. It's a beach, it doesn't belong to anyone.' She bent down again to take a seashell from the hand of one of the children. 'Thank you, darling.'

'Yours?' He gestured to the children, who were now bending over and poking at a piece of seaweed with the huge stick.

She nodded. 'Edward and Lucy.' Both children looked up hearing their names.

'Are we going to have ice cream?'

'It's a bit cold for ice cream,' Beth laughed, rubbing her hands on her arms to warm them.

'But you promised,' said the little girl, and Jack immediately recognised the flashpoint that could trigger the kind of tantrum only a three-year-old could have.

'Hello,' he said, distracting her. 'I'm Jack. I like ice cream in winter, too' he said, glancing at Beth, who raised her eyes heavenward. 'It's like eating snow, isn't it?'

Edward nodded solemnly. 'I like it too.'

'Fine,' said Beth, laughing, 'I promised ice cream, so ice cream it'll be. We'll drive up to Aunty Polly's shop after this and get some. Okay?'

'Yes please,' said Lucy, earnestly. Mollified, they went back to poking at the seaweed.

'Twins?' said Jack, realising as soon as he'd spoken that she'd probably heard that a million times.

Beth nodded. 'Yes. And no, they're not identical, and yes, they're a bit of a handful, and no, I'm not planning any more.'

'I asked for that,' he said, turning his collar up against the biting wind. It didn't feel much like spring here on the beach with the wind whipping across the sea. 'I bet you get the third degree every time you go anywhere.'

'I do,' agreed Beth. 'And now I get the whole *aren't you amazing doing it all by yourself* spiel as well, since getting divorced.' She made a face.

'It is pretty impressive,' he said, watching as the twins scampered up the pale sand, giggling and then falling over dramatically with squeals of glee. 'I mean you've got a lot on your hands.'

'I suppose.' Beth gazed at the twins. She had no make-up on, and her upturned nose was scattered with freckles which made her look very young. 'I'm lucky, I've got lots of help – I couldn't do it without the childminder and the nursery and my ex has them quite a bit of the time, so...' she tailed off. 'Anyway, enough about how amazing I am,' she gave him a teasing look. 'How are you getting on? Did you get an email about the TV show?'

'I did. Not sure what we're letting ourselves in for, but I can't blame you for that as I was the one who pushed for it.'

'Yeah,' she looked down at the ground, tracing a pattern

in the sand with her toe, then looked up at him from under surprisingly long lashes. 'I'm blaming you if they do some sort of hideous expose and my business is ruined.'

Ironic, thought Jack. 'I can't imagine you've got many secrets hidden.'

'Little do you know,' she said, teasingly. 'But seriously, no. I can't imagine what's interesting about a flower farm, to be honest, but I suspect most of my bit will end up on the cutting room floor.'

'I think you're doing yourself down. From what Polly was telling me when I was at the shop the other day you did an amazing job of creating the whole thing from scratch.'

Beth looked embarrassed. 'God, Polly. I love her but she's got such a habit of shooting her mouth off.'

'You should be glad. I think it's nice that you all look out for each other.'

'I suppose we do,' said Beth, starting to walk along the shoreline as the twins ran ahead. 'I think because we grew up here as a close unit with just our dad, it sort of became a habit.'

'No mum?' He'd imagined them growing up in a very traditional unit to match their traditional old-fashioned country estate.

Beth shook her head. 'Not in the water, Lucy,' she called ahead. 'No, our mum left when we were really young. Dad brought us up – it was sort of happy chaos. Cold, happy chaos.'

'Cold?'

'The house was always bloody freezing. The roof leaked. Lachlan's sorted it all now, but it wasn't the cosiest place to live. We basically camped out every winter in the kitchen. No wonder we're all close, when we had to live in each other's pockets.'

'I had visions of you all roller-skating along the west wing as children when I saw Applemore.'

Beth laughed. 'Oh, there was loads of that – we used to ride our bikes on the gallery but Joan – she was the house-keeper – would go mad if we did. But there were no carpets up there and it was perfect for playing in the winter.'

'A bit different to growing up in a flat in Glasgow,' Jack said, thoughtfully.

'A bit,' conceded Beth. 'But I spent as much time as I could at my friend's house – she lived in the village and their place was tiny and warm and cosy. I think that's partly why I escaped as early as I could and moved to the farmhouse.'

'I take it these two aren't riding their bikes around the corridors there?'

'Definitely not.' Beth laughed. 'It's very much an aver-age-sized family house.'

'I'm surprised,' he admitted, as Edward dashed back towards them and Beth swooped him up into her arms, pushing his hair back from his forehead and giving him a kiss, 'I honestly thought you were all going to be a lot –' he searched for the word.

'Posher?' Beth put Edward back down, taking his hand. 'You're heavy, darling. It's because you're three, now.'

'We're having a party,' Edward informed him solemnly. 'We were three. And Aunty Charlotte is making a cake.'

'That sounds good,' said Jack, smiling down at him. 'I like cake.'

'Can you come to our party?' Edward looked at his mother. 'Can he?'

'I'm sure Jack has plenty of grown-up things to be doing,' said Beth, kindly.

'I want Jack to come,' said Edward.

'We'll see,' said Beth, wisely. Jack hid a smile. It was

funny watching toddlers – it didn't seem that long since Anna had been that age, and in another way it seemed like a lifetime ago. He felt a pang of longing for the little girl she'd been, and wondered once again if he'd get back to find she'd replied to his messages. It had been so long.

'Anyway, to get back to what we were saying,' Beth continued, 'I'm glad we've managed to dispel your preconceptions now you know we're not actually dining off gold plates and changing into black tie for dinner.'

'I didn't say that,' he protested.

'I'm teasing you.' She looked at him sideways, a smile playing on her lips.

'I hadn't thought before about how much work there was keeping a place like this going. It's a big change, coming from Glasgow to live in a tiny village like Applemore.'

'How's your second in command doing? Danny, isn't it?'

'He's working hard, which I think is making up for the lack of nightclubs and social opportunities.'

'There's always the pub. And the hotel – Harry's done lots with it, and it's actually quite busy at nights now. Not that I get out much,' she said, as an afterthought.

'Yeah, there's a village meeting coming out. That's something to look forward to.'

'Very funny. He does do a quiz night, that's a good laugh. Miranda – she works with me three days a week – keeps nagging me to go.'

'Danny mentioned it. Maybe we could make up a team?' He was surprised to hear himself saying.

'That sounds like fun.'

'Okay. It's a date.'

Beth looked at him with raised eyebrows and her expression made him burst out laughing.

'Steady on,' she said, putting both hands up in front of her chest. 'I know you city types move a bit faster than us country bumpkins but I don't think we're at the dating stage just yet.'

'Very funny,' he said, shaking his head. 'It's a figure of speech.'

'I know.' She stopped and crossed her arms, looking at him thoughtfully. 'Seriously though, it'll be nice to get out. Between work and these two I seem to have forgotten to have a life.'

'It's easily done.'

She reached into her pocket and pulled out a couple of chocolate biscuits. 'If I don't feed them something now, they'll hit meltdown point before we get back to the car.'

'I remember it well,' said Jack, unthinkingly.

'Oh – you've got children?'

'One. A daughter. Anna.'

'I didn't realise.' Beth looked slightly uncomfortable. 'Is your wife back in Glasgow?'

He shook his head. 'No, no wife. We're divorced. Anna lives with her mum. They're in Paris.'

'That must be hard?'

He exhaled slowly. 'Yeah. It's not great.'

'Has she always lived there? Did you live there before?' Beth stopped herself, putting a hand to her mouth. 'Sorry, I didn't mean to fire off twenty questions at you.'

'It's okay. No, her mum was offered a dream job opportunity in France and I didn't think I could stand in the way. She's better off with her, because – well...' He tailed off. She was better off with her mum, there was no two ways about it. Over there, living on Rebecca's salary, she could have everything she wanted.

'Must be hard for you though, having her so far away.'

He cleared his throat. ''Tis a bit, especially at the moment. She hasn't taken the move particularly well.'

'Oh?'

'I'm public enemy number one for facilitating it.'

'Ah. Yeah, the dads-and-daughters thing is tricky, isn't it? I had some massive fights with mine growing up.'

Jack thought about his own dad for a fleeting moment. Most of the time he tried to put him out of his mind, but right then he could hear his voice in his head and it made a shiver - which was nothing to do with the chill wind – spiral down his spine.

'I guess she'll get over it in time,' he said, a moment later. 'I hope so, anyway.'

They walked back up the track together, taking it slowly to keep pace with the twins, and paused at the fork in the trees which led back towards the log cabin.

'I'll give you a shout about the pub quiz,' he said, putting his hands in his pockets and watching as the twins – re-energised by their chocolate biscuits – gambolled around in the pine needles of the woodland floor, giggling and making silly noises.

'I'll see you before then,' said Beth, 'If you're coming to this village meeting?'

'Wouldn't miss it for the world,' he said, mock-sincerely.

'It's a date,' she said, turning away, but not before he caught the amused expression on her face.

CHAPTER SEVEN

'LET ME GET THIS STRAIGHT,' Miranda tore the wrapper off a packet of chocolate fingers and offered them round, sitting down on an upturned plastic drum before she continued. 'So you bumped into some random person in the street and agreed to be on a TV show without mulling it over for three weeks?'

Beth nodded.

Miranda made a curious face and leaned forward, tugging at her sleeve teasingly. 'And you're definitely still Beth Fraser, and you haven't been body-swapped with aliens?'

'Definitely still me.'

'You've got to admit,' said Phoebe, nibbling thoughtfully on the edge of a biscuit which she stared at intently for a moment, 'It's not exactly your usual style.'

'I thought I'd mix things up a bit.'

'Normal people say that and try a different colour of eyeshadow,' said Phoebe, who was always beautifully – if impractically, one might argue – made up in a rainbow of colours. Today she was wearing a pair of patchwork rainbow dungarees, with one green and one red Doc Marten boot, and eye make-up that wouldn't have been out of place on a catwalk. Her hands, however, were covered in compost and she had a smudge of mud on the end of her nose. Beth smiled to herself at the sight.

'Well I think it's a good thing.' Miranda passed round mugs of steaming coffee. They'd been working hard since before first light, determined to get an unexpectedly big order of tulips packed and ready to be delivered that morning. It was only 8.30 now, and Phoebe stifled a yawn.

'I really appreciate you two coming in this early,' Beth said.

'No probs.' Miranda dipped a biscuit in her drink. 'The alternative was lying in bed listening to next door having a bit of early-morning excitement – I'm not sure who she's met, but they seem to be very hot on before-work sex and the dividing walls in our houses are not thick enough. Seriously, I think I need to get some earplugs.'

'Or if you can't beat 'em, join 'em, as my granny would say.' Phoebe giggled. 'You need to get back on the online dating.'

'I've come to the conclusion that online dating doesn't work in a village this size. You can pretty much guarantee who you're going to see on there because you've bumped into them at the Applemore Hotel bar the weekend before. Plus the jungle drums are so bloody bad round here that as soon as you meet someone everyone has you married off…'

'And you tried to persuade me to do it?' Beth raised an eyebrow.

'Safety in numbers. Anyway, you're sorted now you've got the hot Glaswegian on the case.'

Phoebe did a double take. 'You what?'

'Why d'you think she's signed up for this TV show? We've been friends with her for ages and she's been like a blooming church mouse, keeping herself to herself. The next thing we know she's bumped into Mr SAS rescue and she's agreeing to be on national TV.'

'Hardly.' Beth felt her cheeks going pink. 'I happened to think it was a good business opportunity.'

Miranda and Phoebe exchanged meaningful looks.

'Shut up, you two or I'll find two other suckers who want to get out of bed and grub around cutting tulips at half six in the... oh, wait.'

'My point exactly. So you're stuck with us, and we want all the gossip, don't we, Phoebs?'

'There is no gossip.'

'You've got to admit you wouldn't kick him out of bed, though,' said Miranda, taking another biscuit and licking it lasciviously.

'Urgh, Miranda,' Phoebe said, sticking out her tongue in horror, 'Please never do that again.'

'What?' She licked the biscuit again, eyes wide, making an exaggerated face. 'That?'

'I'm going to be sick.' Phoebe made gagging noises.

'Me too. If I promise to tell you everything, will you promise to never do that to a Cadbury's chocolate finger ever again?' Beth shook her head. How on earth she'd ended up running a business with these two was beyond her. 'More to the point, please don't do anything like that when the TV crew eventually do turn up, or you'll end up getting arrested.'

Miranda shoved the whole biscuit in her mouth and motioned to indicate that she wasn't going to make another sound.

'Okay,' explained Beth. 'So they had two other people

who were meant to be part of this two-part show they're doing about the impact of tourism on Highland communities, and interviewing travellers as well as people who live here. Anyway, for whatever reason they dropped out, and Jack –'

'*Jack*,' said Phoebe, in a silly voice.

'Jack,' continued Beth firmly, 'happened to bump into the producer and get chatting in the village, and he happened to see me and suggest that it might be a good opportunity, and that's why we're here.'

'So when are we expecting the film crew and the whole production thingy? Are they bringing massive big caravans and lorries?' Phoebe looked excited.

'One camera operator, the producer, and a sound person.'

'Oh,' Phoebe sagged. 'I was hoping this might be my big break and I'd be discovered and be whisked off to Hollywood.'

'I didn't realise you wanted to act.' Miranda looked at her quizzically.

Phoebe shrugged. 'I don't. But I wouldn't mind going to Hollywood. Applemore's bloody freezing, and I quite fancy a nice house by the beach.'

'You've *got* a nice house by the beach,' pointed out Beth, 'And I suspect that the chances of being whisked off to find your fame and fortune after being featured for five seconds on a TV show about summer holidays in the Highlands are pretty slim.'

'I can dream,' said Phoebe. She was sitting on the potting table, swinging her rainbow legs, gazing into the middle distance. It was a constant source of amazement to Beth that Phoebe managed to get anything done, when she was perpetually daydreaming. But despite this, she had a smart business head underneath the dreamy exterior – she'd managed to gather a huge following on Instagram where she took daily photographs of her outfits and make up companies sent her expensive samples in the hope she'd show them off in her designs. It was Phoebe who'd pointed out that a daily record of the flower farm on Instagram was an easy way of gaining publicity – well, easy-ish, thought Beth. She scanned around the greenhouse, aware she had to find something pretty to photograph. The pictures were having an effect, though – she'd noticed that the number of orders for the boxed tulips they packaged up on Tuesdays and Fridays were double what they'd been the year before. That was a start, but she still had to work out how to make more money.

'You can dream,' agreed Beth, finally, looking at her phone to see what the time was, 'But you probably better dream whilst driving to college. If you don't get going now, you'll be late.'

Phoebe grabbed a handful of biscuits and scooted off, car keys jingling.

'That girl,' said Miranda, laughing.

'I love her. She's a complete nutcase, but I love her.' Beth threw the now-cold remains of her coffee out of the greenhouse door and rubbed her face. 'I am exhausted. I'm fine if I keep moving, it's if I stop I realise that I could sleep for a week.' She covered her mouth as a huge yawn appeared as if summoned by the prospect of sleep.

'Twins still getting up at hideous o'clock?'

'They weren't even here last night, they were with Simon and Morag. I swear I'm more tired when I get some sleep.'

'That sounds familiar. It only lasts about seventeen years, if it's any consolation. Then you're up half the night waiting for them to come home and they sleep until lunchtime and you still have to get up and go to work.'

'Why does nobody tell you this stuff before you have children?'

'They do,' said Miranda, sagely, 'It's just none of us actually listen. It's why the human race continues.'

'That's comforting,' said Beth, drily. 'Right, I'm going to get on.'

The walled garden of Applemore House had once been the pride and joy of the Fraser family. When the house was built in 1859, Hermione Fraser, wife of one of a long line of James Frasers, had insisted to the builders from Glasgow that yes, she really did want a lean-to glasshouse along the entirety of one wall, and no, she didn't think it was too cold to grow fruit in the chilly climate of the north-west of Scotland. She'd worked hard, training fruit bushes and espaliered trees along the walls, filling the beds with salad vegetables and enough produce that the house was almost self-sufficient. In their father's study there was a huge leather-covered photo album full of pictures of Hermione, her pointed chin (which Polly had pointed out was very similar to Beth's) raised slightly, as she looked at the camera with an expression which suggested she wasn't to be messed with.

Her iron-willed determination ran down through the female line of the Fraser family. It was stamped through Beth Fraser as if printed on a stick of seaside rock. It was just as well, Beth reflected, as she tried later that morning to balance her broken phone tripod on a pile of pale golden stacked bricks. They'd crumbled from the top of the wall and were now piled up on the side of an empty border, waiting for Beth to sort them out.

'So what I'm doing today…' she began, and then swore as the tripod seemed to topple forward of its own accord and her mobile phone crashed down onto the ground. 'What I'm doing today,' she continued, talking to herself, 'is wasting a huge chunk of time that could be spent planting on the second lot of sweet peas, instead of attempting to make a video for Instagram.'

She picked up the phone and turned it over. The screen was covered in a spider's web of cracks, obscuring a cute picture of Edward and Lucy on the beach in wellies and waterproof overalls. She traced a finger across their cheeks. Please, please let them have settled well at nursery this morning. She felt a jolt of longing to squeeze them both onto her lap and cuddle up on the sofa watching *Sarah and Duck*, or one of the other programmes they loved, but – she shook her head, trying to erase the thought – there was no point in focusing on that. They weren't coming home to her this evening. She had a whole day and a night to get work done, and it was the busiest time of the year for a flower farmer. She put the phone in her pocket. Maybe it was a sign that she wasn't supposed to think about such mundane things, but should instead be focusing on what mattered. And what mattered right now was a greenhouse groaning at the seams with young annual plants, which were desperate to be potted on. The twins would be fine with their father – Beth pulled a face. Simon had called the other day and been perfectly pleasant but the subject of his plans hadn't come up, and she'd decided that she was going to deal with things sequentially and not get stressed out.

On a plus note, at least Simon hadn't stayed with the secretary with whom he'd had an affair. That had died out pretty quickly, although he hadn't hung about in meeting Morag – but at least she was nice enough, even if they'd never be best friends. Not like that other woman. Beth reached forward and snipped vigorously at the head of a dying plant with secateurs – there was no way she could have been civil with her. Just the thought of it made her feel quite murderous, even now, when the conflict had faded into the past.

She headed back to the greenhouse. Even in the eighteen months since Lachlan had moved back to Applemore, there had been lots of changes. Growing up in the draughty, slightly leaky big house they'd played as children in the walled garden, where their single parent dad had felt happy to know that the four siblings couldn't get up to much mischief in an acre of confined space where the broken wooden door was jammed stiffly shut against the cracked frame. She paused for a moment, putting a hand against the rough wood of the door that led into the garden. When they'd grown up the paint had peeled away in satisfying shards if you worried at it with a curious finger. Beth had sanded it back last autumn, treating the wood and painting it a pale, sage green. She'd rolled up her sleeves and painted the woodwork of the greenhouses that ran the whole length of one of the walls the same colour.

She leant against the wall, feeling the gentle heat of the bricks through her shirt. The April sunshine seemed to have brought everything to life. Standing still, she could almost hear the rustle of new leaves unfurling. Close by, a couple of early bees were buzzing industriously. She swept her hand along the top of the lavender hedge, eliciting a scent redolent of lazy late summer afternoons. If she closed her eyes and imagined, it could be early on an August morning.

But closing her eyes and imagining wasn't going to get

anything done, and she had just over twenty-four hours before she had to pick up Lucy and Edward from nursery school. She shook her head, bringing herself back to the present. There was so much to do.

When she'd decided to renovate the garden, it had seemed like a fairly straightforward job – cut the grass, tidy the edges, dig over the beds. Only it had been years since anyone had maintained the place, and every single bed had been a snarling tangle of bramble cables and bindweed. Now each bed was dug out, neatly edged, and crammed full of plants and flowers which she used to create the individualistic, hand-tied bouquets she sold through the summer months. They'd helped her to grow her name, but she needed to scale the business up. If there was one thing she'd learned, it was that while pottering around doing the mundane tasks, absorbed in something repetitive, that she found ideas would spring to her. The wicker baskets she'd spent time working on in winter were a perfect example – out of season, she'd been trying to work out a way to make extra money and they sold like hot cakes. Each little wicker basket was stuffed full of pretty miniature narcissi and muscari. which had been planted to come into bloom in time for Mothers' Day, and she'd driven around lots of the local shops offering them for sale as well as selling them direct at the farm shop. Winter had been full of all the usual unglamorous jobs – mulching paths, digging over beds so they could be broken down by the frost, planting late bulbs, all with freezing fingers and an almost permanent drip on the end of her nose. She'd struggled to find pretty pictures to share online in the middle of winter, and resorted to cheering herself up by re-using old photos of sun-drenched beds of astilbe and larkspur, asters and lupins from the year before, which her followers seemed to love. She shook herself. This wasn't getting anything done.

A few hours later, she looked at her work with a glow of satisfaction. The sweet peas were growing at a rate of knots, and the tulip beds were coming on so fast she could swear if she stood still and listened she'd hear the gentle rustle of their leaves shifting and stretching upwards towards the spring sunshine, aided by the warmth of the greenhouse and the heat of the radiator, which was making a huge difference to how things came on this year.

Best of all, she'd had a brainwave, and – she brushed compost from her jeans – Charlotte had sent a message to say that she was heading to Applemore for lunch if she wanted to join her. She put her hands in the small of her back and stretched, realising she'd been bent over for ages. Lunch at the big house was a far nicer prospect than the slightly squashed cheese sandwiches that had been lurking on the passenger seat of the car since six that morning.

She could hear shouts of laughter from across the garden wall as she walked through the trees to the house. It was nice, despite her misgivings, having a bit of life in the countryside around the garden. She often caught a glimpse of Danny and Jack as she worked – they'd be perched in the treehouse that overlooked the garden with a gathering of teenagers, snatches of music or chatter carrying on the wind. They always waved a hello. It had been a few weeks since the outdoor centre opened and so far it had been problem free – she felt a bit guilty that she'd secretly braced herself for trouble. She was also dying to know exactly what they did, but didn't feel that she could turn up unannounced and ask, although – she found herself smiling at the thought – she could always lob half a tree in their direction and use it as an excuse?

'What's the joke?' Charlotte was climbing out of her car when she walked into the back courtyard of Applemore.

Beth shook her head. 'Nothing,' she lied.

'I'll extract it from you over lunch,' said Charlotte, brandishing a brown paper bag. 'I've got some of Anna's amazing new white chocolate and raspberry blondies. If that doesn't get your secrets out of you, nothing will...'

Beth shook her head. 'Honestly, you can't have any bloody secrets in this family, can you?'

'Not one.' Charlotte held the door open as the three liver-and-white spaniels hurtled out from the kitchen in a blur of wagging, wriggling excitement. 'Hello, dogs.'

Beth bent over to stroke their silky ears. 'Hugh's getting a bit podge, isn't he?'

'Don't say that to Rilla,' Charlotte laughed.

'Say what?' Rilla emerged from the boot room, re-tying her hair back in its habitual ponytail.

'Charlotte thinks your dog is a podge.'

'I do not. *Beth* says she thinks you're overfeeding him.'

'Don't,' said Rilla, shaking her head in despair. 'He just has to look at food and he puts on about three kilos. I'm trying to get him to lose weight, but he's clearly got a very efficient metabolism. If he got stranded at the North Pole he'd survive for days on nothing.'

'Think about what he was like when you got him?' Beth rubbed the top of his head and he gazed at her with adoration. 'He was skin and bone.'

'Now he's definitely not that.' They headed into the kitchen and Rilla opened the door of the Aga, pulling out a huge saucepan. 'Lachlan made soup before he left for Glasgow.'

'I still can't believe he ended up being so good at cooking,' said Charlotte, taking a loaf of bread from the deep stone window-ledge, where it was cooling on a metal rack.

'Just as well one of us is,' said Rilla. 'If it was up to me we'd be living on toast and cereal with a side of chocolate.' She got out four plates and laid them on the table.

'So what's been happening?'

'Where's Poll?' Charlotte poked at the butter. 'This is rock hard. If I stick it on the Aga for a couple of moments it might defrost.'

'She's on her way,' said Rilla. 'A delivery turned up just as she was leaving. She said start without her, but I said we'd wait. Meanwhile I want to hear all the news I've missed.'

'You say that like you haven't seen us for a month,' said Charlotte, laughing.

'Well,' said Beth, who'd been washing her hands at the kitchen sink and was scrubbing fruitlessly at her grubby fingernails, 'I've had a brainwave. That's news.'

'Go on?' Rilla lifted an enquiring eyebrow.

'Several brainwaves, actually. You can tell me what you think.' Beth took a slice of bread from the chopping board and tore the crust off, chewing it thoughtfully for a moment before she continued. 'Okay. I've been doing some research. I've planted enough stock that I can do this and still cover what I've already got in the books and the other stuff. If we have people come in and pick their own flowers for their wedding flowers and bouquets, instead of me making them up, which takes ages, I can charge per bucket and they can take them home and make up the sort of little posies I do for the tables, and things like that. That's one. Plus pick your own flowers. Plus I'm thinking I can do a subscription for the flower boxes, and have people pay once a month for them.'

Charlotte whistled in admiration. 'Impressive.'

'Let's disregard the fact that bloody Simon shouldn't be putting you in this position,' said Polly, who'd slipped in unnoticed while Beth was in full flow.

'She's got a point,' said Rilla.

Charlotte and Beth exchanged glances.

'I know,' said Beth, 'but it is what it is.'

'It's shitty, is what it is,' said Polly.

'It's complicated,' said Beth, reaching over and rescuing the butter from the top of the Aga. It was already floating in a pale yellow melted pool on the side plate. 'Oops.'

'Right, so Simon —' ('the knobhead' muttered Polly, under her breath) 'notwithstanding, and with Beth's mega brainwaves, which are going to solve all her financial problems, does anyone else have any exciting news before I serve this soup?'

'Well, I think we've made the best batch of gin ever,' said Rilla, cheerfully. 'Only I'm not going to be able to drink any of it for a while.' She put a hand to her stomach, ducking her head slightly, her cheeks flushing pink.

'Oh my God,' said Beth, looking at her brother's girlfriend with her eyes wide. 'Are you saying what I think you're saying?'

Rilla made a face, wrinkling up her freckled nose. 'I might be.'

'No way,' said Polly, leaping up to give her a hug. 'Oh Rilla, this is so exciting. What's Lachlan saying?'

'It's early days yet, so he hasn't got past the basic shell-shock element. Nor have I.'

'The twins will have someone to play with,' said Charlotte, beaming. 'Oh, this is fab news. Why the bloody hell isn't Lachlan here to celebrate?'

'He told me I should tell you all now, and he'd deal with

the fallout afterwards.' Rilla spooned out soup into bowls warmed in the oven.

'Is that verbatim?' Charlotte said, knowing their brother all too well.

'Pretty much. I think he had visions of being outnumbered by us lot shrieking with excitement over the prospect of knitted baby booties, or something like that.' Rilla grinned. Beth knew her brother and his practical girlfriend well enough to know that was never going to be the case.

She reached over, giving Rilla a kiss on the cheek. 'Well, I think it's lovely news, and I think you're completely insane, obviously.'

'Sleep is for the weak, eh, Beth?' Charlotte gave Rilla a hug, looking at her over Rilla's shoulder and winking.

'You're not joking.'

'It's fine,' Rilla said, taking a spoonful of soup then dropping it quickly as the scent hit her nostrils. Soup splashed all over the table and the spoon clattered to the floor. 'Oh God,' she said, leaping out of her chair and heading out of the door.

'It begins,' said Charlotte, sagely. 'Do you remember how sick you were with the twins?' She got up and found a cloth in the sink, wiping up the soup and moving the bowl away from Rilla's place at the table.

Beth, who'd thrown up every morning for the whole nine months, groaned at the memory. 'It was grim.'

'I am staying single forever,' declared Polly.

'I think I said that,' said Beth, unthinkingly.

'You did not. You galloped off and married the first person you met because you wanted two point four children and a dog,' protested Charlotte, cutting another slice of bread.

'Do me one,' said Polly. 'She's got a point,' she added.

'Weirdly,' said Beth, 'I think when I was little I always thought I'd live on my own with some cats in a nice little house.'

'And here you are – with the twins, admittedly,' Charlotte said, laughing, 'Well on your way to reaching Mad Cat Lady status. Maybe you should get another couple of kittens.'

'She can't be a mad cat lady if she's got the hots for the new outdoor adventure bloke next door,' pointed out Polly, as Rilla returned, looking slightly pale.

'Ooh yes,' said Rilla, who avoided the table and poured herself a glass of water instead. 'The handsome Jack MacDonald.'

Beth tried to play it cool. She was more than aware that she'd spent quite a lot of time gazing in the direction of the treehouse every day she was at the gardens, half-hoping that she'd get a friendly wave hello and find an excuse to chat to Jack. But since he'd roped her into signing up for the TV show, he'd clearly been flat out with work, and so had she. Not that she was interested, she reminded herself, because she was planning to become a mad cat lady. But there was no harm in looking...

While she'd been daydreaming, Rilla and Charlotte had started chatting about her plans for the holiday pods she was building in a strip of woodland that looked over Applemore Bay. The planning permission had taken ages, and finally seemed to be getting somewhere.

'So that's going to take up all my time,' explained Charlotte, 'although I'm still trying to work out how I can get my hands on Midsummer House.'

'What's Midsummer House?' Rilla looked up, tucking a strand of hair behind her ear.

'It's a gorgeous old Victorian place – a big white house

that's hidden away down a mile-long track in the woods. I'll take you for a drive one day and show you it. If I could get a hold of it, I could get it done up and add it to the holiday rentals portfolio.'

'We could rent this place out,' pointed out Rilla. 'Given the size of the place, and how many rooms we currently occupy, it seems a bit ridiculous having them all lying empty.'

'You could do Airbnb,' Polly buttered more bread, dipping it in her soup.

'Dear Lord, no,' Charlotte shook her head. 'People in your house all the time. That's my idea of hell.'

'We're not all wildly antisocial,' said Polly, who was by far the most outgoing of the Frasers. She loved living on the doorstep of the shop, getting up in the morning and spending all day with people. It was Beth's idea of hell, and Charlotte – who was also introverted by nature – glanced across at her, rolling her eyes.

'Some of us are,' she said, finally.

'Although I don't think me throwing up every five seconds would make for a particularly pleasant Airbnb experience,' Rilla pointed out, reasonably. She tipped the rest of her water down the sink, making a face once again. 'Ugh, even water tastes grim.'

'So Rilla's setting up an Airbnb,' Beth said, laughing, 'Charlotte's expanding her business empire, and you're – oh God, Poll, what's happening about this supermarket in town? I saw people going in with clipboards the other day.'

Polly shrugged. 'I can't get stressed about it. At the end of the day, I reckon people will still come out here for all the stuff we sell, and hopefully a little supermarket in the village will help the locals who don't have cars.'

'That's very noble.' Charlotte narrowed her eyes. 'Is this official party line, or do you believe it?'

Polly caved. 'Bit of both. I mean there's not much I can do against the might of a national supermarket chain, is there? And at the end of the day, I'm not meaning to sound ridiculous but really, I've got it easy. I don't pay rent on the shop building, I just waltzed in and decided to make it a thing.'

'Yeah but you worked really hard to make it,' said Rilla.

'I did,' agreed Polly, 'But I'm lucky I could. Most people couldn't. So I decided the other day when I was sweeping up at the end of the day and thinking that I wasn't going to whine about it, and I'd take it on the chin.'

'Very impressive,' said Charlotte. She looked at her reflection in her spoon, thoughtfully.

'Yeah,' said Polly, laughing. 'Doesn't mean I'm not going to bitch to you lot about it, obviously, and I'll be making voodoo dolls and casting spells to make sure it's a complete flop.'

'Obviously.' Beth grinned at her. The thing about sisters, Beth thought fifteen minutes later – full of white chocolate brownies and coffee – was that you had people who had your back, but didn't take any of your crap. It was nice to have people who cut through all the waffle and told you realistically what they thought. And it was nicer still that they all thought her pick-your-own idea was a goer. She headed back to the flower farm with a head full of plans, ready for an afternoon of hard work. On her way, though, she took a detour, strolling the little wooded path which led to the stone memorial they'd put in place for their dad and his partner, David. The ground was thick with the green leaves of wild garlic and the scent rose into the air as she walked. A moment later she heard a crack of a branch underfoot and turned, stopping herself stock still as she saw a couple of deer in the distance. For a few seconds they eyed each other, Beth holding her breath and watching with delight, and then the two deer shot off, almost silently, into the depths of the wood.

'Well that was bloody amazing,' said a voice behind her. She gasped in surprise and spun around, to find Jack MacDonald standing with his hands in his pockets, an expression of awe on his dark features.

CHAPTER EIGHT

'I'M SORRY, I didn't mean to make you jump.' Jack said, realising he'd given her a fright.

Beth's hand was on her chest and her eyes wide with surprise. She stepped backwards, foot twisting on a branch which lay on the soft earth. As she lost her footing and staggered slightly he reached out a hand to steady her. She looked up, eyes meeting his, and a smile lit up her face.

'I don't get out much,' she said, laughing.

'Clearly. You still alright for this quiz night, or d'you think it might tip you over the edge?'

'I think I'll just about manage the excitement.' She let go of his hand and they stood for a moment in silence. He was still listening out for a sound that might help him work out where to go next.

'You okay?' She looked at him quizzically and he realised how odd he must look, half-focused gaze scanning through the tall poles of the pine trees, head slightly cocked as he tried to separate out the usual sounds of the woods from anything unusual.

'I shouldn't be here,' he said, realising he was once again wandering around on the Frasers' land without permission. 'I wouldn't be, it's just – we've got a bit of a problem.'

Normally she had her hair tied back in a ponytail, but today her long blonde hair hung down her back. 'Don't apologise,' she said, shaking her head slightly. 'It's only land.'

She'd said something similar when he'd met her on the beach.

'In any case,' he said, taking a hand out of his pocket and rubbing his chin. 'I'm looking for an escapee.'

'What kind of escapee?' She frowned. 'You don't mean one of your teenagers?'

He nodded. Right now he was still in the 'playing it cool, hoping they'd be back in a moment' stage. Give it another hour and he'd be all systems go, but right now he had a fairly good idea that the teenager in question had decided to take themselves on a wander around the Applemore estate and he suspected – from the trail he was following, where the path was disturbed and the scent of wild garlic was pungent in the air – that if he headed down towards the walled garden he'd find her there.

'I'm on my way back. Do you want me to keep an eye out?'

'I suspect they've headed your way. D'you mind if I walk with you?'

'Of course not.' She fell into step beside him. 'How can you tell?'

He grinned at her, looking at her sideways. 'Ah, it's all those SAS skills they teach us. I could tell you but I'd have to kill you, and all that…'

Beth's eyes widened and she looked at him for a

moment as if she couldn't quite work out if he was teasing her.

'Joke. It's pretty easy. This stuff –' he motioned to the carpet of green '– is a pretty good giveaway. That, and the fact that when we were in the treehouse earlier this morning she was fascinated by the bed of tulips you've got running along the side of the wall.'

'Really?'

'It takes all sorts,' he said, laughing. 'No, seriously, you should come and see how the garden looks from our vantage point. It looks amazing. You could get some really nice photos for your Instagram thing from up there.'

She looked at him with a curious expression and he realised in that moment that he'd given himself away. It was Danny – who was far more of a social media person than he was – who'd looked up Applemore Flower Farm when they'd been cooking pasta for dinner the other night, showing him the pretty photographs of the flowers she grew.

'Danny was showing me. You're all pretty hot on the social media stuff,' he explained, trying to cover his tracks and feeling slightly like a stalker.

'Oh God, I'm nothing compared to Polly,' said Beth, but he noticed her cheeks going slightly pink with pleasure. 'She does a really good job of doing stuff for the shop.'

'And your brother and sister-in-law have the camping site, and there's the holiday cottage business as well. You lot have things sewn up around here, don't you?'

She screwed up her face in thought. 'I hadn't really thought of it that way. God, do you think people think we're lording it over people? How awful.'

He shook his head. 'That's not what I meant at all.' Well, he'd handled that brilliantly. 'I mean you've done a really good job of diversifying – that seems to be the secret these days.'

She seemed to soften slightly, the tension dropping from her shoulders. 'That sounds a bit better. I've always found the idea of this place a bit – well, a bit much, if you know what I mean?'

He nodded. 'It's a far cry from where I grew up, that's for sure.'

A moment later as they approached the wall of the garden he put a finger to his lips. 'Look.'

Beth stopped and shaded her eyes against the sunshine. 'What am I looking at?'

'That apple tree.'

As he spoke, the blossom-laden branches shifted slightly, as if they were being blown by a strong wind – but the air was completely still.

'I think we might be in luck.'

'Remind me not to run away from you,' said Beth, arching an eyebrow in amusement.

'My misspent youth comes in handy once in a while,' he said, forgetting himself for a second.

'Oh really?'

'Joking.' He closed that line of conversation down with a brief smile. God, the last thing he wanted was Beth asking questions. He couldn't deny he liked her, despite himself, but if they were going to be friends he didn't want her probing into his past… that was left behind, a long time ago. 'Just a figure of speech,' he added, for good measure.

'I used to hide in the walled garden sometimes when I didn't want to go to school after my mum left,' Beth said to him as she opened the grey-green door. He stepped aside to let her go in, and then followed behind, heading for the apple tree.

'I'll leave you to it, shall I?' She stood with her hands on her hips, and he felt her eyes on his back as he strode away. He picked up the walkie-talkie he used to keep in contact with Danny, flicking the communication channel button with a thumb.

'Stand down,' he said into the mic, hearing a crackle and fizz from the other end.

'You got her?'

'In a manner of speaking,' he said, marching up a long strip of bark path that led between two beds crammed with fresh green plants, which were staked neatly with bamboo canes and string.

'Millie,' he said, calling into the branches of the apple tree, 'You planning on staying there all afternoon?'

A shower of pale pink petals tumbled onto the grass as response.

'Only I've got plans for this afternoon and I could really do with your help.'

A few more petals tumbled down, and there was a rustling in the branches.

'I tell you what, I'll let Danny know you haven't jumped on the first train back to Inverness, and if you want to make your way back out in the meantime, that's okay by me.'

He turned away, taking a few slow steps back up the path, noticing as he did so that Beth had made her way across the garden and was standing looking – it didn't take SAS training to recognise her posture – extremely cross. He flicked a glance back over his shoulder to see two slim legs hanging down from inside the tree and smiled to himself.

'I just wanted to see what this place was,' said a small voice, and there was a thud as Millie landed awkwardly on the grass, followed by a waterfall of what looked like tulip stems. 'And I saw all these flowers and I thought I'd pick some for the nice lady who runs the bunkhouse because she said it was her birthday tomorrow and that her husband never remembered any, and my mum always said the same thing about her boyfriend, and…' she tailed off, pulling a twig out of her hair and dropping it on the ground.

Listening to her but aware of something in the corner of his eye, Jack looked over his shoulder, realising immediately that it was Beth, who was marching across the grass towards them, an expression of fury on her face.

Jack lifted both hands in an instinctive calming movement, glancing from Millie to Beth, not quite sure how to handle the situation. Millie instinctively knew she was in for it and ducked behind Jack's shoulder, muttering 'uh-oh' under her breath.

As Beth approached, she slowed, taking in the scattered tulips and glancing at his face for a moment.

The walkie-talkie crackled once again. 'You okay?' came Danny's voice, into the strained silence.

'I could do with back up,' said Jack, looking at Beth as he spoke. 'We've got a bit of a – situation.'

Beth surprised him then by breaking into a smile and walking forward, peering round his shoulder. 'Hello,' she said gently. He spun around to see Millie frowning cautiously, a long rope of hair twisted around her finger. She looked at him for a moment as if trying to gauge from his reaction whether Beth was safe. He gave the slightest nod.

'Alright?'

'This is Millie,' he said, stepping back so the two of them could see each other clearly. 'She's from Inverness. I think she's quite taken with your tulips.'

'I think you might be right,' said Beth, with the slightest hint of asperity in her voice. She shot him a look which he recognised straight away as *we'll talk about this later*, but beckoned Millie over towards the fallen flowers which lay on the grass, stooping down to gather them up.

'You're more efficient at cutting than Phoebe, my apprentice,' she said, handing the tulips to Millie. 'She always cuts them too high. The secret is,' she pulled off a discoloured leaf 'that now you've got these, you need to put them in water. Come on, I'll show you.'

Jack stood with his mouth hanging open in surprise as Millie – who'd been the most intransigent of the group all week, causing arguments and deliberately tipping someone out of a kayak at the river – followed her obediently back down the grassy paths towards the greenhouse. After a couple of moments, he caught them up.

Beth opened the door to the greenhouse and the smell of damp, earthy air hit him immediately.

Millie fanned her face. 'It's really hot in here.'

'You should see what it's like on summer days.' Beth bent down under a long wooden trestle table, coming back up with a black bucket. 'I have to block out the sunshine or it gets so hot you could melt. It's nice in winter, though.'

'My grandpa had a greenhouse,' said Millie. 'He used to grow tomatoes.'

'I grow some too,' Beth passed her a pair of long handled metal scissors 'But my children aren't exactly keen. In fact they think I'm trying to poison them.'

'He used to grow the wee cherry ones.'

'My favourites.' Beth picked one of the tulip stems that Millie had taken and cut it neatly across the end. 'Right,' she explained, 'What you need to do is cut each one across like that, and then pop them in a bucket of water. They've had a bit of a shock – as has Jack, I think, with you going missing like that – and this way we can revive them. It won't take long.'

Millie giggled. 'Maybe we should put you in a bucket of water too,' she said, looking at Jack. This was the brightest she'd looked all week, he realised, and it was all down to Beth's kind, open-hearted reaction. He caught her eye when Millie was cutting the stems and mouthed a thank you.

She shook her head, giving a slight smile at the same time.

'So now you know how we condition the flowers – that's what it's called when you get them ready – the next thing we'll do is tie them into a nice bouquet.'

'Millie was picking them for Sandra at the bunkhouse,' Jack explained. 'Apparently, it's her birthday tomorrow.'

'Perfect timing,' said Beth. 'I'll give these a few hours, and then bring them over to the centre at the end of the afternoon?'

'Are you sure?' Millie shuffled her feet, tracing a half-circle in the earth with her toe.

'Of course. We can't have Sandra going without flowers on her birthday, can we?' Beth lifted the bucket of tulips into her arms. 'We'll take them and put them in the shed where it's dark – it's far too warm for them here.'

'But there's loads of them,' said Millie, pointing to the long bed of flowers which were growing in long swathes.

'This warmth is nice for them to grow in, but we need it to be cool for them to be conditioned.'

'I thought you just picked them and made a bunch,' said Jack, giving Millie a conspiratorial smile. She beamed back at him.

'Me too.'

'It's a complicated business, flower farming,' Beth said, as they headed back out of the greenhouse.

They said their goodbyes and Jack headed back round, following the path that led round the walled garden of the flower farm towards the treehouse. Inside, Danny had gathered the rest of the group and they were busy listening to someone's music on a portable speaker while he outlined the plans for the rest of the afternoon.

'Ah,' he said, catching Jack's eye. 'The wanderers return. Right, I've just been explaining that we're going to be doing den building in the woods this afternoon. You up for that, Millie?'

She nodded, slipping in to sit down beside her friend Charly, who whispered something in her ear, making the two of them giggle. It looked like she was none the worse for her little adventure.

An hour later, Danny strolled across the path in the woods to Jack, grabbing an opportunity while the teenagers were all occupied to catch up.

'You going to fill me in?'

Jack shook his head, laughing. 'Let's say it was one of those experiences where pretty much everything you don't expect happens.'

Danny cocked his head. 'How so?'

'I'll tell all later. But the more I get to know Beth Fraser, the more she surprises me.'

'Oh yeah?' Danny lifted a cheeky eyebrow. 'I can't wait to hear all the details.'

'Shut up, you,' he said, shaking his head and laughing. 'The most important thing is Millie didn't do a runner, and nobody got hurt. Well, apart from an armful of flowers.'

'Eh?' Danny screwed up his face in confusion.

'Long story.'

'Come and see this, Jack,' shouted Millie from inside the den they were building. She poked her head out of the gap in the stacked branches which was acting as the door, and he was delighted to see her little face smeared in mud and grinning from ear to ear. Den building always lifted their spirits – it was amazing to see teenagers who'd often been forced to grow up far too fast get a chance to play and mess around like kids again.

'Coming,' he said, pulling his phone out of his pocket. 'Can I take a photo of it?'

'Only if you promise you'll put it on your Insta,' she said, disappearing back into the den again.

A couple of hours later they were back at the log cabin. The sun had dropped lower in the sky now, and the air was noticeably chilly. Sandra had lit the log burner and left a huge urn of hot chocolate for them all to drink, and they were all sitting around chatting when the log cabin door opened hesitantly.

'Hello?' Beth's face appeared around the side of the door.

'Hiya,' said Millie, springing up from her chair. 'This is the one I was telling you about,' she said, tugging Charly to her feet and pulling her across the room.

'I've done the flowers for you,' Beth said, bringing them out from behind her back.

'They're gorgeous,' Jack said in surprise, looking at the colourful bunch of brightly coloured tulips tied in brown paper and long twirls of raffia string. 'I can't believe they've come to life so –'

Beth shot him a very brief look, eyes wide and nostrils flaring slightly, which he recognised immediately as 'Shut up'. He gave her the ghost of a wink.

'–So well.'

'Amazing what a bit of TLC will do,' said Beth, handing them to Millie. 'Pop these in water overnight and you can give them to Sandra in the morning.'

Millie shook her head. 'I'm giving them to her today.'

'I'm sure she'll love them,' said Beth, 'Whenever she gets them. I'd better get back,' she continued, looking at the clock. 'I seem to spend my whole time checking I'm not late for picking up the twins from nursery or something else.'

'It goes with the territory,' said Jack, holding the door open for her as she left. The gaggle of teenagers who'd all been silenced by her appearance had sprung back into life and were chatting and laughing, all crowding around Danny, who had the advantage of being close enough to them in age that they saw him as a sort of middle ground. Beth paused for a moment. 'I'm impressed,' she said, looking at the pile of mountain bikes balanced against the wall of the cabin. 'You seem to be doing a pretty good job.'

'Ah, this lot were deceptively easy, really. Millie's group were from a secondary school over near Inverness – none of them have a particularly tricky background. Next week, though, we've got a group who'll be a bit more of a challenge.'

'Should I expect hordes of them to be abseiling over the side of the wall on a daily basis?' laughed Beth.

He shook his head. 'Hope not. I mean definitely not.'

She made a face. 'That doesn't sound as convincing as it ought to.'

'Let's hope not, considering we've got the TV people turning up. It's the worst timing possible, really. They can't do anything when they kids are on site because it's a safe-guarding issue, but she was most insistent they wanted to come and do some filming. She said she promised they wouldn't get in the way.'

Beth nodded. 'She said the same to me. Trouble is this is when things start ramping up and it gets manically busy, so I'm hoping she's not going to be under my feet tripping me up with cables and things.'

'There goes my idea of sending her your way to keep her out of my hair.' Jack grinned.

'I was thinking the same thing.' Beth swiped at her forehead with the back of her arm, trying to brush a hair out of her eyes. 'Are you looking forward to the quiz?'

He half-shrugged, laughing. 'I've been bracing myself for the disapproval of the entire populace of Applemore.'

'I don't disapprove of you,' Beth said, and then, as if she realised what she'd said, she took a step backwards. 'I mean I'm sure lots of people think you're doing a good thing. I think it's a good idea to come to the meeting and explain about what you're doing, mind you, because –' she laughed again. 'Sorry, I'm rabbiting on. Too much time spent with plants and not enough with people.'

'Don't apologise. I was going to say I really appreciated what you did earlier. You could have just bollocked her – I mean she was trespassing, she damaged your flowers...'

Beth shrugged. 'It's nothing. I mean it's pretty clear she didn't mean any harm, and what she was doing was sweet.'

'And those totally weren't the ones she picked, were they?'

Beth shook her head. He noticed as she cast her eyes down that her cheeks had flushed slightly pink beneath long dark lashes. A moment later she looked up, eyes sparkling with amusement. 'I didn't want her handing over a bunch of flowers that were still tight in bud. She wanted a colourful bouquet. I just swapped a few –'

'– Most of them,' he interrupted, feeling a teasing grin tugging at the sides of his mouth.

'Alright, pretty much all of them.'

'Well, it was lovely of you. I appreciate it.'

'No problem.'

He watched as she set off down the path to her van,

long, jeans-clad legs striding purposefully. Beth didn't seem to do anything slowly. He liked how focused she was, and how decisive.

'You seem to be a bit of a hit with Ms Fraser,' said Danny later, as they bumped down the rutted track towards Applemore. The teenagers were all installed safely in the bunkhouse with their teachers and the support staff, and Sandra had been absolutely delighted with her flowers.

'What d'you mean?'

'Personal flowers for Millie, invites to the quiz night, teaming up for TV shows…'

He shook his head, pausing at the end of the lane with a hand on the gearstick waiting as a tractor rumbled by.

'I'm just saying,' continued Danny, 'didn't have you down as having posh girls as your type.'

'She's not posh,' he said, defensively. 'Just because she grew up in that place doesn't mean she's all la-di-da. You've met her, she's pretty much as down to earth as they come.'

'And you don't have a thing for her, right?' Danny said, scrolling through his phone. 'Just checking out her Insta again. She's not married, is she?'

'Nope.' He wasn't going to admit that he'd noted when they first met – with some pleasure – that she was a single parent like him. Difference was she had her kids living with her, and his was still resolutely ignoring his calls. He'd sent a string of photos through on WhatsApp that morning, showing Anna the mountain bikes all ready to go, in the hope it might spur her into replying. She'd always enjoyed getting out with him before she'd moved away…

'Earth to MacDonald? Come in MacDonald…'

'What was that?'

'I was talking to you and you weren't paying a blind bit of notice. Love sick, if you ask me.'

'I've got no time for relationships,' he said, slowing as they wound down the narrow road towards Applemore village, 'You know that.'

'I know you've told me it repeatedly since we met, and I didn't believe it then and I don't believe it now. We're not supposed to be single, you know. We're supposed to find a mate.'

'A mate?' Jack snorted with amusement.

'A life partner.' Danny had the good grace to laugh at himself. 'I know I sound a bit cheesy, but that is the general idea, man. Meet someone nice, pair up, settle down, have a nice house and someone to share stuff with.'

'You sound like you're getting broody. Something you want to tell me?'

Danny shook his head. 'I'm just saying you're not getting any younger.'

The road curved round and the village came into sight, bathed in the last of the late afternoon sunlight. It looked picture-postcard pretty.

'I'm perfectly happy with all this,' Jack said, waving an arm in the direction of the village. 'I've got work, and I've got Anna, and I think we've all established that relationships and me aren't a good combination.'

Danny sighed and shook his head, but wisely said no more. Jack knew that mentioning Anna was a sure-fire way of shutting him up, because he'd admitted that the whole situation left him utterly perplexed. He had a great relationship with his parents, and he'd made it clear to Jack how much he admired the way he worked with the teenagers at the centre. Jack knew that it made no sense to Danny that despite all of that, he'd somehow failed in his relationship with his own daughter. He pulled up outside the cottage.

'I'm going to nip into the hotel bar for a quick pint. You fancy it?'

Jack shook his head. He wanted a shower and a quick half-hour snooze on the sofa more than anything. Danny jumped out and rapped a goodbye on the roof of the 4x4.

'See ya,' he said, thrusting his hands into his pockets and heading off up the street towards the hotel.

Jack sat in the driving seat for a long moment, staring out at the sea and thinking. The water was as calm as a millpond, only a fishing boat heading off into the distance leaving a trail in its wake. By the harbour rails, a young couple were crabbing with two small children, plastic buckets by their side, laughing and chatting. In the last week, the village had started to come to life as walkers and tourists arrived. Being surrounded by relaxed, happy people enjoying each other's company only emphasised what he'd chosen to give away – he closed his eyes, both hands clamped tightly round the steering wheel as he sat, lost in thought.

No wonder Danny couldn't get his head round what he'd done – it was hard enough for him to do it. But despite everything, Jack still thought sending Anna to live in Paris with Rebecca was for the best. There, she had money, stability, and the sort of designer flat you saw featured in expensive magazines. He couldn't offer her any of that. Living with her mum, Anna experienced the kind of lifestyle he could only have dreamed about when he was growing up in a tiny flat in a deprived suburb of Glasgow. She had riding lessons and extra-curricular French classes, nice clothes and pocket money. In contrast, his house came with the job, he had no savings, no security – nothing. It was a no-brainer. And if she'd ever found out – and eventually she was going to ask why he didn't have any family to speak of – where he came from, and worked out his past… well. He'd risk losing her forever.

He sat back against the driving seat, putting his fists to his forehead. Of course, any sane man would point out that he'd lost her already. It had been months since they'd moved, and he'd hardly heard a word. God, that girl was strong willed, he'd give her that.

Just thinking of you, he typed into his phone, looking at the photograph of Anna on her WhatsApp profile. It was several years out of date – she was eleven there, long hair in two plaits and grown up teeth slightly goofy in a still babyish face. He hit send, knowing as he did so that it wasn't going to make a bit of difference.

Now she was sixteen. Rebecca had sent him a photo of her on her way to a trip at her new French school. No uniform over there – she was wearing a pale blue sweatshirt and jeans, her long dark hair loose around her shoulders, huge dark brown eyes wide and wary. She looked – funnily enough, given she was Glasgow born and bred – very French. He scrolled through his photographs, looking at it for a moment, then went back to WhatsApp and did a double take.

Two blue ticks indicated the message had been seen. His heart thudded unevenly in his chest.

CHAPTER NINE

'You sure you don't mind having them tomorrow night as well?' Beth looked at her ex-husband. Simon stood on the doorstep of his house in his socks, wearing a *Star Wars* t-shirt that had seen better days.

'Not at all,' he said, giving her a strange look. 'You alright, Beth? You look knackered.'

'Cheers,' she said, drily. 'I can always rely on you to make me feel good.'

'Sorry,' he rubbed at his hair so it stood up on end. 'Just saying.'

'We're not all being kept by our partners,' said Beth, hearing herself snipe and regretting it instantly. 'Oh, forget I said that,' she continued, as he opened his mouth, about to start into another long spiel about how he'd be making a fortune once he'd retrained, blah blah blah.

'You're in a weird mood,' he said, bending down and picking up the tiny dinosaur-patterned rucksack that Lucy had dropped on the floor moments before when she scampered inside.

'I've got a lot to think about,' she said, trying desperately not to mind the fact that the twins could be heard inside the house, squealing with laughter with Morag, Simon's new partner. She tended to keep out of the way when they did the swap-overs, returning the twins with neatly pressed clothes folded into their little overnight bags, and notes about what they'd eaten and activities they'd done. Beth – who tended to grab stuff from the tumble dryer and shove it in five minutes before they left – had no idea how she did it, and quietly hoped that a new-born – when it came – might make the wheels come off Morag's hyper-organised, super-efficient life slightly. Discussing it over wine one night, Charlotte had pointed out with her usual calm reason that schadenfreude wasn't exactly the nicest trait, but Beth had told her to sod off. Nobody was perfect, after all.

'Okay, we'll drop them off Sunday after lunch,' Simon said, hand on the doorhandle. 'Lucy, Edward – do you want to come and say goodbye to Mummy?'

Morag hovered at the back of the hall, a pink polka-dot apron tied over her navy blue bank manager outfit. She gave a little wave. 'Alright?'

'Great thanks. You feeling okay?' It was the first time Beth had seen her since Simon had announced they were having a baby.

'Bit tired,' she admitted, 'but at least I'm not feeling sick.'

'You were awful with the twins, weren't you?' Simon looked from Beth to her replacement, apparently completely oblivious to the awkwardness of the situation. God, he was as tactless as a bloody rhinoceros. For a moment she didn't know where to look, but when she glanced up from the doormat where she'd fixed her gaze for a second to gather herself, she saw Morag giving him a wide-eyed glare. Beth hid a smile of relief, swooped Edward and Lucy into a cuddle as they hurtled down the hall towards her.

'Have a lovely time, you two,' she said, kissing their foreheads.

'Morag,' said Edward, twisting in her arms, 'Can Mummy stay and have 'paghetti with us?'

'I think Mummy has lots of work to do,' said Simon, reaching out and lifting him up in the air.

'Lots,' Beth agreed. 'Lots and lots.'

'Okay,' said Edward, sliding out of his father's arms and wandering off, hair mussed up and t-shirt hanging out of the back of his red trousers. Beth's heart melted at the sight.

'See you on Sunday, then, darling' she said, giving Lucy one more kiss and passing her over to Simon. Much as her heart ached to leave them, the prospect of a night out tomorrow and an early – uninterrupted – night tonight was utterly blissful.

She spent the whole evening watching Netflix, eating the remains of a box of chocolates she'd forgotten about, which was lurking in the back of the utility room, and doing a mountain of the day-to-day jobs that took over her life. By the end of the evening she had a stack of brown paper cut to size and stamped with her custom-designed Applemore Flower Farm logo, and she'd stamped and prepared a mountain of the cardboard boxes that she used to send out the postal flowers. All of this meant she hadn't had time to sit down and work out the financial projections she'd promised her accountant, but – she told herself that she needed to do all those things, and that was good enough excuse. The reality was she was beginning to wonder if – even with the planned pick-your-own days and the bridal buckets, and selling flowers at the farm shop, and, and,

and... was it going to be enough? Had she bitten off more than she could chew simply because she was determined to prove a point to Simon?

Full of chocolate and with her brain whirring at a hundred miles an hour, Beth slept terribly. Climbing out of bed at six, she decided she might as well get to work instead of taking the opportunity for a child-free late morning in bed. Downstairs in the farmhouse she surveyed the chaos from last night's work. Grabbing all the brown paper offcuts, she balled them up and shoved them in the recycling, stacking the boxes of paper wrapping, raffia and pale tissue paper by the door so she wouldn't forget them on the way out. Someone on the BBC news was grumbling about long working hours. Beth rolled her eyes, thinking that she'd gone so long without a day thinking about work that she was beginning to think she'd gone slightly mad. Pushing the dishwasher shut with one foot, she flicked on the kettle, tipped instant coffee into her travel mug, and then turned to shove a pile of clothes into the washing machine while the kettle boiled. If she had eight pairs of hands like an octopus, she'd find life much easier.

All her stresses were forgotten when she arrived at the flower farm. There was a magic in the air in late spring – the beds sparkled with diamond drops of dew, early sunlight bathing the place in a soft golden haze. There were a million things to do, but first – Beth popped the lid off her coffee, and set off to walk the path that led around the acre of garden – she was going to take a moment to herself.

Sheltered on all sides by the walls, the beds were thriving. The outdoor tulips – planted in neat rows last autumn – were vivid green, jostling for position as their buds readied themselves. Fluffy delphinium foliage filled a bed lined with lavender, which she could swear had grown about three inches in the last fortnight. It felt as if the whole place was holding its breath, waiting for someone to say *go*. The first year she'd started growing, it had amazed her how one moment she'd been worrying that she'd have nothing to sell and the next she'd been panicking about how on earth she was supposed to manage it all. There was so much to do – the last of the narcissi had to be picked and processed, and there were sweet little forget-me-nots, red campion and cowslips coming through, which she noticed as she strolled down the path past the foliage bed. They'd make cute little posies – once she'd sorted out the tulips and ranunculus, she'd come back and cut some before the sun got too high in the sky. And where the two eucalyptus bushes seemed to be growing like weeds. She made a mental note to get Phoebe on to planting the autumn bulbs when she was in on Monday, and that she needed to get the last crop of hardy annuals sown now that she'd levelled off the old allium bed. And she needed to get a grip on herself and stop worrying. It was going to be fine, somehow. She stopped for a moment, looking over the wall at the huge oak tree where the wooden treehouse Jack and Danny had built could be seen through the acid green of the new leaves. They were growing something new as well. With Charlotte working on the cabins, Polly trying to make a go of the shop, and Lachlan and Rilla working all hours on their various ideas, everyone seemed to be wrapped up in themselves. It'd be nice to have a chance to hang out tonight at the pub quiz – it was ages since they'd all been out. Goodness knows what she was going to wear…

'Hello-oo!'

A few hours later, Beth was startled by a familiar voice at the door of the polytunnel. Pulling off her gloves, she dropped the scissors she'd been holding and stood up so fast that she saw stars and had to close her eyes for a moment to steady herself.

'I came the very minute I got back,' said Joan, beaming from ear to ear.

'Oh it's so lovely to see you!' Beth let herself be wrapped in the warm hug of the woman who'd been the next best thing to a mother for the Fraser family. Joan had been the housekeeper, a strength and stay for their dad after their mum left, and she'd been the one who'd wiped away tears and found plasters for bumps and scrapes when they were children, then handed out painkillers and strong coffee as the tree-climbing accidents were replaced with teenage traumas and then hangovers and headaches as they grew into adulthood.

'I swear I still feel like I'm at sea.'

'A month on a cruise ship will do that to a person,' Beth said, giving Joan's arm a delighted squeeze. 'Oh, I've missed you.'

'And I've missed our chats,' said Joan, looking down the polytunnel. 'This place has come on great guns since last month. It's like a jungle in here. Those tulips look lovely.' She nodded to the long bed of tulips which were ready to pick. She'd have them wrapped and off to the farmer's market in Strathtorron by eight in the morning tomorrow. No chance for a lie-in then, either, she thought, and a yawn slipped out. She put a hand to her mouth.

'Now then, I want all the gossip,' Joan said, folding her arms and looking Beth up and down. 'You're tired, Bethy. Have you been burning the candle at both ends again?'

'Oh you know me, party all day, party all night…'

Joan chuckled. 'I don't want you working yourself into an early grave. You need to make sure you're having some fun as well.'

'I've got the quiz night tonight at the hotel.'

'I was thinking more like a holiday and a bit of time for yourself, but it's a start.' Joan shook her head. 'Anyway, tell me – how are my two wee bairns?'

Joan adored the twins. Beside her siblings, she was the one person who Beth felt safe leaving them with. Simon's parents were both dead, as were hers, so Joan was the nearest thing they had to a grandparent and they adored her.

'They're with their dad and Morag.' Beth nodded thanks as Joan – who never arrived empty-handed – opened a packet which contained some of the delicious brownies from the farm shop.

'I stopped to say hello to Polly on the way. I gather she's got some competition on the way.'

'She's trying to tell herself that it won't make any difference to business.'

'I think there's room enough for a supermarket and a farm shop in Applemore, to be honest,' said Joan, settling herself on the edge of the table by the entrance to the polytunnel. 'Are you needing to work while we chat?'

'If we go to the greenhouse, I can pot on the dahlias once I've eaten some of this,' said Beth, through a mouthful of brownie.

'I'll give you a hand,' said Joan, following Beth across the garden towards the big greenhouse.

'So, tell me what else has been happening,' said Joan, once they were settled. Beth got to work, deftly tipping out the dahlias which had outgrown their pots and re-potting them with extra compost so they had space to grow and thrive. Later in the summer they'd form the mainstay of the bouquets she sold, taking over from the midsummer flowers. She caught Joan up with all the village news, what the rest of the family had been up to, and Simon's bombshell.

'And you're just going to let him drop you in it?' Joan shook her head disapprovingly.

'I can manage on my own,' Beth protested.

'You sound exactly the same now as you did when you were a wee girl. I'm sure you can, Beth, but there are only twenty-four hours in a day and you work far too hard as it is.'

'If I employ anyone else, the cost of paying them will wipe out any extra profit I make.'

Joan tutted. 'So you're going to work your fingers to the bone to prove a point.'

'Something like that.' Beth couldn't help smiling. 'It'll work out. I've got the farmers' market, two new shops taking bouquets twice a week, and the flowers-by-post thing is working out really well.'

'What time did you get to your bed last night?'

Beth looked at her phone. 'Gosh, is that the time? I must get on.'

Joan gave a snort of laughter. 'Don't come that nonsense with me, young lady. I know you far too well. I think it's great that you're determined to make this work, but you've got to have a life as well. Anyway, you haven't told me what's going on with your new neighbours.'

Beth, who knew that if Joan caught one look at her face she'd work out something was going on, busied herself with scooping up the spilt compost into her cupped hands and tipping it back into the big plastic bucket where she stored it.

'Oh, they're nice enough,' she said, dusting off her hands and turning away to put a stack of pots on the shelf. 'This place really needs a good tidy,' she added.

'Polly said the guy in charge of it has the hots for you,' said Joan, in the casual-not-casual tone Beth knew all too well.

'Oh you know what Polly's like,' said Beth, feeling a heat creeping onto her cheeks that had nothing to do with the warmth of the greenhouse.

'Aye,' said Joan, 'I do, and I also know when you're being deceptively cool about something, young lady.' She gave a chortle of laughter and Beth turned around.

'I hardly think he's got the hots for me,' she said, 'Given the first time we met I bollocked him for doing his best to trash the polytunnel.'

'I hear you're going to be starring in a TV show together.'

'Yes,' Beth was going to kill Polly when she saw her later, 'But it's not *Love Island*, it's a documentary thing about living on the west coast and the effects of tourism and stuff like that.'

'Mmm,' said Joan. 'Well, I think it's no bad thing if you've got a bit of love interest going on. You can't stay on your own forever.'

'I'm not on my own. I've got the twins, I've got a business, and…'

'Take it from one who knows,' said Joan, firmly. 'It's not as much fun being independent as you might think, especially as you get older. You deserve the right to be happy, you know.'

'I always thought you liked being on your own,' Beth rubbed a bit of dust from her eye and settled back against the low staging of the greenhouse, hitching one hip up to rest herself against the shelf.

'Well I did,' said Joan, with a mischievous look, 'And

then I might have met someone on the cruise who made me think differently…'

'Okay, enough about me, I want to hear everything.' Beth crossed her arms and waited expectantly.

'He's called George, he's a retired science teacher from Aberdeen, and he's very nice. He's coming over to visit the week of the summer fair.'

'But that's not for a month!' Beth shook her head. 'How are we going to survive that long without meeting him and checking him out?'

It was Joan's turn to turn away and act casual. She rifled in her handbag for a moment, eventually pulling out a neatly pressed linen handkerchief which she used to dab away imaginary crumbs from the brownies they'd eaten ten minutes before. Beth waited patiently, eyebrows slowly migrating northwards, a look of expectation on her face.

Joan shook out the hanky, folded it neatly, and put it back in her bag.

'I'm waiting.'

'Well,' Joan said, and burst into the most uncharacteristically girlish giggle, her apple cheeks going quite pink with delight. 'I'm driving over to Aberdeen to see him next week, but I don't imagine you'll be wanting to come along and play gooseberry.'

Beth, who'd known her all her life, looked at her with amazement.

'What?'

'I just never –'

'Och,' Joan said, shaking her head. 'That's what I mean. You don't want to end up like me, all on your own at sixty, with nobody to talk to but a couple of cats. Just because you and Simon didn't work out doesn't mean you have to be on your own for the rest of your life.'

Beth made a vague noise of assent.

'Anyway, I really ought to try and get a bit of sleep. I'm all over the place.' Joan looked at her watch. 'These Caribbean cruises are all very well, but the jet lag is no blooming joke.'

'My heart bleeds for you,' Beth said, leaning over and giving her a kiss.

'I'll be back over to see the babies at the beginning of the week. Maybe you can get out for a wee night out with this handsome outdoor adventure chap?'

'You're pushing it now. Shoo.'

Cackling with amusement, Joan headed home. Beth got back to work, scrubbing out the buckets she'd need for the next morning's blooms. Tomorrow morning Beth – who she suspected might be slightly hungover after the quiz night – would be grateful. She mulled over what Joan had said as she worked. Unbidden, a vision of Jack, broad-shouldered and hugely apologetic as he filled the doorframe of the polytunnel the day they met popped into her head. Was she closing herself to the idea of another relationship on the grounds that her marriage to Simon had been a disaster? If she was honest with herself, she and Simon had bumped along more like friends for years – she'd only married him because she was so desperate to get away from Applemore and live a more normal life. She shook herself back to reality. She needed to get finished up, and get home and in the shower, or she'd be turning up to the village meeting and the quiz night looking like she'd been rolling in compost. Not – she told herself firmly – because she wanted to look nice because Jack was coming. Absolutely, definitely not because of that.

CHAPTER TEN

'YOU READY FOR THIS?'

Danny nodded. He was standing at the door of the cottage, shrugging on a hoody over his navy blue t-shirt. Jack watched as he checked his reflection, running a hand through his hair, which lifted slightly then fell neatly back into place.

'This place absolutely honks of aftershave. Are you hoping you might get lucky?'

Danny winked. 'You never know. There's a lassie who works behind the bar – she was there last night when I went in for a drink. Phoebe, I think she's called?'

'Right. And you've got your eye on her.'

'She's got her eye on me, I reckon,' he said cheerfully. Jack laughed and shook his head. To have the confidence of a twenty-three-year-old Danny, who'd had no knocks in life and was comfortably certain in his own skin.

'Just don't go trying to chat her up when we're trying to do a charm offensive at this village meeting,' Jack warned, as he locked the cottage door behind them. Danny jigged from one foot to the other as if warming up.

'I won't. Don't worry, we'll have them eating out of our hands by the time we're done with them.'

'I bloody hope so,' said Jack, who was painfully aware that they'd been lucky to get away with an uneventful week. When the staff had climbed out of the minibus on Monday, they looked like they'd gone ten rounds in a boxing ring with Tyson Fury. The group they'd had had been hard work, and he was utterly knackered – it was one of those weeks where he'd had every sense stretched to the very limit and he'd half expected every morning to get to the centre and discover that one of the teenagers had absconded with a tin of contraband spray paint and desecrated the high street with graffiti. But despite his misgivings, and several challenging incidents (the terminology used to describe what everyday people would call utterly hair-raising near-disasters) they'd made it to Friday and even had a really good bonding session following their final kayaking experience on the river. He was absolutely desperate for a drink and a chance to switch his brain off from being responsible for a bit.

It had been a genius idea by Greta, head of the village committee, to decide to relocate the bi-monthly meeting from the cold and draughty memorial hall to the welcoming environs of the Applemore Hotel. Tempted by the prospect of a pre-dinner pint and a chance for a catch up with friends and neighbours, turnout had doubled the first month. Then Harry, the owner, had decided it was a perfect opportunity to combine the evening with their popular quiz night and as a result, when Jack and Danny walked in – expecting the place to be half-empty – they were surprised to find that there was already a throng of people waiting to be served at the bar, and almost all the tables – which had been shifted around slightly, so they could accommodate more people – were already occupied.

'Pint?' Danny looked through the crowd towards the bar as if he was checking to see if someone he knew was there – oh, of course, Jack realised, as a tall girl with pink hair gave him a shy wave – that must be the Phoebe he'd been talking about.

He felt a tap in the small of his back and turned around to see Polly Fraser smiling at him, a half-drunk glass of wine in her hand. 'D'you want to join us?'

He took in the rest of the group. Charlotte, the oldest sister, who he'd met on their first day, was frowning into her phone, typing furiously. She looked up. 'Hi. Yes, join us. It's going to be heaving in a moment, and you won't get a seat otherwise.'

'Alright?' Lachlan shifted over onto the banquette beside his pretty dark-haired girlfriend, making space for Jack and leaving a stool free for Danny.

'You sure you don't mind?'

Lachlan shook his head. 'It'll make a change not to be outnumbered,' he said, laughing. 'So how's it going?'

'Great.' Jack settled into the chair and they chatted comfortably while waiting for Danny to return with drinks. It was strange how happy they seemed to be to welcome them. Locals arrived, nodding a hello in the general direction of the table. Danny made his way back over with two pints and a couple of bags of crisps.

'While I'm up,' he said, putting them down on the table, 'anyone want anything else?'

'I've planned this in advance,' said Polly, pointing to a

second glass on the table. 'The secret to getting through the village meeting is anaesthetic.'

'It's not that bad,' said Lachlan's girlfriend. She reached across the table, putting out a hand. 'I'm Rilla, by the way.'

'Oh sorry,' said Lachlan, looking embarrassed. 'I assumed you three had met.'

'Not officially,' Rilla said, taking a sip of her drink. She made a face and put it down.

'Ladies and gentlemen,' said a very small woman with short, neatly swept back hair. She was holding an iPad and standing on a bar stool. She clapped her hands, then when that had little effect on the noise levels, shouted 'LADIES AND GENTLEMEN' at the top of her voice. The clamour settled to a dull murmur. Jack scanned the room, wondering where Beth was. She'd said she was going to be there, but there was no sign of her. On the other side of the room she could see Miranda, the woman with dark reddish brown hair who worked alongside her. She caught his eye and gave him a brief wave. The woman started talking about the village improvement society and plans they had for floral baskets along the harbour. Half-listening, Jack took the opportunity to look around the bar. He recognised several of the faces from nights he'd spent with Danny having dinner here, and several who he'd bumped into walking around the village in the evenings, getting his bearings. It was surprising to see what a range of ages had turned up – not just older people but young ones of Danny's age, too, who were leaning against the wall by the pool table, chatting quietly under their breath. One glance from the woman who was chairing the meeting silenced them, and it was a moment before Jack realised that she'd stopped focusing on them and was now looking at him.

'Sorry?' he shook himself. 'I didn't quite catch that.'

The man standing beside her – who he recognised as Murdo, the old man they'd met the first night they arrived, gave a chuckle.

'I was saying that it's nice to have some new blood in the village, and that it's been a pleasant surprise how well it seems to have gone.'

There was a general murmur of assent, but all Jack could hear was the chuntering of disapproval from another table. Rilla shook her head very faintly, muttering 'Dolina's off on another rant' to Polly, who giggled.

Greta fixed her eyes on the woman, who stopped grumbling and instead scowled at Jack, who picked up a beer mat and flipped it between his fingers, trying to pretend he hadn't noticed.

'I was thinking it might be nice if you came up and gave us a wee description of the sort of thing you do. If you don't mind, that is?'

Jack could see a wry smile tugging at the corners of Murdo's mouth but stood up, murmuring 'I'll take one for the team, shall I?' to Danny.

'Excuse me,' he said, edging past Polly who shuffled her chair sideways to let him pass. 'You wait there,' he said to Archie, who was sitting under the table hoping someone might drop some crisps. He gave a tail wag of acknowledgement, his bright button eyes looking up at Jack innocently.

The good thing was he had the whole spiel off pat. He made his way through the mass of people, aware that all eyes were on him, and headed towards the bar. Even standing on a bar stool, the woman was still about half a head shorter than him.

'I'm Jack MacDonald from Wildcat Adventures. We're a

not-for-profit independently funded social initiative and our primary role is providing outdoor adventure and activity for young people who've had some challenges in their lives.'

'Aye, tearaways, you mean,' said a ruddy faced blond man of about forty-five. His friends – all of whom had the same slightly bullying rugby player look – all snorted with laughter as if he'd said something wildly original. Jack gave them a flat stare.

'What we do is offer kids that wouldn't have experienced anything like this a chance to spend four nights on a residential trip doing physical activities. Most of them haven't had the chance to mess around outside. Many of them come from backgrounds where they've experienced trauma and this sort of thing helps them to look outside the environment they're living in and see there's something more out there.' He felt the familiar sense of passion rising as he spoke. It wasn't just a job – it was a passion, a way of life. 'We give them a chance to take measured risks – to make decisions about unfamiliar situations, faced with challenges they wouldn't normally experience. This measured risk-taking has been proved to increase their self-esteem and confidence, and most importantly it gives them an increased awareness of the consequences of their actions on other people. So it might look to you like they're messing around on the river, or building a den in the woods, or making a camp fire, but they're learning communication skills, motivation, and concentration.' He stopped, realising that the entire room had fallen silent.

'Sorry,' he said, turning to Greta. 'I didn't mean to go on.'

'Don't apologise,' she said, a broad smile of approval on her face. Murdo gave him a nod. 'You've managed to get this lot listening far better than I ever could. Even my husband's paying attention.'

Murdo gave a chuckle and tipped his glass towards Jack, eyes twinkling as the room erupted in laughter. Jack gave a quiet sigh of relief – it looked like he'd managed to get them on side – for now, anyway.

'So while Mr MacDonald has got your attention, I'd like to talk about the plans for the tourist season, unless anyone has any questions for him?'

She scanned the room. Jack – used to these situations – wasn't surprised that there was a deafening silence. A moment later, there was more laughter as – like a tiny, scruffy little missile, Archie darted his way between the tables, hurtling up to his feet where he made a fruitless but hopeful leap in the direction of the bowl of crisps which sat on the side of the bar.

'I think you've been upstaged,' said Greta, with a smile, bending down to scratch behind Archie's bristly brown ears.

'Always.' Jack smiled, and – picking up his dog – made his way back across to the table, realising as he did that his seat had been taken by Beth, who was sitting beside Danny. Her long hair was loose around her shoulders, clipped back on one side with a clasp. There was a slim silver chain around her neck from which hung a delicate hammered silver locket. She looked up at him and he thought once again how pretty she looked when she smiled, noticing that her freckles had been darkened by the week of sunshine they'd had. They dotted the bridge of her nose and looked as if they'd been sprinkled across her cheeks.

'Have I stolen your seat?'

He shook himself inwardly. Get a grip, man, he told himself, and stop behaving like a lovesick teenager.

'I'll find another.' In his attempt to pull himself together he sounded unnecessarily terse. She'd think he was being deliberately unfriendly if he carried on like that.

He borrowed a stool from the next and turned to find Danny had shifted to make a gap between himself and Beth at the table.

'That was a pretty impressive speech,' she leaned in towards him, her voice low. He felt the hairs on the back of his neck rise as he felt the whisper of her breath on his cheek. There was so little room at the table that his leg was brushing against hers, and he could feel the warmth of her skin through his jeans. The locket swung forward and he pulled his eyes away from it, as if fearful it would mesmerise him somehow.

'All part of the service.'

'And an impressive finish by Archie.'

He'd returned to his original spot under the table, and Jack could feel the warmth of his little terrier body as he curled up to snooze at his feet.

'You're going to show me up on TV if you're that calm under pressure,' she continued. Charlotte gave her a wide-eyed look, putting a jokey finger to her lips and whispering across the table 'You're going to get us thrown out for insurrection.'

Jack laughed. Beth gave him a mischievous look, and sat back in her chair, long fingers wrapped around her glass. He noticed she'd scrubbed her hands clean, and remembered the first time they met and how she'd curled her fingers away from him, conscious of how grubby and compost-stained they'd been. He smiled to himself.

The meeting went on for another fifteen minutes, with a much-debated vote about the design for new recycling bins, a complaint about people walking their dogs and not picking up after them, and a proposal that the village streetlights should be dimmed after ten o'clock at night to prevent light pollution. Polly rolled her eyes at him.

'It's always this exciting, if that's what you're wondering.'

Once the meeting had come to a close, Lachlan and Rilla stood up.

'Are you not staying?' said a returning Polly, who'd gone to the loo.

Rilla shook her head. 'I'm so tired I think I might fall asleep sitting bolt upright.'

'I was exactly the same,' said Beth, looking up at her. 'It does pass.'

'Pregnant,' explained Polly. 'It's very exciting.'

'I'll be excited when I'm awake,' said Rilla, covering her mouth as she yawned widely.

Jack nodded. He had a memory of Rebecca being so wracked with exhaustion that she'd come in from work and sleep until dinner, wake up to eat it, then climb into bed to sleep for twelve hours before waking, still exhausted, the next morning.

'Shh,' said Lachlan. 'It's supposed to be a secret, isn't it?'

'What is?' Miranda appeared, coming over to say hello to Beth. She smiled a hello at Jack. He liked her, despite her slightly scatty nature – she clearly adored Beth, and she was a hard worker, which he appreciated. Every time he saw her in the gardens she was flat out, digging or cutting or trundling back and forth with a wheelbarrow. They'd had a good chat about working outdoors and how beneficial it was for mental health, and he'd surmised that for Miranda the job was as much about keeping herself on an even keel as it was about helping Beth run the flower farm.

'Lachlan's latest gin recipe is a secret,' said Charlotte, quickly. She tapped the side of her nose knowingly, and Jack noticed her brother shoot her a look of gratitude as he turned to leave.

'Oh,' Miranda seemed oblivious to the subtext. 'I bloody love their gin. Talking of which, does anyone want one? I'm going to the bar.' She bobbed her head in the direction of Harry, who could be seen pouring pints behind a post-meeting throng of locals.

'I'll come with you,' said Danny, who'd been keeping a close eye on the bar for a chance to chat to Phoebe. 'Same again?'

Jack nodded. 'I'll get the next couple.'

'Don't sweat it,' said Danny, over his shoulder.

A couple of older teenagers wearing Applemore Hotel branded polo shirts were busying themselves putting the tables and chairs back in order. The crowd had thinned out a bit now, and people were getting themselves drinks and getting ready for the quiz, which started in half an hour. In the corner of the room, a serious looking man of around fifty with hair the colour and texture of straw was setting up a laptop and a projector in preparation.

'That's Jimmy, the quiz master. He takes it very seriously,' explained Beth.

'So who have we got in our team?' He felt now that people had left that he should shift his chair over, but sitting close to her, aware of the sensation of her body a breath away from his, he really didn't want to. He cleared his throat and stood up for a moment, sorting out the chairs so they were arranged neatly around the table.

'You'll end up with a job here if you carry on,' teased Harry, the owner, who appeared from the kitchen with a tea-towel over his shoulder. 'How's it going?'

'Not bad,' admitted Jack.

'And I see you've been permitted entry to the crack

RACHAEL LUCAS

Fraser quiz team,' he said, kissing Beth, Polly and Charlotte hello. 'Is he aware how crap you all are?'

'You're kidding,' said Jack, looking at Beth, who was laughing. 'I was under the impression we were sure-fire winners.'

'Umm,' said Polly, shaking her head in amusement, 'About that...'

'We're hoping you're going to be our secret weapon. Or Danny is.'

'I'm okay on sport, but I'm pretty hopeless on famous people,' Jack admitted.

Danny returned, with the pretty pink-haired girl following.

'Hi Phoebe,' said Beth, shifting her chair sideways so she could sit down.

'I've filled up the ice and the fridges,' Phoebe said to Harry.

'Thanks, Phoebs.' Harry ruffled her hair. 'You're an angel.'

Danny looked at her fondly. Jack, who was feeling slightly confused as to who was who and how everyone knew everyone, sat back in his chair and observed. Beth noticed.

'Phoebe works at the bar two nights a week. She's also doing a placement with me as part of her apprenticeship – she's training to be a florist. So she's learning about flowers at the moment, and I'm hoping that when she qualifies she's going to stay on and make us our fortune by selling wedding flowers for millions to deluded people who think that the secret to happiness is a hideously expensive bouquet.'

'My God you're a cynic,' said Polly, laughing. 'She doesn't mean that, do you, Beth.'

Jack, who liked Beth's dry sense of humour, turned to

look at her. Her eyes were dancing merrily in her pretty face.

'Of course I don't.' She lifted a sardonic eyebrow. 'Or do I…?'

'You don't,' said Charlotte, finally. 'Nobody who loves the hideous mush that is *Love Actually* could be anything other than a romantic at heart.'

'Oh no, please don't get onto *Love Actually*,' said Polly, downing the second half of her second glass of wine. 'Or if you're going to, please let me get a vat of gin to drown myself in first.'

'Make sure it's not Applemore,' said Beth, laughing. 'Lachlan and Rilla don't need the bad publicity if they've got a baby on the way.'

Jack watched the realisation of what she'd said hit a split second later. Her eyes widened and she put a hand to her mouth as if to catch the words, nostrils flaring in horror.

'A *what?*' burst out Phoebe, wide-eyed. 'Oh my God,' she said, grabbing a passing Miranda, who spun slightly so her drink slopped over the side of her glass. 'Did you know Rilla's pregnant?'

'Ha!' Miranda plonked herself down on one of the stools, pulling it in and leaning forward with her chin on her hands and a conspiratorial manner.

'I bloody knew something was up,' she said, giving Beth an old-fashioned look. 'All that waffle about new gin formulations earlier.'

'Shh,' said Beth, putting a finger to her lips. 'It's still early days. I shouldn't have said anything. This is why secrets and alcohol don't mix.'

'Don't worry, I won't breathe a word.' Miranda put a purple-tipped finger to her lips. 'I didn't hear a thing.'

Danny caught Jack's eye. 'Definitely feeling the whole small town thing right now, how about you?'

Jack grinned at his workmate and murmured a reply. 'Yeah, you get the feeling that if you sneezed in this place the entire village would know you had a cold before you'd even had a chance to do anything about it.'

'Right, I hope you lot are feeling brainy,' said Miranda ten minutes later, taking a pen and a sheaf of paper from one of the pub staff who was handing round the photo round for the quiz. She looked down at the printed photographs. 'Is that Jodie Foster?'

Phoebe leaned over, frowning in thought. 'I dunno. Who's Jodie Foster?'

'Phoebe…' said Miranda, laughing and shaking her head.

The first round of the quiz flew by – Danny more than made up for Phoebe's lack of knowledge about famous faces, and Charlotte was a whizz on film titles.

'She's always been a film fan,' Beth explained to Jack as they watched Danny and Phoebe heading up to the bar together. 'When I was escaping into the countryside and growing my own little patch of flowers, Charlotte used to be curled up on the sofa watching movies with our Dad.'

Jack felt a pang of envy at Danny's easy manner – he was standing by the bar, Phoebe smiling as she looked up at him, their body language saying everything. In contrast he was torn between the fact that he really liked Beth and the fact his head was ringing warning bells and reminding him that he'd sworn off relationships.

'Must be nice having so many siblings,' he said, twirling a beer mat between his fingers.

'Hmm,' said Beth. She cupped her face in her hand and

looked at him thoughtfully. A couple of drinks in, she was more relaxed than he'd seen her before. She wrinkled her nose in thought, two fine lines etched on her forehead. 'I always felt a bit like the one who didn't quite fit. Lachlan was the oldest boy so he was given lots of responsibility, Charlotte ended up being the one who looked after us when our mum left, Polly was the baby. I was the middle one. How about you?'

He shook his head. 'Just me.'

'I always fancied that. Funny I ended up having twins.'

'Anna – that's my daughter – always wanted a wee brother or sister.'

'You didn't…' Beth said, tailing off as if she sensed something in the air. 'Sorry, I don't mean to poke my nose in.'

'Oh you're not. No, Rebecca and I split not long after she was born.'

'That must've been hard.'

'Awful,' he said, and then raised one eyebrow, making her laugh. 'Not really. Rebecca's a good person, but she and I were pretty much as incompatible as it's possible to be. Plus the age gap didn't help.'

Beth burst out laughing. 'I bet I can outdo you on the ex front. At least she doesn't spend all his weekends playing Warhammer.'

'Oh,' he said, the smile disappearing from his face. 'I'm a massive Warhammer fan. In fact I was about to ask you if you knew anywhere in the village where I might be able to get together with some players.'

Beth looked at him suspiciously.

He looked at her, face deadpan. 'What?'

'Oh my God, you're serious,' she said, eyes widening. Across the room, he could see Danny, Miranda, Phoebe and

Charlotte all standing by the bar, laughing and chatting to Harry.

'I'm not,' he said, after a moment. 'I will admit to a fondness for *Star Wars*, but everyone has their faults.'

'It's fine, I've got a terrible cheesy romance film habit, but don't tell anyone. It'll completely ruin my street cred.'

She pulled a lock of hair over her shoulder, absent-mindedly twirling it around her finger. 'Simon isn't actually all that bad. I just got married really young because I wanted to escape.'

'Yeah, I can see why you'd want to escape the enormous castle and your own private forest…'

'It's not as amazing as you'd think,' Beth said, shaking her head and laughing, 'I realise that there is literally no way I can say that without you thinking I'm a complete arse, so I'm going to stop talking.'

'I'm teasing you,' he said, giving Danny a nod as he came back across the room carrying their drinks, Phoebe following behind. 'If there's one thing this job has taught me it's that you can't ever judge what someone's family life is like from their background. You have to take everyone on their own merits.'

'You talking about work again?' Danny pulled up a chair. Phoebe sat down beside him, opening a bag of crisps and offering them round.

He shook his head. 'No, believe it or not, we weren't.'

The crack team at the next table by the fireplace were racing ahead – by the end of the second round they were twenty points in front. Jack watched the way that Charlotte and Beth related to each other – she'd said there were only a couple of years between them, but while Beth joked and laughed with Miranda and Phoebe, it was interesting to notice that Charlotte seemed distracted. She wasn't drinking, and she kept an eye on her phone all evening. Maybe it was that big sister thing Beth had mentioned – the dynamics of family life intrigued him, because he hadn't ever experienced it. Growing up, he'd pretty much been left to his own devices a lot of the time. It surprised him that Beth had been brought up with only one parent around, as he had.

'Jack?' Danny nudged him a moment later.

'Sorry, I was away in a dream,' he said, shaking himself. 'What's up?'

'Miranda and Phoebe were saying they'd love to see what we do,' he said, looking across the table at Miranda, who was folding an empty crisp pack into tiny squares.

She looked up and nodded. 'I'm dying to have a go on a kayak.'

'You are?' Beth looked at her with surprise.

'Aren't you?'

Beth shook her head. 'I prefer staying on dry land.'

'We don't just do water sports,' Jack said, turning to look at her. His knee brushed hers and he felt a jolt of desire. Beer plus a pretty girl was a really terrible combination. He could feel his resolve weakening. 'We've got the nightline, if you three want to do some team bonding?'

'The what?'

'It's a rope course through the woods... we use it for the teenagers as a confidence building exercise. You have to wear a blindfold, and you need to use your senses to get around the course. It's really simple, but it takes a lot of co-operation and it really makes you think.'

'I'm intrigued.' Miranda leaned in, keen to hear more. Phoebe stole a glance at Danny, who flicked an eyebrow upwards, giving her a half smile. She looked down. The two of them were like something from a Flirting 101 guidebook.

Beth saw him watching and her lips curved upwards in a smile. She caught his eye, amused.

'Alright,' she said, surprising him. 'I'm game if you lot are.'

'Why don't we go the whole hog,' said Danny, turning to Jack, 'We could do a bushcraft session? Take them camping? We can do it in a few weeks when we've got a long weekend off.'

Charlotte shook her head with a snort of laughter. 'I think I'm busy that day.'

'You don't know when it's going to be,' said Beth, giving her sister a dig in the ribs. 'Oh go on, Char,' said Miranda, taking a swig of her drink. 'You can't be the sensible one all your life.'

'I *am* the sensible one,' said Charlotte, drily, 'Which is why I have no desire whatsoever to camp out overnight on a bed of heather and get bitten to death by midges when I have a perfectly comfortable memory foam mattress at home.'

'Chicken,' said Beth, folding her arms.

'I am not,' said Charlotte, sitting up slightly.

'*Sisters...*' sang Miranda, tunelessly. Phoebe glanced at Danny again. Across the other side of the bar, the quiz master was preparing for the music round. A snippet of Kylie Minogue blasted out, clearly surprising him. He jumped, and snapped his laptop shut. Harry roared with laughter behind the bar.

'Fine,' Charlotte said, after a moment. 'Okay, let's do it. Beth, if this results in disaster I'm blaming you.'

'It won't,' said Jack. If he was completely sober, he'd probably have come up with a million and one reasons why doing this was seriously dodgy, but they had weekends free, and nothing better to do, and if there weren't some advantages to being in charge, what was the point of being the boss?

Plus, he told himself a while later, as he watched Beth leaning over their quiz sheet, blonde hair falling over her shoulder, forehead creased in concentration as she tried to remember the answer to one of the questions he'd missed, it would mean he'd get to spend more time with her. Not – as he reminded himself, firmly – that he had any intention of them being anything more than friends.

CHAPTER ELEVEN

THE NEXT DAY was one of those mornings for Beth. She'd woken up to the alarm, snoozed it twice, and then rolled out of bed looking like she'd been dragged through a hedge backwards, stopping in the kitchen only long enough to make a coffee and take two painkillers for the headache that came with that final – unwise – glass of wine she'd had last night. As she waited for the kettle to boil, she'd thought about the evening, running back through the night as if it was a film in her head, skipping over the good bits and remembering the bits that made her cringe. Why on earth didn't brains focus on the bits where you looked cool and sophisticated?

She and Jack had been standing outside the hotel with his little dog Archie at the end of the evening, the rest of the pub quiz people having spilled out of the bar fifteen minutes before. Phoebe and Danny were standing on the opposite side of the road, leaning against the harbour rail, looking out to sea. The sounds of their laughter carried through the still evening air. Miranda and Charlotte had stood chatting to Harry for ages as he and the staff cleared up, persuading him to wrap up some leftovers from that night's service in the restaurant. Beth had felt suddenly shy, standing there, him on one side of the door, her on the other, both looking at each other. The easy chat they'd shared seemed to have dried up completely.

'Are you working tomorrow?'

She'd wrapped her arms around herself against the cool of the night air.

'Yeah, up ridiculously early to get all these flowers over to the farmers' market – I share a stall with a friend. You?'

Jack had shaken his head. 'I'm going to drive over to Inverness. We've got an order of equipment which was supposed to be here today but it's gone AWOL, so I said I'd go and pick it up.'

'That's a long drive,' she'd said, thinking to herself as she did that she'd somehow developed the conversational skills of someone who'd been locked in an attic for twenty years. If she'd been Polly, she'd have been bright and chatty, and Charlotte's calm self-possession meant that she wouldn't have found silence awkward. But she was there, simultaneously feeling like she'd run out of things to say and also desperately trying not to sound like a complete twit.

Fortunately at that point Charlotte had reappeared, handing her two warm parcels.

'Chips,' she'd said. 'D'you want some?'

'I'm okay, thanks,' Jack had said. Archie had been far more interested, and he'd had to scoop him up into his arms, laughing, as he set off for the cottage and they'd headed back to Charlotte's car. 'I'll give you a shout about some dates for this weekend idea on Monday,' he'd called after them.

145

'Can't wait,' said Miranda, jogging up behind them. 'Sorry, I forgot my bag.'

Charlotte had driven her home from the pub quiz, dropping Miranda at her little cottage on the way out of Applemore village. The night sky had been the faded denim blue of late spring, Jupiter glowing bright. Beth had gazed out of the window, sitting in silence, until Charlotte had broken into her thoughts.

'You like him,' she'd said, with her usual calm simplicity.

'Who?'

'Don't come the innocent with me,' Charlotte had said, slowing as they approached the tight bend in the road at the top of the hill before home.

Beth bit her thumbnail, and didn't say anything. Her phone buzzed with a reminder she'd set herself earlier. *Remember to put paper in boot*, it said. She had to be up at half five to get the flowers ready to go for the farmers' market. Tomorrow morning Beth was going to hate 'let's stay a bit longer' Beth. She groaned faintly at the prospect. Luckily it wasn't her turn to be there for six to get set up – that was her friend Fliss's job this time. She yawned, as if her body had remembered that it was going to be hauled summarily out of bed six hours later.

'He likes you, too, incidentally,' Charlotte continued, passing the narrow driveway that led to Applemore House and heading on through the countryside to the farmhouse.

'Don't be silly,' Beth said, and then a moment later 'Do you think?'

'Ha,' said Charlotte, sounding pleased with herself. 'I knew it!'

'Look, I have enough going on in my life. I've got work, twins, a house to run, a failed marriage, and did I mention work?'

'Doesn't mean you're not entitled to a life,' Charlotte had said, pulling up outside the farmhouse.

As Beth drove down to the flower farm the words echoed in her head. She took a mouthful of still-too-hot coffee and winced as she swallowed. There was loads to do. Thankfully she'd taken the car seats out and folded down the seats of the car, and the back of the pick-up was ready to go. The sky was a vibrant orange-pink – it was going to be a gorgeous day later, but right now the air was crisp and fresh. Hopefully she'd make enough money to make it worthwhile. She loaded up the flowers, shivering as she took them from the dark, chilly outbuilding where she stored them overnight to keep them fresh. She'd worked so hard prepping the day before – processing, arranging, labelling – that her fingers were red and stiff in the cold, and she was thankful for her fingerless gloves. She worked fast, and an hour later was heading along quiet roads towards Strathtorron.

Her friend Fliss was already there, and the market square was bustling with stallholders getting organised. Land Rovers and battered white vans jostled for space in the narrow streets. Tarpaulins flapped and the air was filled with the clang of metal poles as people assembled the stalls, shouting and laughing to each other as they worked.

'You look knackered,' said Fliss, giving her a kiss of welcome.

'Thanks,' said Beth, drily.

'I hope it was worth it.'

Beth couldn't help smiling. 'I had a lovely night.'

'Nice to see you getting out. You can tell me all the hot goss once we've got set up.' She kicked at the leg of the folding trestle table so it clicked into place.

Beth started carrying the buckets of flowers from the

back of the pick-up and putting them to one side. Fliss fastened their signs up with bungee cords, humming to herself as she worked.

They covered the table with a gingham cloth, and together set their stall out. Beth had met Fliss, who was a baker, at a part-time college course on business building the summer before – both of them single parents, they'd bonded over coffee and cake after class, and when the chance for a stall came up at the thriving farmers' market where Fliss lived, it seemed the perfect chance. Doing it together made it more fun, and made the juggling a little bit easier to manage. Not that there hadn't been unscheduled disasters – one weekend Fliss's ex hadn't turned up to collect their son the night before, so she'd had to bring him along where he'd managed an hour of behaving beautifully before he'd started howling with boredom in his pushchair. In the end they'd taken it in turns to keep him occupied, Fliss fudging it and managing to waffle about flowers in such a way that the buyers didn't seem to notice, and Beth doing the same and hoping nobody would notice that she didn't have a clue about artisan sourdough bread.

'Looking good,' Billy, the market inspector, strolled past, stopping to peer over the buckets of flowers at the delicious array of cakes and breads that Fliss was arranging in the wicker baskets on the table. 'Save me a couple of those banana loaves, will you? The missus was fuming that I forgot to get her some last month.'

'You should probably make it up to her with some flowers,' said Beth, giving him a knowing nod.

'You're probably right. I tell you what, put that nice bunch of – what are they? The pink ones?'

'Ranunculus,' explained Beth. 'And tulips. And the little pale cream ones are a scented narcissus.'

'Ah,' said Billy, laughing. 'I think it'll stick with just calling them the pink ones. Anyway, put that big bunch aside. I tell you what, this job is going to bankrupt me. I'm no' supposed to end up buying my way round the market when I'm doing an inspection, but there's so much good stuff on offer.'

'You're not joking.' Fliss put a hand to her stomach. 'My tummy has been growling since Nick and Jenny over there started cooking the meat for those fresh roast pork rolls they make.'

'I thought it was just me.' Beth lifted the bouquet out of the metal bucket and placed it round the back of the stall so it wouldn't be picked up by an unsuspecting potential buyer. 'I tell you what, I'll nip over and get a couple of their bacon rolls before we get started.'

She handed Fliss over her coin purse and the contactless payment gadget. 'In case there's a mad rush in the next five minutes.'

By the time she returned, despite the fact that it was only half past eight, the early-bird customers had already started appearing, baskets over their arms, peering with interest at the stallholders' wares. Strathtorron was a little town which was on the road to Inverness, and the brightly painted signs seemed to tempt people in on their way to the city for a weekend trip.

'Morning,' said an elderly couple in unison.

'Hello!' Fliss beamed a greeting.

'So who grows the flowers, and who bakes these lovely cakes?'

'I do the flowers,' said Beth, motioning to the Applemore Flower Farm apron she was just tying around her waist, 'And Fliss is the whizz in the kitchen.'

'What a lovely combination, don't you think, Bill?' the

woman bent down, picking up a bunch of tulips, their stems wrapped neatly in brown paper. 'Actually, I think I'll take three of these. One for me, and one each for the girls. We're going to visit our grand-daughters in Inverness,' she explained, as her husband pulled out his bank card. 'I'm doing the shopping, he's doing the paying.'

'Wouldn't have it any other way,' chuckled her husband. 'I tell you what though, I'm not leaving without a couple of those nice-looking ginger loaves.'

The next hour flew by, with hardly a second to spare. Beth had just nipped back to the van to replenish her stock of tulips which seemed to be selling at a rate of knots when she heard Fliss laughing, and then the deep rumble of a familiar-sounding Glasgow accent followed by a sharp terrier bark. Her stomach knotted. She picked up the bucket, and with it in her arms, rounded the side of the stall to see Fliss passing a pack of her cheese-topped sourdough buns across to Jack.

'Fancy meeting you here,' he said with a grin.

'I thought you were off to Inverness to pick up some equipment.'

Fliss looked from Beth to Jack, her eyebrows shooting skywards. 'Am I missing something here?'

'Fliss, this is Jack. Jack, I mentioned Fliss last night.'

'Fame at last,' beamed Fliss. 'Hello, you,' she said, bending down to stroke Archie. 'So how do you two know each other?'

Beth put the bucket of flowers down, picking up the empty bucket and swinging it in her hand. 'Remember I told you about the outdoor centre?'

'Oh, the place you were —' Beth shot her a look, remembering that the last time they'd spoken she'd been grumbling about it to her. Fliss, thankfully, pulled herself up short. '– I remember,' she added, giving Beth a sideways glance.

'Jack runs the centre.'

'Oh I see,' said Fliss, putting her hands in the back pockets of her jeans and arching her back. 'I set off without breakfast this morning and saw the signs as I was coming along the road, and I thought I'd investigate,' Jack explained. 'And I thought it'd be nice to see you in action.'

Beth looked at him for a moment, his dark eyes catching hers. The fan of wrinkles at the edges crinkled as he smiled and she felt the knot in her stomach untangle slightly. But – she told herself very firmly – she was just glad to see him because he was a friend, and it was always nice to see friends in unfamiliar situations. She shook herself inwardly. Honestly, this was ridiculous.

'The flowers look amazing,' he continued, casting a glance at the masses of brightly coloured blooms in their stainless steel buckets. 'You've been working hard – again.'

'Always.' Beth smiled.

'Has Beth told you she's coming on an adventure with us?' Jack paid for the rolls, then pocketed his wallet. He hadn't shaved, and the day-old stubble emphasised the line of his jaw. As if aware she'd noticed, he rubbed his chin briefly, still looking at Beth while talking.

'No way,' Fliss snorted with amusement.

'Cheek,' said Beth. 'I am more than capable of a bit of outdoor adventure.'

Fliss gave her a sceptical look. 'I'm aware you spend all your working week outside grubbing around in the mud, but I didn't have you down as the mountain-climbing sort.'

'No mountain climbing,' Jack assured them, 'But I've been musing on what we can do, and I think a bit of bushcraft might be fun.'

Beth groaned. 'Are we talking rubbing two sticks together to make fire?'

'That sort of thing, yes. I bet you can't wait.'

'I'm counting the days.'

Fliss had turned away with a bright and welcoming smile on her face as a sudden influx of potential customers appeared, asking questions about the ingredients of her cakes.

'I better let you get on,' Jack said.

'Have a good trip.'

'Thanks. Hope you have a sell-out day – although by the looks of it, you're not going to need much luck.'

'Fingers crossed.'

With a wave, he was gone. Beth stood watching him as he strode across the marketplace, tall and broad, long legs clad in jeans. He had – objectively speaking, she told herself firmly – a very nice bum.

'Ahem,' said Fliss a moment later, elbowing her in the ribs.

'What?'

'Don't give me *what*,' she snorted, putting her hands on her hips.

'Hi,' said Beth, smiling with gratitude at a girl in her early twenties who had picked up a couple of the sweet little posies of purple alliums and pale lilac anemones she'd tied up late yesterday. 'Can I help?'

'I'd like to take these, please,' she said, handing over the exact change. Beth popped it in the coin purse that hung around her waist.

'I want to know what's going on with you and the hot Glaswegian.'

'Nothing is going on,' said Beth, firmly. 'We're just – neighbours.'

'Right.' Fliss paused again to serve another customer. The sun was shining in a cloudless blue sky now, and the market square was filling up fast. 'He looks really familiar though, I'm sure I've seen him somewhere. He's not been on TV or something?'

Beth shook her head. 'Not as far as I know.'

'You know me, I've got a really weird memory for faces. It'll come to me in the middle of the night tonight and I'll text you.'

'Please don't,' joked Beth.

'Okay, I'll text you in the morning.' She scratched her head. 'Maybe he used to be a male model or something.'

'Hardly.'

'Oh come on, he's gorgeous.'

'He doesn't look anything like a model.'

'He's tall, dark, looks a bit dangerous… what's not to like? Which brings me to my next point – you realise he's got the major hots for you.'

Beth shook her head. She busied herself with re-arranging the flowers to fill in the gaps, moving buckets around and straightening the pile of business cards which she handed out with each purchase. Then she took out her phone and took some pictures, sharing them on Instagram.

'You can put your head in the sand all you like,' said Fliss, persistently. 'But I want to know all the gory details when there are some. You realise he couldn't take his eyes off you?'

Beth felt a heat rising in her cheeks. 'You're imagining it.'

'Let's see,' said Fliss, smugly. 'Outdoor activities.' She snorted with amusement at her own joke. 'That's one word for it.'

'Felicity!' said Beth, laughing.

153

But no matter how she tried to keep herself from thinking about it, she couldn't ignore the jolt of longing that she'd felt when he gazed at her. For half a second, she allowed herself to imagine how it would feel to snake her arms around Jack's neck and feel the graze of stubble on her cheek. Her heart thudded unevenly and she felt her breath catch in her throat.

'You okay?' Fliss looked across at her. Beth nodded, but felt certain that her feelings were written all over her face.

CHAPTER TWELVE

'Hi Jack,' Gina from the TV production company was on the phone, and Jack felt a vague sense of unease. He shifted from one foot to the other, standing on the ridge of the hill that looked out across the water toward the islands. Ahead of him, Danny and a couple of the other members of staff were giving last minute instructions before the group set out onto the loch on their rafts. 'Just calling to firm up the dates for filming. We're going to be heading down your way on the fourteenth of June – hoping to get in before the mad rush of the school holidays starts – so we'd like to pencil in some time to have a chat with you, do a bit of pre-work, that sort of thing.'

'Of course,' he said, absently. He was only half-listening, mind wandering as he watched the teams clamber onto their rafts, wondering what activities he and Danny would be showing Beth and the others for their bushcraft experience. In an ideal world, he'd be taking Beth out to dinner, but – he shook his head. 'Sorry Gina, I missed that bit. What did you say?'

She laughed. 'I've spoken to Beth – thought it might be nice if we could do a bit to camera with both of you, seeing as you're neighbours, so to speak. I've been having a look at your website – maybe we could do it in your little treehouse? That way we could get a bird's-eye view over the flower farm as well.'

'You have been doing your homework,' said Jack.

'Once a journalist, always a journalist,' said Gina, sounding slightly smug, and the hairs on the back of his neck prickled uncomfortably. He shook himself. She was a TV producer, not a hack looking for a story.

They sorted out times and dates and he hung up. He'd more than enough to be getting on with without worrying about what she might dig up – at the end of the day, he was probably making something out of nothing.

All of that was forgotten that evening, though, when he called Rebecca for his once-weekly catch up. While Anna was still refusing to talk, it was the closest he could get to keeping in touch with what she was up to.

'You've got to give Anna her due,' he admitted, crossing one leg in front of the other as he stood, leaning against the harbour wall, watching a busload of tourists climbing out and making their way towards the Applemore Hotel. 'She's bloody determined.'

Rebecca gave a wry laugh. 'Can't think who she gets that from.'

'I was thinking you,' he said, thinking of Rebecca's drive to get to the top of her career despite numerous setbacks. She'd worked incredibly hard, and while their relationship had foundered early on, he admired her as a person and as a mother.

'Don't do yourself down,' said his ex, generously. 'You've done pretty well for yourself.'

'Apart from the obvious,' he said, with a heavy sigh. 'None of that actually means anything if I have a daughter who'd rather pretend I don't exist.'

'She's just angry that you didn't stand in the way of the move.'

'I wish she'd take it out on you instead of me,' he said, laughing and picking up a stone from a little pile that was balanced on top of the wall. He threw it into the water, watching as a gull swooped down in its wake then flew off in disgust realising it wasn't something delicious discarded by a tourist.

'Oh, believe me,' said Rebecca, with feeling, 'She's making her views well known. Who knew sixteen was going to be such hard work?'

He smiled. 'I think we thought we'd missed the teenage thing when she was easy up until now.'

'Too blooming right. Turns out she was storing it up waiting until she had enough explosive power in her armoury to make a massive impact.'

'How's she doing at school?'

'Oh, she's great there, apparently. No problem at all. She's a veritable delight.'

'That's fairly standard, y'know.'

He heard Rebecca sigh. 'I know, I know. You're about to tell me it's a sign she feels secure at home, and all that stuff.'

He shrugged. The gull landed on the wall a few metres away and stared at him beadily.

'It's great in theory, isn't it? I've sent messages, photos, videos of the beach... I've told her I love her. I've done everything by the book.' Even as he spoke, he knew that the answer didn't lie in a book. He'd done everything he could and Anna's actions – or lack of them – told him everything he needed to hear.

'I'm going to sort out some time off, and get over to you for the weekend. I'll have a look at flights.'

There was a pause before Rebecca spoke.

'This weekend... I can't do this weekend.'

'You can't, or Anna can't?' He was careful to keep the edge out of his voice. He'd worked bloody hard to keep things amicable with Rebecca for Anna's sake – for all the good it had done, he thought, shaking his head slightly – but that had meant doing everything her way.

'Neither of us. I've got a friend coming to stay. We've got plans.'

'Okay, fine. I'll come the weekend after. How's that? It's been two months and I've had a handful of messages from her in that time and she's still refusing to take my calls half the time, and being offhand the other half. I know she knows her own mind, but I'm beginning to think that my hands-off approach looks like I don't give a damn.'

'She knows you do.'

'Okay.' He wasn't convinced. 'I'll give you a shout once I've got more of an idea about timings. It's going to have to be a bit of a flying visit, but hopefully it'll work.'

'Sure.'

He put his phone back in his pocket and turned, hands on the railing that surrounded the harbour, looking out to sea.

'Penny for them?'

He spun around, a smile breaking across his face. Beth was standing there, twins holding her hands, and he'd never been so glad to see a friendly face.

'Oh hi,' he said, looking down then at Edward and Lucy. 'Hello, you two. Have you been somewhere exciting?'

Edward had smears of blue paint all over his face. Lucy was holding onto a pink and yellow helium balloon in the shape of a unicorn, her tiny pudgy fist clutching on as if her life depended on it.

'We went to a birthday party,' said Lucy, looking at her brother. 'Is that your doggy?'

He nodded. Archie wagged his stumpy tail and rolled over, making Lucy giggle.

'Can we pat him?'

'Gently, darling,' said Beth, lifting a finger in warning. 'He might not be as friendly as Uncle Lachlan's dogs.'

'He's fine,' said Jack, squatting down to the twins' level and rubbing Archie's stomach to show them he was friendly. 'Look.' Lucy put her hand on the dog and patted vigorously. 'So, a birthday party. That sounds exciting.'

'A bit too exciting,' said Beth. He straightened up and watched as she let go of Edward's hand for a second to push up the sleeve of her cardigan. The little boy scampered off towards the grassy patch where there were a couple of picnic tables. 'Go on, you can have a play for five minutes,' she said to Lucy, taking the balloon ribbon from her hand. 'I'll hold that so you don't lose it. Hopefully they might burn off some of the sugar,' she added to Jack, watching as they climbed onto the table and sat, legs swinging, chatting away happily.

'I remember Anna at the same age. Seems like about five minutes ago.'

'How old is she now?'

'Sixteen. I was just on the phone to her mother,' he went on, as they strolled towards the twins. 'I'm still persona non grata for not putting any barriers up to her mum's move to Paris, or that's how she sees it.'

'Were you tempted to?' Lucy stood beside him, evening sunlight turning her hair a dark gold.

He scratched his chin. 'Yes and no. I mean how could I

stand in the way of her having pretty much everything she could ever want?'

Lucy gave him a shrewd look. 'Materially?'

'Riding lessons, tennis lessons, a massive house, private school. All that stuff.'

'D'you think that matters?'

'I think maybe that's easy for you to say when you grew up in a place like Applemore. If I showed you where I grew up, you'd see.' He realised he was sounding chippy and gazed across the water at the distant islands for a moment, wondering as he did so if the past was always going to weigh so heavily on his present.

'Maybe you could take me one day,' she said, and then stopped herself, as if she'd spoken without thinking. 'I mean if you really wanted to make your point.'

He laughed. 'I'd take you. You'd get a shock, though.'

'I'm fairly unshockable,' Beth said, bending down to pick up Lucy, who'd tottered over rubbing her eyes. 'I think these two might be hitting the wall. Come on Ed, let's get you two home.'

'Did you get a call from Gina about the filming?' He wished for a moment that she didn't have to leave, and that he could stand chatting to her for ages. He turned, falling into step beside her as she headed back to her car, which was parked along by the bookshop. A couple of exhausted-looking walkers with poles in hands dodged them, stepping off the pavement and onto the road to let them past.

'I did. She seemed very keen we should do a bit together in the treehouse? Seems a bit weird to me, but I said yes, whatever. I just hope it's going to make my fortune.'

'I'm sure it will. I noticed the other day that everything seems to be growing at about a hundred miles an hour.'

Now he sounded like he'd been spying. Cool, MacDonald, he thought to himself. Effortlessly cool.

'Yeah, it's that time of year. You should come over and have a look – I mean you could, if you like?' She shaded her eyes against the sun, turning to look at him.

'I'd love to. I promise solemnly not to drop any trees on you, and I'll make sure there are no errant teenagers crashing around helping themselves to your prize flowers.'

She smiled. 'Okay, come over tomorrow evening. Simon has the twins, and I'm going to be working late. You can get the guided tour and tell me what you think of my plans.'

'It's a deal. If you play your cards right,' he said, lifting an eyebrow, 'I might let you in on what we've got planned for you lot.'

'Oh God,' Beth groaned. 'Go easy on me. I might've grown up here, but I don't fancy sleeping under the stars and freezing to death. I like my home comforts.'

Jack shook his head, laughing. 'I promise you won't freeze to death.'

'That leaves quite a lot of scope for other stuff,' Beth opened the car door and watched the twins climb in.

'That's the plan.'

'I can't wait. No, wait – I very definitely can. Okay, I'll see you tomorrow.'

He headed back home. He'd been in for an hour and was sitting on the sofa – Danny having disappeared off for a date with Phoebe and instructed him not to wait up – when a notification buzzed on his phone. He picked it up, expecting it to be either Nathan, the charity boss, who seemed to spend all night thinking about work and texting at inopportune moments, or Danny sending a jokey text about the amazing night he was having while Jack sat at home like an old git. He stared at the screen in surprise.

Hi Dad…

His heart thudded against his ribs. Finally.

Hello AB, he typed. *You okay?*

Keep it casual, he told himself. Don't come in all heavy.

Yeah. Sorry I was arsey with you.

He shook his head. Only in the world of teenagers – completely wrapped up in their own feelings, oblivious to those of their parents – could a teenager go off the grid for nearly two months and casually apologise with a brief sentence.

Don't be. It's ok. Love you.

There was a pause. He could see she was typing, but then she stopped and the screen went blank. Then she started to type again.

Dad?

Yes darling?

Can I come up and see you?

Course. We can have a look at flights. I can pick you up in Inverness.

Okay.

AB? She'd been Anna Banana ever since she was a tiny baby, and it had stuck as their private name for her.

Yeah

It's lovely to hear from you.

You too. Need to go, apparently we're going out for dinner.

He lay his head back against the sofa pillows and closed his eyes. God, he'd missed her. But he'd done what he thought was the right thing, sending her down there – he had his reasons. One day when she was older, he'd explain. He just hoped that before that, she didn't work it out.

~

The next day seemed to drag on forever. They had a particularly objectionable group of middle management bods who'd come in for a team building day – the sort of day they charged a fortune for, the profits of which meant that they could keep the costs down for the groups of teenagers they worked with. But he always struggled with the pseudo-alpha sort of idiot who turned up to these things determined to prove that they were the bigger man than their work colleagues. Danny, who didn't get wound up by them, had been detailed with taking them on a raft building experience. Jack sorted stuff out back at the log cabin HQ, and kept in contact by walkie-talkie. At the end of the afternoon he went down to show face, making polite conversation with the quietest member of the group, who'd – as he suspected – ended up being the one who'd come up with the plan for the raft that was now bobbing successfully on the loch, with the loudmouth bloke who'd rubbed him up the wrong way standing on top, legs akimbo, looking proud of himself. These sort of days taught you a lot about people, he thought, watching. He took some photos for social media, and then headed off with a brief wave – Danny and the others could take it from there. He'd pretty much given up trying to pretend to himself that he wasn't desperate to go and see Beth – he'd liked talking to her last night, and she actually listened, which seemed to be a rare quality.

She was digging over a flower bed when he got there, face scarlet and damp with sweat.

'Sorry, I'll be two secs. I needed to get this done, it's been bugging me for ages.'

'D'you want a hand?'

'It's okay, I'm nearly done. It's not actually difficult – the soil isn't heavy, it's just hot.'

'Hopefully it'll be nice and warm like this when we're

camping.' He couldn't resist teasing her, knowing he'd get a reaction.

'Oh God, don't.' She straightened up, pushing her hair out of her face. 'Please tell me you're joking.'

'You'll have to wait and see.'

'I tell you what you can do,' she said, after a moment. 'If you go into the greenhouse you'll see the kettle and a packet of chocolate digestives. If you want to make us a coffee, I'd be eternally grateful. Then I can give you the guided tour.'

'Deal.'

'Milk and one sugar, please,' she called after him as he turned to walk away.

He headed across the garden. In the last few weeks since he'd been there, everything seemed to have shot up. There was a long bed of tulips, the buds of which were still green and tightly closed, and he recognised the neat bushes of lavender which released their scent as he brushed past. They weren't flowering yet, but there were long stems shooting up from the bushes – it wouldn't be long.

Inside the greenhouse, he switched on the kettle and found a jar of instant coffee, making them both a cup. It was fascinating to see Beth's workplace – it wasn't spotlessly tidy, but there was a place for everything – heaps of pots stacked on the shelves, and bags of compost lay on a wooden pallet to one side of the door. There were rolls and rolls of string and raffia, and piles of the brown paper she used to wrap her simple bunches of flowers were stamped with **Applemore Flower Farm** and a row of little daisies. She worked harder than anyone he'd ever met – it seemed to verge on an obsession.

'Here you are.' He handed her a cup. She'd finished digging, the spade stuck in the soil. She wiped her muddy hands on her jeans. 'D'you want a biscuit as well?'

'Please.' She took one, glancing at her fingernails which were filthy again. 'Sorry, that's a bit grim. I work on the principle that all this grubbing around must mean I have a really healthy immune system.'

'A good principle.' He raised his mug to hers in a jokey toast.

'Cheers.' She took a sip. 'Oh God, that's lovely. I know when it's hot you're supposed to want a cold drink but I have been dying for this for ages. It's so nice to have someone make me a cup.'

'Yeah,' he nodded. 'That's the thing about living on your own.'

'Nobody to bring you a cup of coffee in bed.' Her gaze met his and he thought, with a sudden stab of desire, how much he'd like to wake up beside her. She looked away, and he shook himself. 'Anyway, I'm looking forward to the guided tour.'

'Okay, you can be my guinea pig.' She started walking, mug in hand. 'So the thing is, I need to get more money coming in, and –'

He turned to look at her, wondering why she'd stopped talking. Beth stood still, eyes wide, and motioned subtly with a pointing finger to her left, pointing across his body towards the wooden door in the garden wall.

'Hellooooo,' called a familiar voice. Gina the TV producer was standing in the doorway with one hand on her hip, another waving frantically.

'Oh God, I completely forgot she was coming today.'

He shook his head. 'I thought she said next week.' She was rushing towards them, a huge smile on her face, enormous sunglasses balanced on the top of her head. 'Big plans, treehouse, all that jazz?'

Beth giggled. 'That's a surprisingly accurate impression.'

She made a face. 'I must've got the dates muddled somehow. Or she did. I need this like a hole in the head today.'

'I thought it was only me having second thoughts.'

She shook her head. 'I know it's good for the business, and all that jazz – as she would say – but I don't know if I'm cut out for being on TV.'

Jack pasted on a welcoming smile as Gina reached them. She had a phone in one hand, and was typing something in with one finger.

'There,' she said, with a flourish, putting it back into her expensive-looking handbag. 'Right. Well this is a turn-up for the books. I was hoping I might get you, Beth, but here we are and I've bagged two for the price of one.'

Beth smiled cautiously. 'I think we've got in a mix up over dates – Jack thought you weren't here until next week?'

'Well yes,' said Gina, taking off her sunglasses and wiping them on the hem of her blue and white striped shirt, 'That was the plan, but then we saw the weather forecast, and thought we'd take advantage of this glorious weather to get as much in the can as we can, so to speak.' She gave them a bright smile. 'Make hay when the sun shines, and all that. Isn't that rule number one of farming?'

'Probably,' admitted Beth, glancing up at the sky. 'I've been hoping if I don't think about it, this nice weather will continue. Basically I'm going for the ignorance is bliss approach.'

Amused, Jack shot a sideways glance at her. She was absent-mindedly scratching a midge bite on her forearm. She had a smudge of dirt on her cheek, her hair had come loose from its plait and long tendrils were curling around her neck, and he realised with alarming certainty that he was falling for her.

'Well, anyway,' said Gina briskly, 'Here we are, and here

you both are. It's fate. Gregor – he's the cameraman – and Bill the sound man are on the way.'

'But…' Beth opened her mouth to protest.

'Only take twenty minutes. Half an hour at most,' said Gina, with a winning smile. 'I know you're not busy,' she went on, looking at Jack, 'because I saw your people heading off in a minibus, and I bumped into your co-worker – the handsome young one? Anyway he said that as there was nobody about he'd be happy for us to do a bit of filming of the centre. He looked jolly good on camera, actually.'

Jack groaned. Danny had been dying to get in on the filming since he'd first heard about it.

'You could have got him to do the whole thing,' he said, 'In fact if you want to just use him, I'm more than happy to take a step back.'

'Oh gosh no,' said Gina cheerfully. 'The more handsome chaps we have the better. You've got a good face for television.' She frowned at him for a moment. 'It's funny, when I showed Gregor your photo he said he thought you looked familiar, and I've been racking my brains trying to think who you remind me of.'

A breath caught in his throat. 'Lots of people say that,' he said, lightly. Gina looked away, turning to watch as her crew lumbered in carrying heavy equipment over their shoulders.

'So you're happy to go ahead? Oh please say yes,' she said, putting both hands together in a gesture of prayer, eyes huge and lashes batting, 'It would make my life so much easier.'

'If you put it like that,' he said, feeling sorry for her – she had a job to do as well, after all, and as far as he could gather she'd spent the best part of the last month driving up and down the North West coast of the Highlands trying to persuade diffident, naturally uncommunicative Scots to share their feelings and talk about things to camera. It didn't come naturally to them.

He looked at Beth, who gave the ghost of a nod.

'Caught bang to rights,' she said. 'Okay, fine. I'm game if you are.'

'Saying that is what got us into this mess in the first place,' said Jack a moment later as they followed Gina back across the stone path towards the greenhouse.

'Cheers for this,' said the older man, who was balding, with a salt-and-pepper beard. He was sweating in the late afternoon sunshine, dark patches in the armpits of his checked shirt. 'Bloody hell it's hot for the beginning of May, isn't it?'

'It's always lovely up here this time of year,' said Beth. 'That's why we get so many visitors at the beginning of the season.'

'Okay, save that for when we're talking to camera. I've got some questions to ask you, but what I want to do is use them as prompts so it looks like you're chatting happily. If you'd like to give us a bit of a tour of the flower farm, Beth?' Gina spun on her heel, taking in the beds crammed with plants of all shapes and sizes.

'You said you wanted a tour,' she said to him under her breath as they waited ten minutes for Bill and Gregor to get everything set up.

He'd been hoping for a bit of time alone with her, not a live studio audience, but he was hardly going to admit that.

'Okay, Beth, let's go. I'll ask you some questions, you chat away naturally as if you're talking to a friend – ignore the camera – and when we come to the edit we'll make you and the gardens look fabulous.'

It turned out that Beth – who seemed cool and confident the rest of the time – was completely incapable of stringing a sentence together without stumbling over her words when there was a camera pointing in her face.

'So these are the peonies,' she said, pointing to a row of dark green bushes where fat crimson streaked buds could be seen beginning to show their heads. 'And they're, um… oh no, sorry, let me start again.'

'Why don't you take me for a walk round,' Jack said, as Beth dropped her head into her hands, shaking with laughter. 'Just pretend you're giving me the guided tour we were planning. Would that work?'

Gina looked questioningly at Bill and Gregor, who nodded emphatically. It'd been well over the half an hour they'd promised, and he suspected they were desperate to head home – it was a long drive back to Glasgow, if they were heading back there tonight.

'Okay. Try and pretend we're not there. Jack, if you want to ask any questions, we'll sort it in the edits.' Gina's calm demeanour had slipped slightly and she looked slightly wild-eyed and desperate.

'Alright.' Beth took a deep breath. He longed to take her hand, squeeze it and tell her she looked beautiful and sounded perfect. Instead he smiled encouragingly, and said 'Lead on, MacDuff.'

'So what made you decide to do this anyway?'

'The flower farm?' Beth started walking. 'Well, it was an overgrown jungle and it had been for years. I didn't have the same hankering that Lachlan had to leave Applemore and get away from everything – Polly was the same, too – she went off to uni and only came back after Dad died. I don't know, really – I think I wanted to make my mark. I always had a little patch of garden of my own when we were growing up, and I used to grow sweet peas because they were my mum's favourite flowers. So it was a sort of reminder of her.'

'How old were you when she died?'

'Oh she didn't die, she left –' Beth reached across, snapping a faded bloom with her fingers and putting it in the pocket of her apron. 'Anyway – I think I wanted to prove that I could make something out of this huge jungle.'

They turned, walking along the grassy path alongside colourful clumps of lupins, which he recognised from his granny's garden when he was young.

'It looks amazing,' he said, as they paused to look at a long bed of neat green bushes, the leaves feathering out over a bed which was covered in a deep layer of some sort of mulch. 'I assume these will be something pretty in a few weeks?'

'These are part of my new plans,' explained Beth. 'I'm expanding this year so my plan is that we have a cutting patch, where people can come along two weekends a month and cut their own flowers.'

'Oh that's a gorgeous idea,' said Gina, forgetting that she was supposed to be being unobtrusive. Beth turned to her, smiling.

'Do you think it'll work?'

'Absolutely. It's glorious.' Gina gestured to the garden. 'This is heaven. I'm sure it's hard work, but it looks like bliss being out here surrounded by flowers all day every day.'

'Shame this isn't going to be on TV until later in the year. It'd be perfect publicity for you.' Gregor stepped to one side, shifting the camera slightly. 'The light is gorgeous. Just stand there a sec, looking over towards the trees?'

Jack stepped to the side so Gregor could shoot some footage of Beth. Birds were almost deafening with their evening calls, and there was a drowsy hum of bees which sounded wonderful, but he guessed it wouldn't show up on the finished film.

They wandered along the paths, chatting and laughing, and after a while it seemed that Beth had managed to completely forget she was being filmed.

'This is TV catnip,' Gina said, as they reached the far corner of the flower farm. 'I think we've got enough here, don't you?'

'Deffo,' said Gregor.

'So interesting to see how people are diversifying to make money up here,' she said, scratching her forehead. 'If only there was a way of getting rid of these damned midges it'd be heaven on earth.'

'Vitamin B,' Jack said. 'That's the secret, or so I'm told.'

'Everyone seems to have the secret, but as far as I can see –' Gregor slapped his arm as another cloud of them threatened to drain his lifeblood '– the secret is some sort of full body netting.'

'Don't knock it,' Beth said, laughing. 'I've seen people camping in exactly that. I bet they don't have to cover themselves from head to toe in calamine lotion every night.'

'You don't get used to it, then?' Bill, the quiet sound man, put down the huge fluffy boom microphone and rubbed at his head so his hair stood on end.

'You learn to live with it. Don't put that in the programme,' Beth added, hastily 'Or nobody will want to come up here and we won't make any blooming money.'

'Don't worry, we won't breathe a word.'

'I tell you what,' Gina said, checking the time on her phone, 'Let's take advantage of these lovely long light evenings and get some footage of you, Jack – maybe round in the treehouse?'

'You don't think you've got enough with Danny?' He'd been half hoping that he'd be able to duck out altogether.

Gina gave a small shrug. 'Between you and me, he was a little bit… too exuberant.'

'Fancies himself on *Love Island*,' said Gregor, with a snort of amusement.

'Ah.' Jack, who'd suspected Danny might go a bit over-board, could picture exactly what he meant. Right. He needed to man up and get over himself – the chances of anyone seeing him on TV and putting two and two together were non-existent, and he needed to put the charity first. This sort of publicity was invaluable. He squared his shoulders. Might as well get it all over and done with in one go, then he'd never have to go near a camera again.

'I'd better get on,' said Beth, but he thought he caught a note of reluctance in her voice… or was that wishful thinking on his part? He was about to turn away when she put a hand to his arm.

'Give me a shout about the weekend. You've got my number?'

He nodded, feeling hopeful all of a sudden. 'I have.'

'We can't leave it to Phoebe and Danny to sort. They're on another planet – well, Phoebs definitely is.'

'Danny too,' he grinned. 'I'll message you later.'

With a spring in his step, he headed round the perimeter wall towards the treehouse, leading the way.

Fifteen minutes later, he, Gina, Gregor and Bill were sitting one at each corner of the treehouse. Archie was curled up at his feet, casting the occasional disapproving glance through one half-open eye at Gina, to whom he'd definitely taken an irrational dislike. The sparkling solar fairy lights twinkled around the wooden frame and he'd put down the sheepskins for them to sit on, but even so it amused him to see these professionals reduced to sitting cross-legged on the floor, looking incongruous and slightly out of their comfort zone. He, on the other hand, was feeling remarkably cheerful. His phone buzzed in his pocket several times, but he let it go, knowing he'd be able to deal with whoever it was after he'd got this over and done with.

'So we want a quick rundown on what you do, why you do it, that sort of thing. And why you chose to come up here, rather than focusing on the centre you have in Glasgow and near Inverness.'

Jack felt himself relax. It was going to be the usual spiel. He could trot that off without even having to think – he'd done it the other night at the pub quiz. Once they'd sorted out the sound levels and set everything up, he leaned forward, elbows resting on his knees, and the filming was over – painlessly – in no time at all. All that time he'd spent tying himself in knots worrying about it, and suspecting Gina of having some sort of ulterior motive had been a waste of time. He was so cheerfully relieved that he didn't even mind taking them back to the log cabin, running through some of the activities they did, and showing them round while Gregor did some extra filming. As he jumped into the truck to head home he remembered the calls he'd missed, but his phone had run out of battery and the screen was dead. Whatever it was would have to wait until he got home.

'What kept you?' Danny was sitting with his feet up on the coffee table when he got back to the cottage.

'Oh you know, the usual – bit of filming, bit of showbiz, the usual.' He strode across the sitting room and picked up the missing phone wire, plugging his phone in and leaving it sitting on the mantelpiece. 'I'd have rung to tell you but someone had nicked the bloody phone charger out of the truck again.'

Danny grinned sheepishly. 'Soz. Mine died and I grabbed it this afternoon. Forgot to tell you.'

'It's fine.' Jack picked up one of the sofa cushions and lobbed it at Danny's head.

'You're in a suspiciously good mood.'

'Am I?' Jack said, casually, sitting down on the armchair and folding his arms behind his head. In a moment, when his phone was charged, he was going to text Beth. He had an excuse now.

'I recognise that look.' Danny sat up, peering at him.

'What look?'

'You look like you're feeling chuffed with something. Or is it someone?'

'Don't know what you're talking about.'

'Right.' Danny's tone was sceptical. He picked up the TV remote and flicked through the channels, not giving any one station a chance.

'How can you see what you're doing at that speed?'

'Fast-moving brain, mate, fast-moving brain. Not like you. It's age that does it.'

'Watch it, you.' He shook his head, laughing. 'Anyway, I've got to message Beth in a bit about the weekend. Have you checked with Phoebe? She seemed to think she'd probably have forgotten.'

'Nope, she's all set. Got the night off from the pub, and I bumped into Miranda coming out of the outdoor shop half an hour ago with a pair of brand new walking boots, so she's taking it very seriously by the looks of things.'

'Right well we'd better get everything sorted. I'll message Beth.'

His phone buzzed as it came back to life, and then a second later it buzzed again. And again. 'Someone's popular,' said Danny, cocking an eyebrow as he watched Jack from across the room. 'And again,' he added, as the phone buzzed another three times.

But Jack wasn't paying attention. He was looking at the screen, which was filled with notifications.

Rebecca: 3 missed calls

Anna: 4 messages

Rebecca: voicemail

'Just got to make a couple of calls,' he said, walking out of the room.

CHAPTER THIRTEEN

MEANWHILE, over at Applemore, Beth had stopped by to drop off a couple of buckets of flowers for Charlotte, who liked to decorate the holiday cottages she rented out with some personal touches. She wandered into the kitchen, but there was nobody to be seen. The dogs were sitting on the flagstones of the floor, having assumed their summer positions where they avoided the heat of the always-on Aga. They didn't move, simply beating a welcome with their tails. Beth bent down, giving them a scratch behind the ears, and stood for a moment listening out for sounds of anyone about. Applemore acted as a sort of hub for the family, but she was always conscious that firstly it was Lachlan and Rilla's house, and that if it had been hers she'd have found the constant dropping in irritating. She loved the feeling of closing the farmhouse door at night and knowing nobody was going to turn up. She put the flowers down on the big scrubbed table that sat in the middle of the kitchen, and was pulling the porch door closed behind her quietly when she heard Lachlan's voice.

'Where are you sneaking off to?'

'Nowhere.'

She turned to see him standing barefoot on the huge rug in the hall, hair standing on end, a blue t-shirt with a hole in it over torn jeans. He put a hand to his mouth to cover a huge yawn.

'Am I keeping you up?'

Her brother shook his head, laughing. 'Rilla's gone shopping in Inverness. I went into the study to do a load of very boring paperwork and the sun was shining on my back and the next thing I knew I'd woken up with my face on the desk.'

Beth laughed. 'Come outside and get some fresh air. Fancy a quick dog walk?'

'I'd love that.'

Lachlan grabbed some shoes, and they whistled the three spaniels. Mabel, the oldest of the three, was quite portly now. She trundled along, settling herself between Lachlan and Beth, content to be surrounded by the people she loved while Martha, the younger springer, together with Rilla's rescue dog, Hugh, careered ahead, noses to the ground, chasing the scent of rabbits in the undergrowth.

They walked along in comfortable silence for a while, then chatted about Rilla, Beth asking how she was feeling with morning sickness.

'Can't believe you're going to be a father,' she said, shaking her head.

'You're a parent,' Lachlan said, pulling at a long piece of grass.

'I know, but you spent so long avoiding this place. Now you're jumping in with both feet.'

'I'm thirty-seven,' he said, stepping aside to let her through as the path narrowed. 'Got to grow up sometime.'

'I'm not saying you're not a grown-up,' Beth said, falling into step beside him again. The sun threaded through the trees, warming the carpet of pine needles and releasing their scent into the air. 'I think we all had to grow up pretty damn fast when – well, when she left.'

'True.' He looked at her sideways. 'Anyway, what's happening with you? I bumped into Jack the other day when I was walking the dogs. I think you've got a bit of a fan there.'

Beth shook her head so her hair hung across her cheek, aware that her brother knew her well enough to read what she was thinking with only a look. 'Nothing much. Just trying to find a way to make my fortune.'

'I can't believe Simon has dropped you in it like that.'

'It hasn't happened yet, I'm basically trying – to use a good bit of corporate speak – to future-proof myself.'

'Presumably his baby will be on the way not long before ours.'

'You'll be hanging out at the school gates together.'

'Hardly,' said Lachlan, robustly. 'For one, he cheated on you, which is a one strike and you're out, and now he's pulled this crap on you. I mean what kind of man ducks out of paying for his own child?'

'Yeah, I know.'

'You seem less pissed off about it than I am. Honestly, I could knock his bloody block off.'

'Then he'd definitely not be paying anything,' said Beth, laughing.

'Seriously though, how come you're so sanguine about it?'

She shrugged. 'Not sanguine. I'm... the thing is I don't want to ever be the sort of mother who isn't there for her children. And if he wants to behave like that, at the end of the day there isn't much I can do to stop him.'

'You could take him to court.'

'And say what? Force him to carry on working? I can't make him do the right thing. All I can do is make the right choices myself.'

'You're amazing, you know that?'

She felt colour rising in her cheeks. 'Shut up.'

'Seriously. You've always been so bloody determined.'

'I want to do the right thing. It matters.'

They turned, as if in silent agreement, and wandered down the grassy track that led to their father's memorial stone. It stood in a clearing, a slender beech tree they'd planted growing to one side. She ran a finger over the inscription.

Hector Fraser and David Clark - Together in Eternity

'D'you ever wonder what life would have been like if they'd been honest about their relationship?' Beth stood back, turning to look at Lachlan. He ran a hand through his dark hair, which flopped in an untidy way back onto his forehead.

'Sometimes. I wonder what it'd be like if Mum hadn't left. If she hadn't been cheated on. I mean, it must have been pretty shitty for her.'

Beth frowned. 'I suppose. I think growing up I was always so busy being angry she left, because I didn't know why. And since we found out what happened, I've been so wrapped up in bringing up the babies and work and – well, Simon and me splitting up, and everything.'

Lachlan gave a slight shrug. 'Yeah. When you actually stop and think about it, it changes everything.'

Beth narrowed her eyes in thought. 'Maybe.'

They wandered back to Applemore then, chatting about Lachlan and Rilla's plans for their gin company, Lachlan asking how the TV filming had gone.

'No pressure,' he said, as they crunched across the gravel of the driveway outside the big house, 'But if your TV show could put Applemore on the map, that'd be great, thanks.'

'I'll try my best. I don't even know when it's on yet.'

'I better get on. I've got to get this bloody paperwork done.'

'You still okay to have the twins the weekend of the fourteenth? Is Rilla up to it?'

'Course. We can call it training.'

'I'll make sure I keep them up all night on Friday then, so they can scream the place down so you get the full life-with-a-newborn effect.'

Lachlan fixed her with a horrified stare. 'If you do that, I'm going to accidentally spray your flowerbeds with Roundup.'

'You wouldn't dare.'

'Try me.' He gave an evil grin.

CHAPTER FOURTEEN

'Dad.'

'Hi darling,' he said, leaning back against the kitchen counter. It was such a relief to hear Anna's voice after so long.

'I hate her,' she said, furiously. 'I hate her, I hate living here, and I hate him.'

'Who?'

'Karl.' Anna snarled the name of Rebecca's new boyfriend, a Danish architect. 'He's a sanctimonious pig and he thinks he can tell me what to do and I don't want to ever speak to him again.'

'You're going to have to run this by me again, sweetheart. What's up?'

The phone buzzed in the silence as Anna gathered her thoughts. Another message from Rebecca. *Call me asap*, it said.

'No I will not,' Anna shouted. 'Tell her I don't have to.'

Jack exhaled slowly. It was pretty bloody hard to deal with a furious teenager when she was on the other side of the English Channel, and harder still when he had her mother texting at the same time, presumably telling him exactly what she'd done to cause the current explosion.

'Darling,' he began, cautiously, 'I've got your mum messaging me, and you yelling at her. Do you want to tell me what's going on?'

'Tell her to leave me alone,' Anna said, and there was the sound of a door slamming.

'I might,' he said, trying to calm her down, 'if you can explain to me what's happening. Who do you hate?'

'She told me we had plans this weekend, and that I wasn't allowed to go out. Then she took me out for dinner, and *surprise* along comes Karl, and I'm supposed to be happy that she's met someone new.'

He sighed. Rebecca had always had a habit of approaching parenting in the same way she approached business. No doubt she'd thought that taking Anna out for dinner was a neutral way of introducing someone into her life.

'I assume you're not happy she's met someone new.'

'I've been dragged away from my friends, my school, from –' her voice choked slightly, and he felt a lump forming in his throat '– from you… and now the next thing is I'm supposed to be pleased to meet someone. It's alright for her, isn't it?'

'It's a lot,' he said, gently.

'I will *not*,' Anna yelled at her mother. 'No. You can forget it.'

There was a sound of scuffling, and then silence. He looked at the phone, and realised that the call had ended. A moment later it rang, but it was Rebecca this time.

'Jack.' She sounded slightly out of breath. 'For goodness sake, you need to listen.'

'Where's Anna?'

'I told her to go to her room because she swore at me.'

He recoiled slightly. Anna, his easy-going, laid back girl, had barely lost her temper in her life.

'She's impossible right now. Impossible. I don't know what to do with her.'

Rebecca launched into a furious tirade, explaining that she'd been in trouble at school, been caught truanting, and then to top everything off had been appallingly rude to her new boyfriend over dinner in an expensive restaurant and stormed off into the night, thankfully returning an hour later, soaked from a rainstorm but otherwise unharmed. He felt sick with guilt and remorse.

'D'you think we've done the right thing?'

'Honestly?' Rebecca had calmed down slightly. 'I'd like to think so. But I wish we weren't in this situation.'

He closed his eyes. All of this was his fault. 'I'm sorry.'

'You can't blame yourself. It's the situation, it's not you.'

'Maybe she just needs time. If I come over, that might help. It'll give you a break, if nothing else. At least she's talking to me now.'

'That's a start.'

'Let me ring her back.' He chewed his lip, thinking. 'And Bec?'

'Yes?'

'I think – look, it's not for me to say. But maybe she's got enough going on without you pushing the Karl thing.' He almost managed to conceal the hurt he was feeling. He picked up a cloth and absent-mindedly wiped the kitchen table, for something to distract himself. 'I don't want her thinking you've moved away and now I'm out of the picture altogether.'

'You're her dad,' she said gently. 'Nothing is going to change that.'

Rebecca might have been abrasive and driven, with a manner that rubbed people up the wrong way when they didn't get her, but she was a decent person. It helped to have an ex who was on side, especially under the circumstances.

'Thanks.' He screwed up his eyes, feeling them stinging for a moment. 'That means a lot.'

He called back, but Anna wouldn't pick up. Instead, he sent her a long message, explaining that he knew that she'd had a lot to deal with and that maybe her mum's timing wasn't great, but that in the end moving to Paris was going to be a good thing for her – for all of them.

Even as he wrote, there was a nagging voice in the back of his head pointing out that maybe – just maybe – everything he'd believed to matter really didn't. He read back his words, shaking away the doubts that he felt, and hit 'send'.

The next couple of weeks flew by, and the weekend of their camping trip arrived. Jack was feeling slightly better after a long chat with Anna who seemed to have had – in the way of teenagers – some sort of sea change, and who'd seemed quite cheerful.

She'd asked him what his plans were, and had been interested to hear all about the new centre in a way that she hadn't been in ages. Knowing she was a bit more settled, Jack felt able to return his focus to his own life for a while.

CHAPTER FIFTEEN

BETH WASN'T COMPLETELY sure what to wear. She'd stood in the bedroom, hair wet from the shower, peering into her wardrobe. Why on earth – she pulled on a pair of jeans, stuffing some leggings and her swimsuit into a rucksack – hadn't she thought to ask before the fateful day arrived? She was pretty sure there was a rule about not wearing jeans because they took ages to dry, but then it was gorgeous sunshine for one thing and she had no intention of getting wet for another. Hopefully dressing for the occasion she wanted to have – with minimal rock climbing or goodness knows what else – would be the way forward.

She'd dropped the children off at Applemore and headed back to the farmhouse to get organised. Charlotte had been suspiciously off the radar for the last couple of days, so it was no surprise when she cried off by text, telling Beth that she had the opportunity to meet up with an old friend in Thurso. Beth had frowned at the screen of her phone, and texted Miranda, who at least she could rely on to be there and act as moral support.

'So, where's Miranda?'

An hour later, she was standing alone outside the cabin, rucksack at her feet. Jack was leaning against the wooden rail of the porch, a smile playing at his lips. His long legs were crossed, as were his arms, as he surveyed her.

'She couldn't make it. Something about her son at uni needing to come home – she's gone to pick him up from St Andrews. And Charlotte wasn't ever going to come – she'd made every excuse under the sun, and now she's disappeared off to Thurso for the weekend to see someone she used to work with.'

Jack narrowed his eyes in thought. 'That's a bit weird. Danny's just rung to say that he and Phoebe can't make it until later and that we should go on ahead without them.'

Beth met his gaze with a matching expression of suspicion. This was feeling decidedly like some sort of stitch-up.

'I'm game if you are.' She squared her shoulders. This had all the hallmarks of one of Miranda's bonkers schemes. On a plus note, at least it wasn't online dating and she had to admit – looking at Jack, standing there in the sunlight with the muscles of his shoulders evident beneath the navy blue t-shirt he was wearing, dark grey trousers showing off the length of his long, strong legs – there were definitely worse people to spend an enforced solo afternoon with…

She gave a slight shrug, as if spending weekends doing this sort of thing was totally normal for her.

A brief smile crossed Jack's face. 'I don't think we'll be doing den building – bit tricky when there's only two of us.'

'Oh, that's annoying. It's the one thing I thought I'd get an 'A' for – we used to spend ages in the woods making dens and hiding when we were little.' She pouted slightly, making him laugh. 'Tell me this means we can skip the white-water rafting?'

Jack raised an eyebrow. 'Let me get this straight. Basically, you want an outdoor adventure which isn't really outdoorsy and not very adventurous.'

Beth nodded. 'I spend all blooming week outside. I'm more of a Sunday stroll and a pub lunch sort of girl, given the choice.'

'You're going to tell me you'd rather sleep in the tree-house than camp, next.' He shook his head, laughing again, then came towards her, picking up her rucksack and shouldering it, before gesturing towards the mossy path that led into the woods.

'Is that an option?' She was still hopeful, but there was a bit of her that was thrilled – secretly – at the chance to do something different and to push herself out of her comfort zone.

'Don't even go there, Fraser,' he growled. 'Right, we're going to do the rope walk.'

They strode on into the woods. Birds were singing above them and the sunlight filtered through the tall branches of the pines, warming her skin as she followed behind Jack, trying – and failing – not to notice once again what a good bum he had. She thought irrationally how much she'd like to grab it, just to see how firm it was, then gave a little snort of laughter which made him turn to look at her, wide mouth quirking in a half-smile.

'You okay?'

'Just thinking out loud,' she said, quickly.

'Okay,' he said, stopping as they reached a broad tree trunk. He reached into his pocket, pulling out a long strip of soft, black fabric. 'Come a bit closer, and I'll put this on.'

'You want me to wear a blindfold?'

'I do.' His body was close enough now that she could feel the warmth of it against her, as if there was some sort of magnetic charge between them. His fingers brushed against the side of her cheek as he reached forward, covering her eyes.

'Sorry,' he murmured, his mouth close to her ear, 'That didn't catch your hair, did it?'

Beth felt her eyelashes brush against the soft material of the blindfold, and realised that all at once she couldn't see a thing. She took a breath in, which caught in her throat.

'You okay?'

She nodded, feeling strangely vulnerable. 'This is weird.'

'Can you see anything?' She heard a slight rustling. 'I'm moving to the side of you – if you stay there for a second, we'll get started.'

'All I can see is darkness.' She took a tentative step to one side, feeling the soft spring of the forest floor underfoot.

'That's the general idea.' There was a smile in his voice.

She sensed the nearness of his body, and the faint woody scent of his skin as he stepped behind her again. She felt suddenly vulnerable, aware that she was having to place her trust completely in Jack's hands.

'I'm going to put your hands –' She felt his touch as he lifted them and placed them on top of a slender piece of rope '– on here.' He closed his fingers on top of hers, so she was gripping the rope tightly. For a moment she felt his hand linger and she held her breath, still conscious there was only a few centimetres between them. Beth stood stock still, hearing the thud of her heart in her ears and feeling the slight breeze blowing through the trees, lifting a thread of hair which tickled the side of her neck. She shook her head to move it away but it fell back again. A moment later she felt the brush of his fingertip on her neck as he tucked it behind her ear.

'Better?'

She nodded, not trusting herself to speak.

'Right. You're going to follow the line. I'll guide you. The first bit's easy, so you can get your bearings a bit.'

The forest floor was springy underfoot. Cautiously, each step taking twice as long as it would normally, she made her way forward, still holding the rope with both hands.

'Feels strange, doesn't it?'

'I keep expecting to lose my footing.' She felt as if she was stepping high in the air, not trusting the ground beneath her feet.

'You won't. You have to listen, and use your senses, and trust me.'

'You mean put my life in your hands?' She was joking, mostly.

He laughed. 'I promise you, you'll be safe. Okay, there's a little dip here, so feel with a foot −'

Carefully, she extended a toe, leaning forward. Without thinking, she reached out, catching his strong forearm with her hand to steady herself. 'Sorry.' It was broad, rock hard with muscle, and felt reassuringly safe.

'Don't be,' he said, gently.

'Ah but that's cheating, isn't it?' Reluctantly, she reached across and put her hand back on the rope, stepping like a new-born foal as she made her way down what felt like a huge incline. They moved along for a few more minutes, Beth concentrating hard.

'Take your blindfold off for a sec,' he said, standing in front of her so she stopped dead, bumping into the solid wall of his chest.

'Oops.' She looked up at him, and saw the crinkled laughter lines around his eyes as he smiled down at her.

'Turn around,' he instructed. She spun round.

'I thought that was a huge hill. I was trying to work out how I'd never noticed it before.'

He shook his head. 'Perception. It's interesting, isn't it?'

'Weird how taking one sense away makes everything feel so different.'

'Do you want to carry on?'

She cocked her head to one side. Part of her wanted to say yes, because she loved the feeling of awareness of him that it brought, and how her senses had been heightened so she'd been conscious of the woody, fresh scent of his skin as he touched her, and of the warmth of his body as he guided her hands onto the rope. But – she looked down the trail, seeing the rope slung taut between a huge pine tree and a slender silver birch, then disappearing into the darkness of the forest – it felt almost uncomfortably intimate. If the others had been there, they'd have been teasing and joking and the atmosphere would have been completely different.

'Or you can chicken out,' he said, lifting a challenging eyebrow.

That was it. She pulled the blindfold down again. 'I am many things,' she said, grabbing the rope and lifting her chin in a determined fashion, 'But I'm not a chicken.'

'Okay. I tell you what,' Jack said, and there was a rustling and then she felt the rope shifting in her hands. 'I've done this a million times over this summer. Let's make it interesting. I'll go in front, and I'll wear the blindfold too.'

'How will you know what's coming up?'

'Call it a memory challenge.'

She sensed him moving forward.

'I know this trail. Let's see if I can put my money where my mouth is.'

'Isn't it dangerous?'

There was a crack of twigs. In the silence of the wood,

it sounded deafening. 'Bit crunchy underfoot here,' he said, 'Watch your footing.'

'You didn't answer the question.'

'I wouldn't be risking you if it was.'

Something in his tone made Beth's heart skip a beat. She jumped a moment later as a branch brushed against her arm.

'Logs,' said Jack. 'Just here.'

She felt a bump in the rope as if someone had tied a knot, her fingers running over it. Her toes knocked into the base of a fallen log and she felt the soft moss giving against her shins. She reached down, getting more confident now, and measured the height of it, putting one hand on the damp moss to balance herself as she climbed over it. This was all so far out of her usual comfort zone that it felt completely alien.

'You can see –' Jack broke off for a second '– there's a sort of step here, then you need to duck because there's a low branch.'

She put one hand out in the air, feeling for the branch, aware that she must look like she was pawing, cluelessly – but there wasn't anyone looking, and she didn't want to get walloped on the head. A couple of steps further and her fingers were prickled with pine needles, the air filling with the fresh scent. She stopped for a moment and heard the gentle rain of needles falling onto the forest floor.

'Stop for a sec,' he instructed her.

She stood, still blindfolded, for a moment.

'You can see,' he started again, 'how this works so well with teenagers. It takes away all the bravado – they're forced to focus on listening to each other and working together.'

She felt his fingers as he lifted the blindfold, gently

pulling it over her head. Beth blinked hard, taking a step backwards.

'Weird, isn't it? Takes a moment to get your bearings.'

Beth nodded in silence. She had the strangest sensation, looking around at the tall pines she'd played in as a child, the shafts of sunlight weaving between the trees, that she'd stepped into a new world.

Jack looked at her, a curious expression on his face. 'You okay?'

'Mmm,' She nodded again. 'It's funny how completely absorbing it is. You can't think about anything else at all when you're doing it.'

'I think that's why I like stuff like this.'

As if he could read her thoughts, he inclined his head toward a path lined on either side with fresh green ferns. 'Let's take a wander down here.'

They walked down, stepping carefully over the jagged rocks that led to a clearing where the sun shone down on a wide stream, which gathered in a pool of dark brown peaty water.

'We used to swim here when I was little,' she said, sitting down on a stony outcrop by the edge.

'It's gorgeous, isn't it? Every time I see it, it takes my breath away.'

'Doing that rope thing – even a bit of it – took mine away. It's weird how it changes the way you see things.'

Jack sat down, pushing up the sleeves of his checked shirt. His skin was tanned. She noticed freckles under the dark hairs.

'Not many people wear a watch these days.' She touched it with a finger.

'You can't rely on a phone up here,' he said, glancing down at her hand then looking up to meet her eyes.

'You can now. We've joined the twenty-first century at last. But there were years when a walk like this would mean you were completely out of touch with everyone.'

'Now people can get a hold of you anywhere.'

She shook her head. 'I'm not sure it's a good thing. I quite liked being able to escape. When I was little I used to come up here for the day, take a picnic and a book and hide.'

'It must've been busy, living in a house with three siblings.'

'You don't ever get time to think. I think that's why I like the job I do. It's a chance to escape and I don't have to talk to anyone.'

'Yeah,' Jack gazed across the water, frowning as he noticed something moving in the grass on the other side. 'Shh, look –'

Beth sat very still, following his gaze. 'An otter!' she whispered, delighted.

'Can't believe you grew up with all this on your doorstep.'

'I'm guessing you didn't have many otters where you grew up.'

'Not a whole lot.' He flicked a glance at her, amusement in his eyes. 'The only wildlife we had was drug addicts hanging around outside the local chemist waiting for their methadone prescription.'

'What made you decide to become an outdoor instructor?'

'As opposed to a drug addict?' He grinned. 'I mean I was tempted, but…'

'Sorry, that was a really stupid question.'

'And I'm being glib.' He leaned over, picking a long strand of grass then shredding it as he spoke. 'After I finished school, I – well, I ended up coming to a place kinda like this and I realised that I liked the way it made me feel.'

'I realised as we were walking that I'd forgotten about all the stuff I was worrying about earlier today. There wasn't room in my brain to remember it while I was focusing on trying to get from A to B without falling over.'

'Exactly. That's what I like about it. It gives you a chance to clear your mind. So I trained, and I volunteered, and I ended up working for the charity on their project on the banks of Loch Lomond, and then when – well when things changed at home it seemed like perfect timing to come up here.'

'You didn't want to be in Glasgow with Anna not there.'

He shook his head. 'That's the short version, yeah. It's a bit more complicated than that, but it's a long story.'

Beth took a sideways look at him. For a moment, Jack looked troubled, as if he was about to say something. Then he shook his head and stood up.

'I'll show you where we do the bushcraft stuff, if you like?'

'Yes please.' He reached a hand down to pull her up. When she straightened up, they were standing face on, so close that Beth looked up and their eyes met again. He held her gaze for a moment that seemed to go on forever, then stepped back, motioning the trail ahead of them.

'You go ahead,' he said.

CHAPTER SIXTEEN

GOD, he could have kissed her in that second. It would have been the easiest thing in the world. It felt like the strangest thing to be showing Beth – who'd grown up wandering this countryside – as if he had some sort of right to it. And yet here she was, walking along in front of him, blonde ponytail swinging, perfectly cheerful. He couldn't help but notice the way her hips curved in the dark jeans she was wearing, or the way they moved as she dodged the overgrown foliage as they wandered down towards the forest trail. He shook himself, trying to bring his focus back to practicalities. The last person in the world she'd be interested in was him – they had nothing in common, after all. He'd grown up – basically left to his own devices, with his mum absent more often than not – in a tiny, grim little flat. She'd grown up in what was effectively a castle. He needed to get a grip and remember who he was and where he'd come from.

They trudged up to the top of the ridge, where huge boulders jutted out, surrounded by heather and gorse. The coconut scent of the flowers filled the air and he stopped for a moment, getting out two bottles of water and passing one to Beth, who sat on a rock and drank thankfully.

'Look at that.' He followed her gaze, looking across the water, where huge bruised purple clouds were gathering over the island hills. 'That wasn't forecast for today, was it?'

'Nope, I checked before I left the cottage this morning.'

'Maybe we should head back now?'

'Scared of a wee bit of rain?' He shot her a teasing look.

'Hardly,' she said, laughing. 'But I don't fancy camping in soaking wet clothes.'

'Fair enough.'

They walked along accompanied only by the sound of the skylarks flying overhead and the indignant two-note call of the pheasants, flushed in a whirl of ungraceful flapping out of the heather as they approached.

The skies were darkening with every minute, huge banked clouds seeming to follow in hot pursuit. By they made their way back to the centre, rain had started to fall, landing with huge splashy drops on their faces. Beth looked at the sky again.

'It doesn't look like camping weather, does it?'

On cue, there was a low rumble of thunder. Of all the days for the long spell of good weather to break... God, it was typical. It had been so good to spend time with her – even if (he reminded himself firmly) nothing was going to happen between them. They could at least be friends, if nothing else. His phone buzzed.

Weather looks crappy, Danny messaged him *I think we should take a rain check, yeah?*

'That's Danny calling off. I think that's probably our sign we need to put this off for another time.'

'I'm looking at the weather app – this storm wasn't due

until tomorrow afternoon but it seems to have changed its mind.'

'You're not kidding.' Jack wiped a hand across his brow, mopping away the now constant stream of raindrops that were dripping from his hair onto his face.

Beth made a face. 'I'd better be practical. If this storm is turning up unexpectedly early, it might well be worse than we thought. I need to go and check everything is staked in safely and make sure I've got stuff protected.'

'Of course,' he said, wanting to roar at the sky in frustration. For once he'd wanted to do something for himself – life had been focused so completely on work and other people for as long as he could remember.

'You can give me a hand if you like?' Beth's expression was hopeful.

'Course I can. I mean I can't tell a daffodil from a dandelion, but as long as you direct me, I'm happy to.'

'Don't worry, it's more a case of making sure the stakes I've got in place are all secure enough to withstand the storm.'

'Lead on, then,' he said, locking up the log cabin and double checking the equipment at the side was tied down securely. They had been blessed with the weather since they'd opened the centre, but he knew all too well how quickly it could change up here in the Highlands, and the last thing he wanted was to wake up tomorrow morning to find all the activity gear blown halfway across the countryside when he had a really important group coming on Monday first thing.

'It's nice to have someone to give me a hand,' said Beth a while later, once he'd driven them back over to the gate of the walled garden in the centre's pick-up truck. The rain was coming down relentlessly, her hair plastered to her head. Drips were trickling down the back of the neck of his t-shirt. They were both soaked to the skin. He was holding a roll of twine as she unravelled it and wound it around stakes which were driven at two-metre lengths across a bed of tall plants. 'I mean obviously in the week I've got Miranda and Phoebe's here a couple of days as well, but when stuff like this happens generally it's me making the best of it. Always has been.'

'Your ex wasn't much of a flower person?' He passed her the scissors and she cut the twine, pushing her hair back behind her ears to stop it hanging in her way as she worked. Beth shook her head.

'Simon?' She laughed. 'No, this was very much my baby. He's an office sort of person, not outdoorsy at all.'

'Can't imagine you in an office.' He looked at Beth, watching as she strode on to the next bed of flowers, tossing him the ball of twine and starting to repeat the whole process, this time criss-crossing it between the long stems of flowers. Even he could recognise them as sunflowers, their buds still tight, but their thick, spiky stems growing tall. It was amazing that Beth seemed to be able to coax even the most incongruous flowers to grow up here in the Highlands. If he'd been asked before he'd met her, he'd have been convinced that nothing much more than thistles and heather would thrive.

'We didn't have that much in common really. Not at all, in fact.'

'Sounds familiar.' It was a mystery to him how he and Rebecca had ended up together – one of those weird nights out in Glasgow where you bump into someone, then think it's a one-night fling, and somehow opposites attract and the next thing you know, a year has passed... he gave the faintest shake of his head. Anna had come out of that relationship, and that made it all worthwhile.

'Weird isn't it, how you end up in a relationship with someone and you don't actually have anything that holds you together.' Beth shivered slightly. 'I'm freezing now. Not long to go.'

By the time they'd finished fifteen minutes later, both of them were drenched. The storm was almost overhead by now and the wind was buffeting the sides of the polytunnel, which rattled but – he was relieved to notice – seemed to be staying put.

'Let's hope your repair job holds up,' said Beth, noticing him looking up.

He smiled. 'Fingers crossed. I think we both need a hot bath and a stiff drink now.'

'Okay,' said Beth, and an uncharacteristically wicked smile crossed her face. 'Your place or mine?'

He took a step backwards and looked at her, thrusting his hands in the back pockets of his jeans and laughing. 'Careful, or I might take you up on that.'

She looked at him for a moment and he felt a jolt of longing that was strong enough to compete with any of the lightning bolts shooting from the dark grey clouds.

A brainwave struck him. 'I tell you what, we've got a shower and loads of spare clothes up in the cabin, if you want to come and get changed before we swap the cars over?'

Beth nodded. 'If you throw in a coffee, you've got a deal.'

'Come on then,' he said, pulling the keys out of his pocket. 'I'll light the fire as well, if you're lucky.'

'You really do know how to treat a girl.'

'Oh, you have no idea.' He kept his tone light, mainly

because he was struggling to get his head around what he was feeling.

As they bumped across the track that led back through the woods to the log cabin, his mind was racing. In the time since he and Rebecca had split he'd had plenty of casual relationships – it wasn't as if he'd lived like a monk for fifteen years. But the way he felt about Beth was different, and it unnerved him. Increasingly he was finding himself making light of things in an attempt to cover up the intensity of his desire for her, despite the fact that there was no way she'd be interested. He was damaged goods, after all – hardly the sort of person she'd want in her life. He shook himself. No, he had to accept that whatever feelings he had for her would have to go on the back burner, and he'd enjoy their friendship. That was better than nothing.

'We always keep spares up here,' he explained, as they went into the cabin and he flicked on the lights against the darkness of the storm outside. Outside the shower room, he grabbed a couple of big bath towels and led her towards a cabinet full of old pairs of jeans, woollen sweaters, and soft old T-shirts that had been gathered by staff as emergency supplies. 'There'll be something there for you. Might not be the poshest outfit you've ever worn, but it'll be warm and dry.'

Beth shivered. 'Right now, I'd put on a sack if it meant I could take off these wet things.'

He was all too aware how wet they both were. Her purple t-shirt clung to her body, outlining the swell of her breasts and the curve of her waist. Her long blonde hair hung in soaked tendrils, her long eyelashes starfish-like. She could be a mermaid stranded on dry land.

'The shower's pretty straightforward,' he said, gruffly, 'you warm up and I'll get that coffee on.'

She gave him a thankful smile and closed the door, leaving him standing in the passage, eyes closed, exhaling slowly. Get a grip, man, he told himself firmly.

By the time that Beth returned, flushed from a hot shower and dressed in a grey sweatshirt and a pair of faded pale blue jeans which she'd folded over at the hem – her legs clearly too long for them to be worn in the usual way – he'd lit the log burner and the coffee pot was giving off a delicious aroma.

'As promised,' he said, holding a spoon in his hand. 'You take sugar, don't you?'

'I do,' said Beth, coming to stand beside him, smelling of the hand-made, fresh lemon scented soap they'd bought from the farm shop, 'but I think I can wait until you've had a shower. You must be freezing.' She put a hand to his bare arm, and his skin burned at her touch. Their eyes met, and he found that no matter how hard he tried, he couldn't look away. His heart was banging so hard against his ribs that he was certain she must be able to hear it. The room was silent, but for the muffled thud as the kindling burnt away in the log burner, and a log slipped down against the glass. He shook himself inwardly, lifting his chin slightly – and the moment was broken.

'Okay,' he said, thinking at the same time that if he wasn't such a bloody idiot he'd have done what any sane man would have done in that moment and kissed her, 'I'll have a quick shower. I'll be two minutes.'

Closing the shower room door, he leaned his head against the glass of the mirror and groaned. He was a bloody grown man acting like a lovesick teenager and he needed to either pull himself together, or give in to his feelings, which was something he'd trained himself to avoid. He switched on the shower, turning up the heat so stinging needles of hot water burnt his skin. No – he closed his eyes as the water poured down his body – he had to get a grip. He showered quickly, towelled himself dry, and dressed in some of the spare clothes he kept up there for occasions like this one.

'Coffee?' Beth jumped up from the sofa by the log burner when he walked back into the room, barefoot, his hair damp and standing on end.

'I'll get it. You stay there and keep warm.'

'Okay, I'm not going to argue with that. I can't believe this storm,' said Beth, gesturing to the window. Wind was howling and torrential rain was hammering against the glass, and it looked almost like a winter night under the sodden dark clouds outside. He poured coffee into two mugs, added sugar and milk, and passed her one, joining her on the sofa.

'I hope your flowers are okay.'

She shrugged. 'I've learned that the thing about farming – whatever it is you're growing – is you have to accept that you can't control the weather.'

'That's a pretty good way of looking at it.'

A huge clap of thunder boomed overhead, making Beth jump.

'I swear that's right over the top of us,' he said, as lightning lit up the room a second or two later. A gust of wind blew the tarpaulin which covered the kayaks up in the air so it rattled and flapped, banging against the wall of the cabin.

Beth looked worried for a moment, frowning and looking at her phone.

'You okay?'

'I know it's silly. Just want to make sure the children are okay.'

'No, I get it.'

She relaxed slightly as he said this, sitting back against the cushions of the battered second-hand sofa they'd brought from Glasgow to make the cabin more homely. 'I might quickly ring Lachlan and check.'

'Go for it. I'm going to nip out and secure that tarp.'

He pulled on one of the big waterproof coats which hung on a rail by the front door of the cabin. Despite the cover of the porch, the rain was coming in sideways and the wind whipped through the trees, wrenching the door from his hand so it banged hard against the wall. Beth looked at him, phone to her ear, eyes wide.

'Be careful out there,' she said.

'Don't worry,' he reassured her, as he pulled the door closed before the wind could chill the just-heated room, 'I'll only be two secs.'

He worked quickly, tying down the tarpaulin and making sure everything else was secure. Thank God they'd come back when they had and not hiked further into the forest and got caught in this – not only would they be freezing and soaked, but how would it look if someone who ran an outdoor adventure centre wasn't even capable of judging the weather before setting off on a hike? He knew that he'd been so wrapped up in the idea of spending time with Beth that he'd forgotten to do a final assessment of the weather – which was essential at the best of times, but especially up here where it could change without much notice. There was a creak from the woods. The thunder rumbled again, but from over the forest this time – at least it was moving, even if the storm itself showed no sign of abating.

'Are you serious?' Beth was standing up by the log burner when he went back inside, talking to Lachlan on the phone. She gave him a welcoming smile as he headed across the room and picked up the mug of coffee he'd left sitting on the top of the fire to keep warm, sitting down on other side of the sofa.

'Well there's not much we can do right now, unless we walk over to – no, I don't think it's a great idea either. We'd have to go round the long way, and I'm still defrosting after our soaking.' There was a pause. 'Very funny.' Beth rolled her eyes. 'Yeah, okay. Keep me posted. We've got biscuits. No, no, there's coffee as well. Okay. Bye. Message me if you hear anything.'

'What's up?' He rolled up the sleeves of his checked shirt and then pushed his hands through his hair, watching as she stood by the fire for a moment, her forehead crinkling as she thought.

'There's a tree down on the road to the house, so we can't get back that way even if we take your pick-up truck.'

Jack frowned, thinking. The little road from Applemore led to both the outdoor centre and the walled garden, forking off at right angles beyond the big house, leading to dead ends in either direction. 'It's too dangerous for someone to get out with a chainsaw in this weather, isn't it?'

'Yep.' Beth chewed her lip. 'This sort of thing used to happen all the time when we were growing up, but it meant we got to skip school so it was a lot more exciting then. But I'm fairly sure the last thing you want is to be stuck here with me.'

'Oh, I don't know.' He tapped his fingers on the arm of the sofa, gazing at the flames behind the glass of the log burner. 'There are far worse people I could be stuck with.'

'Very funny.' Beth shook her head, giving a small smile. She indicated the little kitchen area with her head. 'At least we won't starve to death.'

'Better still,' he said, crossing one leg over the other and watching as she sat down on the opposite end of the sofa, cupping her mug between both hands, 'We've got a bottle of decent whisky in the safe if you fancy a drink later. One of the corporate guests left it as a thank you the other week, and I forgot to take it back to the cottage.'

'Well this evening is picking up,' said Beth, curling her legs underneath her and turning to face him. 'And on a plus note I've managed to get out of camping.'

'Did you place a special weather request somewhere?'

'Ah,' she waggled her eyebrows. 'That's my secret.'

'How are the twins?'

'They're fast asleep, apparently. Lachlan and Rilla seem to have filled the entire day with more activities than they get in a week of nursery, and they both conked out in front of the television at four.'

'At four?' He shook his head, laughing.

'I know. I didn't like to point out that they'll be awake all night.'

'It'll be a steep learning curve, then. Still, better they work this stuff out now than when their baby comes along. When's it due?'

'Five months, I think? Six? End of November?' Beth counted on her fingers. 'Or beginning of December. I have to admit I was juggling work and toddlers when Rilla was telling me and it sort of went in one ear and out the other.'

'I don't know how you do it.'

'Fear of failure and deep-rooted psychological issues.' Her tone was arch.

'The usual, then.' He cocked an eyebrow.

'Love me, love my neuroses.' Beth laughed. 'No, seriously – I dunno. It's a case of juggling – badly. How does your ex do it? She's got your daughter all the time, hasn't she?'

'It's not what I would have wanted,' said Jack, quickly.

'Oh God,' Beth said, standing up and heading back over to the kettle, filling it up again. 'I didn't mean to make it sound like I was judging.'

He shook his head. 'You didn't. I guess I have a bit of a sore spot. Watching her go, knowing I was doing it for the right reasons even if it didn't look like it, was the hardest thing I've ever done.'

She leaned over, taking his mug from his hands and as she did so her arm brushed against his. He closed his eyes and set his jaw. God, this evening was going to be bloody hard work when he felt the way he did.

'So we've got all the major food groups,' she said, changing the subject, opening the fridge and clattering about in the cupboards. 'Pasta, cheese, bread, butter, tinned tomatoes…'

'We're not savages,' he said, laughing. 'Contrary to popular belief not all single men spend their live eating pot noodles and watching Netflix.'

'I must be a single man,' said Beth, giving him an amused look as she handed him a cup of coffee. 'Left to my own devices, when I don't have the children I pretty much eat like a student. It's hard finding the enthusiasm to cook for one.'

'I'll make you dinner in a bit,' he said, running through what they had in the cupboards. 'You can be my commis chef.'

'Do you mean tear the lids off the Pot Noodles?'

'Watch it, you,' he said, laughing, and pulling his phone out of his pocket as it started to ring.

'Danny,' he explained, as he accepted the call. 'Alright mate?'

'Where are you?' It sounded from the buzz of chatter in

the background as if his friend had already repaired to the Applemore Hotel bar.

'At the centre. In the cabin.'

'Not camping then?' He gave a chuckle. 'Phoebe's here, and I've just bumped into Beth's sister Charlotte, who says – I quote – that she's feeling completely justified in her decision to avoid our day of adventures given the weather and that her sister must be certifiable.'

'We had a perfectly nice afternoon,' Jack said, amused at Danny's teasing, 'Until the heavens opened, that is.'

'Rule number one: always check the forecast. I've got Archie here, by the way. He's fine.'

'Aye,' Jack shook his head. 'Well, I had other things on my mind.'

There was a snort. 'I bet you did. I did mention to Phoebe that you were probably thinking your lucky stars we couldn't make it until later. Anyway, I was ringing to tell you there's a tree down on the –'

'Yep, I heard.' He made a face at Beth. 'Lachlan rang. We're going to have to hole up here for the duration. I reckon once the storm passes we can head back on foot to Applemore, and we'll work things from there. No, not if it's the middle of the night, no,' he said, as Danny began to protest.

'Are we expecting any more calls from concerned friends and relations?' Jack said, putting the phone down on the arm of the sofa.

'I think that's us,' said Beth. 'So, as we're stuck here for the night, we're going to have to find something to do.'

He looked at her directly and she stared back, dark eyes challenging.

'I noticed you've got a chess set. Are you any good?'

'How are we defining good?'

'Well, on the scale between utterly dreadful and Grand Master?'

'Mediocre. Not completely hopeless. You?'

'I'd put myself at a solid five out of ten, despite a misspent youth growing up in the sticks with three competitive siblings and nothing to do on the weekends because the cinema and the shops were bloody miles away.'

'The perfect match.' Once again, their eyes met.

Beth dropped her gaze first this time. 'Okay, let's see what you're made of, MacDonald.'

He looked across at the little kitchen. 'I tell you what, why don't I put something on for dinner first. It takes a while, so it can cook while I thrash you at chess.'

Beth raised her chin slightly, an amused expression on her heart-shaped face. 'I'll give you a hand to get it sorted before I thrash *you*.'

'Challenge accepted.' He got up and headed for the kitchen.

Half an hour later, a tomato sauce for pasta was bubbling gently on the stove and he had wiped the kitchen clean. Beth, who'd chopped the garlic, was now setting out the chess pieces on a little wooden table that she'd placed halfway along the sofa.

'Shall we have that whisky now?' Jack looked at the clock. 'It's seven, I think that's a respectable time, don't you?'

Beth nodded. 'It's not like anyone's going to come and expect us to drive now. I can't imagine Lachlan getting someone from the forestry to come out at this time of night.'

'In this weather?' Jack looked outside. The storm was still battering the windows, and the wind moaned down the chimney, making an unearthly groaning noise. It could have been November, and not June.

'I feel a bit sorry for all the tourists. Lachlan and Rilla have their campsite fully booked. All those poor buggers sleeping in campervans in this weather.'

'They'll all have heaters and be sitting inside watching Netflix on their laptops,' shrugged Jack. 'Everyone I know who has a van has all mod cons in there.'

'Yeah, Rilla and Lachlan even have a little shower in theirs.'

'Right then. Whisky.' He eased himself out of the sofa.

'And then I'm going to finish this game and take my rightful crown as chess champion of Applemore,' said Beth, leaning forward to look at the board and contemplate her next move.

Jack opened the safe, retrieving the bottle of single malt he'd been given a couple of weeks before. He was locked up for the night in a cabin in the Highlands with a log fire, a bottle of whisky, and a beautiful, intelligent woman who made him laugh. It was almost perfect.

CHAPTER SEVENTEEN

Two GAMES – and two large whiskies – later, Beth was feeling warm, slightly fuzzy headed, but most of all more relaxed than she'd felt in forever.

'This is nice.' She waved her glass in the general direction of the chess board, the fire, and the little kitchen, from which a delicious scent of garlicky tomato sauce was emanating.

'It is.' He leaned forward, moving his knight towards her end of the chess board.

Beth screwed up her face in thought, then echoed his move. 'Check.'

Jack gave a low whistle. 'I'd say you were more than five out of ten.'

Laughing, Beth flipped her hair over her shoulders and made a jokey model pout. 'Thanks.'

'I meant at chess.' Jack shook his head.

'I know.' The two drinks had put them both at ease, and they were comfortably curled up on their respective sides of the sofa. 'I was only teasing you.'

'Lulling me into a false sense of security so you can hammer me at chess, more like.'

'Well, that too. You know, this is the first time in ages when I've actually felt like I can relax.'

'Me too.'

'I think it's because I know there's literally nothing I can do. I can't go anywhere, I can't do anything about anything, I'm just – stuck.'

'It makes me wonder if being marooned on a desert island would be that much of a bad thing.' He lifted a chess piece, brow knitted in thought, then put it back down without moving it. 'I think you've got me.'

'I'm not sure I want to be marooned on a desert island, though. I'd miss the children. And my family, even though they drive me insane half the time.'

'You all seem to look out for each other,' said Jack, rubbing the scruff of stubble on his chin. Beth had a sudden and irrational urge to reach out and run a finger along his jawline, to feel the touch of his skin on hers. She folded her hands around her almost-empty glass of whisky before she spoke.

'We do. I suppose we do.' She looked at him sideways. 'You said you don't have any siblings. Are you close to your family?'

She watched as Jack seemed to struggle with something, as if he was deciding whether or not to speak. He took a long draught of his drink then closed his eyes for a moment, a thoughtful expression written on his dark features.

'My family is… complicated. It's part of the reason why I didn't put up a struggle when Rebecca was offered the job in Paris.'

'I think all families are complicated, aren't they?' She was trying to be sympathetic, but the look of pain on his face was unmistakable and she felt a wave of guilt at being so tactless. 'I'm sorry, that was a bit *all lives matter*, wasn't it?'

He shook his head, smiling slightly. 'No, you're right. That line from Tolstoy says it all, I think – *'All happy families are alike; each unhappy family is unhappy in its own way.'*

'I haven't heard that. But yeah. I mean I wouldn't say we were unhappy, more… well, growing up with one parent missing isn't exactly ideal. It's why I was so determined to make things work even when I realised there was no future with Simon.'

'Yeah.' Jack flicked a glance at his phone, and she guessed he was checking for a message from Anna. 'Thing is, it was pretty clear early on that Rebecca and I weren't going to make a conventional family, but I'd do anything for Anna. It's why I stayed in Glasgow, so I could do the school runs and be there. I never wanted to be one of those every-second-weekend dads.'

Beth tapped her lips with a finger. 'And yet now…' she began, looking at him with a gentle expression. 'You're here, and –'

Jack let out a long breath and looked skywards. 'Alright.' He got up from the sofa, walked across to the kitchen, stirred the pasta sauce, uncorked the whisky bottle, and brought it back over, tipping a couple of fingers into her glass, and his.

'I don't want you to think I'm giving you the third degree,' she said, picking up her glass and warming it in cupped hands.

He shook his head as he sat down, turning to face her. 'I don't think you are. It's not something I really talk about because people don't – well, I never know how people are going to take it. And of course now I've got to think about Anna.'

'Go on.' Her voice was gentle. She didn't want him to feel she was prying.

'So my mum and dad weren't ever together. He was this big, scary looking bloke on the periphery of my life for a long time when I was growing up. Mum worked long hours, and I was pretty good at fending for myself. I had a key, I used to let myself in after school and get a snack and sit and read a book or watch TV or whatever.'

He rubbed at his temples, as if the act of remembering brought him genuine discomfort.

'Anyway, as I got older, he started coming round more. Looking back, I can see that mum was frightened of him. There were rumours at school, lads saying they'd heard he was involved in some pretty dodgy stuff, but whenever I asked my mother she said he worked away a lot because he was a long-distance lorry driver. If she'd been honest –' he hauled in a long breath, and shook his head, '- anyway. She had her reasons. So when I turned fifteen, he said he'd teach me to drive. Took me to the industrial estate where a mate of his worked, gave me lessons, so by the time I was sixteen I could've passed my test with no problems. It still hadn't occurred to me why he wanted to help – back then I thought I was finally having the sort of relationship dads and sons had, and I held onto it as if it was something worth having.'

Beth unthinkingly shifted towards him on the sofa, as if to offer some sort of physical support by her proximity. He didn't say anything, but glanced down at her legs, folded underneath her, which were now only a few inches from his long crossed ones.

'Anyway, you maybe can see where this is going. He wanted me to do a bit of driving for him, told me it was a favour and I didn't need to worry about the police, that he'd sort everything. I was a bit dubious, but mostly I was just grateful to have my dad give me the attention I'd been missing for years. I'd wait outside a bookies, or a shop, or whatever, and he'd disappear inside and return a short while later, and he'd tell me to put my foot down and show his mates – there were always a couple of others – what I could do.'

'Oh God.' Beth was putting two and two together. She reached out a hand, putting it on his knee. 'I'm sorry, this must have been awful.'

He shook his head. 'It wasn't awful then, because I was young and naïve and at that point I still hadn't realised what was happening. But then things seemed to go up a level, and he stopped being – well, he wasn't exactly warm and encouraging, but until then he'd seemed like he actually gave a damn how I felt. Then he seemed to harden, round about the time I figured out that I wasn't driving for him because he'd lost his licence. I realised that I was driving without a licence of my own and that I was risking myself in the process. He didn't like that, and that's when he made it clear I didn't have any choice.'

Beth put a hand to her mouth, looking at Jack.

'He used you as a getaway driver?'

'I was a kid. I had no-one to tell.' He nodded, face bleak. 'And when they got caught, I was as guilty in the eyes of the law as they were. The police don't accept "I was only doing it because my dad told me to" as an excuse for being involved in organised crime. Especially when it's armed robbery.'

'But you didn't pick up a gun?'

Jack shook his head. 'I didn't, but my dad did.' He dropped his gaze, looking across at the log fire, his eyes dark with regret. 'A man was killed. I couldn't forgive myself for that. They sent me to a young offenders' institution.'

'Jack,' Beth flattened her hand on his knee, looking directly into his eyes as he turned to face her. 'You were coerced. Didn't they see that?'

'They did,' he conceded. 'The judge acknowledged that I hadn't had the capacity to make the sort of decisions needed to get out of the situation, but at the same time he wanted to make an example of me. Anyway, I got put away for two years, and my father was charged with aggravated burglary and attempted murder, and then – well, lots more, when they put two and two together.'

'And where is he now?'

'Still in jail.' He sighed heavily. 'But the trouble is he's up for parole soon, for good behaviour, ironically.'

'And you're worried he'll come looking for you?' Beth felt sick at the thought.

Jack nodded. 'I received an anonymous note when I was still in Glasgow, warning me I was still a grass, and that I should watch my back – and so should my family.'

'My God, that's horrible.'

Jack nodded. 'I wouldn't care if it was just me, but I can't put her at risk. That's why when Rebecca was offered the job as all this happened I told her she had no choice but to take it.'

'But you're being punished over again – not just for what happened, but now you've lost your daughter.'

He sighed. 'I haven't lost her. She's talking to me again, at least. But yeah, it's not great.'

'And that's why you work with the kids you do?'

He nodded. 'I wanted to give something back. I was sent to our centre at Loch Lomond for a five-day break like the kids I work with have. It turned everything around for me, made me realise that there was another way of living that bore no relation to that small, insular life I'd led when I lived in Glasgow.'

Beth's heart ached with sadness for Jack. He was a genuinely kind, truly good man, and here he was having to live without his daughter in his life because he still felt he had to do penance for something that had happened years before.

'And look at the difference you've made.' She realised that she still hadn't moved her hand from his knee.

'It's a bit ironic that I've made a difference to all these kids and I seem to be failing wherever I turn with my own daughter.'

'I don't think you are, are you?'

He gave a half-shrug, frowning slightly. 'She's not happy. Moving school and country at this age isn't ideal, but I couldn't put her at risk.'

'Do you think she's safe now?'

'Pretty much. There are very few people who know about my past – I mean obviously Nathan who heads up the charity does, and Danny – but despite his age he's one of the most level-headed people I know. I changed my name when I came out of prison. It was a chance for a new start. And then not long after that my mum passed away, and I was on my own, and –'

'And you've been that way ever since?'

A look of understanding passed between them.

'More or less.'

'Never wanted to find someone after Rebecca?' She cast her eyes down for a moment, feeling her heart thudding unevenly. When she looked up, he had turned slightly, and was looking directly into her eyes, meeting them with an expression she couldn't quite read.

'Not until now.'

There was a long moment of silence, broken only by the howling of the wind overhead, and a spattering of rain on the windows. Beth looked on transfixed as his fingers curled around hers, his thumb gently grazing the skin of her hand. She looked up again, lips parting as she went to speak, and Jack lifted a hand to her face, his thumb catching her chin and raising it slightly before he moved towards her with a kiss that made her forget everything in that moment.

She pulled away, breathless, meeting eyes which were dark with desire.

'Yes.' She meant yes, she felt the same way. But also she was giving herself permission. Yes, she wanted him and yes, this was what she needed – they both did. The muscles of his back were solid beneath her hand as she leant into him, her mouth brushing over dark stubble on the edge of his jaw, eliciting a low groan of desire. He pulled her into his arms, their bodies entwining.

Beth stirred first, waking to the pale midsummer morning light. For a moment she lay, luxuriating in the sensation of being wrapped in Jack's arms, and then carefully twisted Jack's wrist, checking the time – 4.30am. For the first time in forever, she wanted to stay exactly where she was, and hide away from the world, work and responsibilities forgotten. She traced a finger along the line of dark hairs on his wrist, then stretched like a cat, feeling the hardness of his body against hers.

'Morning,' he murmured, into her hair.

'Hello.'

He caught his hand at the nape of her neck, pulling her

mouth gently towards his, running one hand down her back so she sighed with desire and surrendered herself to the sensations she was feeling, sleepily half-aware that this was like nothing else she'd ever experienced.

The first buzz of Jack's phone in his jeans pocket barely gave them pause. Only when it became insistent – first message notifications, then an insistent ringing, did he pull back reluctantly, giving a long, slow exhale and fixing Beth with a look which filled her with an actual ache of physical longing. He shook his head, half-laughing.

'I'd better check this.'

As soon as he glanced at the screen, she knew the moment was lost forever. His eyes darkened again, but this time the expression on his face was one she couldn't quite recognise. He sprang up from the sofa, pushing a hand through his mussed-up hair, and hit the call button, not even looking in her direction.

CHAPTER EIGHTEEN

'WHAT THE HELL'S GOING ON?'

'Jack. Oh God, I'm sorry. I honestly thought I was doing the wrong thing and now –'

There was a silence, and then a muffled gasp, and Jack realised that Rebecca – calm, unruffled, super-efficient – was in floods of tears.

He lowered his voice, moving across the room, aware that he'd left Beth sitting by the fire with no idea what was going on. He glanced across, seeing her sitting, shoulders squared and back straight, as if she was bracing for impact.

'Bec? What's going on?'

'I thought she was with a friend. I was so bloody happy she was settling at last, particularly after how she was the other day with Karl. She told me she'd been invited to stay for the night, and that she'd be going straight from school because they had a training day on Friday.'

A wave of dread hit him as he stood stock still by the cabin window, looking out at the wind-whipped trees. The storm had dropped, but everything had changed utterly in the course of one day – trees fallen, branches strewn across the grass where they gathered each morning.

'And?'

'Don't shout,' Rebecca said, her voice brittle.

'I'm not shouting.' He was being terse, he couldn't help himself. The gnawing sensation of fear was like a solid stone core which was setting through his body as he stood, one hand pressed against the window, set apart from the storm.

'She didn't answer my call that evening. I thought it wasn't a big deal, because – well, I assumed they were busy or off to the cinema or something. But then the next day she didn't get back to me and I got this feeling... instinct, I suppose.'

'She hasn't been in touch with me, either.' Could his father have got to her somehow? He had no way of knowing his official prison release date, but – no, he didn't have any way of knowing she was in France.

'I searched her room.' Rebecca's voice was tight with anxiety. 'She's taken a bag, and her passport is missing.'

Beth, sensing trouble, had come across to the other side of the cabin to join him and was standing, an expression of concern on her face, arms folded. He looked at her as he spoke to Rebecca.

'What the hell?'

'I think she might be on her way to you. It's the only thing that makes sense. Where else would she be?'

'Why on earth would she decide to do that? I told her I was coming over.'

'She's sixteen, Jack. And she's strong willed, and she's not happy. I blame myself.' And Rebecca started crying again. 'What if something happens to her?'

'Don't, Bec.' He was pacing now, thinking as he walked up and down the cabin, already making plans. He'd have to call Danny, leave him in charge, grab the truck, drop Beth back at the flower farm…

'Jack?'

'I'm thinking. Two secs.'

There was a clattering sound and muffled swearing from Rebecca's end of the line.

'I can't find my passport. Oh, hang on – it's here beside the printer. What on earth?'

'She can't fly without authorisation,' said Jack, bleakly. 'I looked into it before. If she wants to come over here alone, she needs a printed form – *authorisation de sortie* I think it was called.'

'Authorisation from who?'

'One of us. All she needs to do is fake your signature.' He shook his head, as if to clear his mind and give himself space to think, still pacing back and forth. Anna wasn't stupid – it wouldn't take her long to figure out this stuff.

'Okay, I'm going to call the airlines, see what I can find out. Oh God, Jack…'

'She'll be okay.' He closed his eyes. Someone had to be the calm one in this situation and he knew Rebecca well enough to tell that she was on the verge of losing it.

'Promise me, Jack.'

'I promise.'

He pocketed his phone and turned to look at Beth, who was leaning against the cabin window biting her thumbnail, her face drawn with concern.

'I'm guessing you gathered most of that.'

Beth nodded. Half of him wanted to gather her in his arms, to feel the warmth and security that he'd felt that morning when he'd woken up in the half light, dozing gently by the glowing embers of the log burner. But the reality was that Anna was out there somewhere, and while she was at risk of being harmed that was his only focus.

'I've messaged Lachlan. He's got Jimmy and his sons out with the tractor to pull the fallen tree off the road so we can get you out of here as soon as we can.'

Calm and capable, Beth had switched into coping mode.

They drove round through the storm-ravaged woods, bumping over fallen branches as they approached the huge toppled pine tree that lay across the fork of the road. In the distance, towering in the pink-streaked morning sky, stood the turreted roof of Applemore. As he killed the engine he could hear shouts and then the chug of a tractor approaching. They climbed out of the car. The air was clean and fresh, taunting them with its promise of a new day and beautiful summer sunshine.

'Morning,' shouted Lachlan, who could be seen through the branches, a good twenty feet away. 'Beth filled me in. Jack, you don't want to hang around – this could take ages. Jimmy has to secure chains round the tree and we don't even know if we're going to be able to move it.'

Beth tugged his hand. 'This way.'

He followed her around the tree, climbing through the undergrowth and ducking branches as they went, in a strange echo of their adventure yesterday. It felt like a million years ago.

'I need the truck,' he said.

'You don't,' said Beth, and Lachlan was walking towards him, the keys to his Land Rover in his hand.

'Take mine,' he said, tossing them to Jack, who caught them in one hand and looked at them for a moment, as if what Lachlan was saying hadn't quite filtered into his brain.

'I can't,' he said, automatically.

'Yes you can,' said Lachlan and Beth, in unison.

'Keep us posted,' said Beth.

'I really appreciate it,' he said, standing for a moment, nonplussed.

'Go.' Beth motioned towards Lachlan's battered Land Rover.

The car was filthy, covered in dog hair, and scattered with papers and leftover coffee cups. Jack drove towards the village, realising as he did so that he didn't have the faintest idea where he was supposed to do. Where did you start when your daughter was missing somewhere between Paris and the Highlands? Pulling into a layby to let a lorry pass, he quickly checked his phone – one message from Rebecca, telling him she'd spoken to the police and they were calling her back. Where was their sense of urgency?

His natural antipathy towards the police had kicked in – ever since his experience as a teenager, he'd been wary of them. He didn't trust that they'd keep the information to themselves – he didn't really trust anyone, if he was honest with himself. He started driving again, scanning the road as he headed into the village.

Applemore was deserted – it was still early in the morning, and while the sky was already as light as day, there wasn't a soul around. He pulled over for a moment, his mind racing. First things first. He needed to calm his mind, think of this the way he would one of his bushcraft activities. There was no point in blindly driving in hot pursuit when she could be anywhere – he needed to work out how she could have got from Paris to Inverness, and track her back from there.

CHAPTER NINETEEN

'RILLA'S FINE with the two of them,' Lachlan said, firmly, as they watched Jimmy's tractor hauling the fallen tree out of the way of the single-track road. 'You need to get up there and see if you've got a business left.'

'Don't even joke,' Beth groaned, putting her hands over her eyes and shaking her head.

'You've got so much protection from the garden walls,' said her brother, reassuringly. 'It'll be fine.'

'I've got a huge order to fulfil for a wedding tomorrow.'

'Best go and face the music. There's no point standing here pretending it's not happening and fretting over what's happening with Jack.'

Beth loved her brother for not being Charlotte or Polly in that moment. If they'd been there, they'd have been giving her the third degree – despite the awful circumstances – dying to know what had happened between her and Jack. Lachlan wouldn't ever pry, and he – like Beth – was completely focused on the situation in hand.

'Try not to stress.' He put a hand on her shoulder.

'Remember what you were like at sixteen. She's not a baby, she's basically an adult.'

'Yeah but we didn't have people catfishing us on the internet, or grooming, or any of that stuff. What if she's been lured into some awful trap?' Beth bit her lip, thinking about the look of terror that had passed across Jack's face when he'd heard the news. His dad's behaviour all those years ago had cast a long shadow. No wonder Jack had done everything in his power to keep Anna safe.

Beth worked long and hard, salvaging broken stems, cutting them cleanly and plunging them into buckets of deep, cool water. The tulip bed she'd planned for her first pick-your-own Saturday session had come off badly, many of the stems flattened and their leaves damaged by the intensity of the storm. If she stripped them and conditioned the flower stems, she could probably save quite a lot of them and process them for sale at the farm shop, but she'd have to work out what to do for the pick your own – the nature of the event meant that she needed the flowers to be further on in their growth than they were for picking – it wasn't going to be easy to explain to passing visitors that the tight budded flowers they were picking were going to last twice as long as the Instagram-friendly rows of colourful flowers they were probably expecting.

She knew that she was worrying about that for the simple reason that it stopped her focusing on what was really on her mind – what had happened last night with Jack, and what was happening right now. She wanted to call him and see how he was doing, but she didn't want to look like she was hassling him. Naturally reserved, it didn't come easily to her to put herself out there, and as the sun rose up in the sky, bathing the garden in warm yellow light, she became increasingly convinced that she'd made a horrendous mistake in allowing herself to fall for Jack's charms. Not that he was exactly a lady-killer… he'd clearly been torn last night as well. Maybe it was better if it was left as a one-off. She pulled up a tangle of sticky willow which had grown between the tulip stems, tossing it onto the grass. She'd explain the next time she saw him that she understood it had been a mistake, and they could go back to being friends. It was easier all round.

The weather seemed to be almost mocking – the sun was warmer than it had been all year so far, the sky a brilliant cerulean blue. She sat down on the little wooden bench which faced south, closing her eyes for a moment and feeling the heat on her face. They'd had very little sleep, staying up talking and – she felt a wave of longing and tried to suppress it – making love all night, and she was exhausted, physically and mentally. If she closed her eyes for a few moments…

'Mummy!'

What felt like two seconds later she was woken by the sound of Edward and Lucy, faces once again sticky with chocolate, rushing towards her. Rilla and Lachlan followed behind, looking exhausted. She glanced at her phone – no messages – and shoved it back in her pocket.

'Hello darlings,' she said, scooping them both up to sit one on either knee. 'Have you had an adventure with Uncle Lachlan and Aunty Rilla?'

'We made these for you,' said Lucy, handing her a squashed, slightly melted piece of flapjack.

'Just what I needed after all this work.' She kissed them both. 'What else have you been up to?'

'We got into bed for cuddles this morning,' beamed Edward, hauling up his T-shirt to scratch a deliciously round little tummy.

'Oh yes?' Beth caught Rilla's eye. 'What time this morning?'

Rilla, who had suspiciously bruised-looking dark shadows under her eyes, smiled. 'Oh, not too early. Just 4.45, when Lachlan left to sort out the fallen tree with you. What's happening?'

'Still waiting to hear.'

'Is Jack's daughter in the habit of absconding?' Rilla took Lucy's hand as she jumped down from the bench, looking down at her and smiling.

'I don't think so.' It was so bloody hard not being able to tell them the full story. 'It's a bit – complicated.'

'Things usually are.' Rilla lifted an eyebrow. 'You okay?'

Beth nodded. 'I'll be better when I've heard what's happening.'

'But you've got reason to believe she's on her way up here?' Lachlan pushed his floppy dark hair back from his forehead in his habitual gesture.

'It seems the most likely thing, yes.'

Beth scanned the flower beds. There was still so much to do. Of all the times for Miranda to be away, meaning she had to handle everything single handed – a sigh slipped out, unbidden. Rilla and Lachlan exchanged a look.

'I think,' said Rilla, reaching out a hand to Edward and smiling at him, 'That Mummy has lots and lots of things to do after that big storm, and maybe it might be fun if we go down to see Aunty Polly at the shop? Then we can get some potatoes and do some nice potato print pictures at Applemore. What d'you two think?'

The twins jumped up and down, cheering with excitement. 'Yay, yay, yes!'

Oh, to be that easily amused.

'And I'll give you a hand.' Lachlan pulled her up to standing from the bench. 'You look knackered.'

Beth opened her mouth to protest.

'No arguments.'

She looked at Rilla, who shook her head.

'What he said,' she said, firmly.

Together they returned the pots that had flown up in the air, strewing themselves across the gardens, and staked and tied the flowers that had been storm-battered, working together in the easy, quiet way that came naturally to them.

'I'm glad you came back,' she said, a couple of hours later, as they stood surveying their handiwork.

'Back from where?' Lachlan arched his back with a groan. 'Bloody hell, I have no idea how you do this every day. I'm knackered.'

'From Edinburgh.'

It took him a few seconds to catch on. 'Yeah.' He looked across, unthinkingly, in the direction of Applemore. 'It took me a while to get my head round the idea of being responsible for this place. It doesn't feel like a millstone round my neck anymore.'

'That's because you've got Rilla,' she said, leaning down to pick up a stray dandelion from the edge of the lavender bed. 'And the next generation of Fraser babies.'

'I guess we all get there in the end.' He turned to look at her. 'So, what's the story?'

'What story?'

'Oh come on, Beth, it's glaringly obvious that you two are a perfect match.'

'We're just friends.'

'Friends don't look at each other the way you two do. I mean for God's sake, I'm a man, with the emotional intelligence of one of your daffodil bulbs, and I can see it.'

'Unfair to daffodils.' Beth ducked, laughing, as he swiped at her. 'Anyway, like I said before, it's complicated. I've got the twins, he's got a daughter in France who clearly has more than a few issues.'

'I'm just going to point out that you told me that life was too short, etc, etc, when Rilla left Applemore for Paris eighteen months ago. And now look where we are.'

Beth shrugged. 'I dunno. I haven't even heard from him.'

'He's got quite a lot on his plate, remember.'

'Oh God I know.'

'Have you messaged him? Called?'

She shook her head.

'Maybe he'd like a word from someone he cares about.' Lachlan looked at her sideways. 'Just saying, as Polly would say.'

'Okay.' She pulled her phone out of her pocket. 'I'll try ringing.'

'I'll stick this stuff back in the greenhouse,' said Lachlan, striding across the path. 'Then I suggest that you and I head back in Jack's pick-up, get your van, and you get home for a hot bath and a bit of a kip. We'll keep the twins for a bit longer, let you get some rest. You look like you haven't slept for a week.'

The thought of a bath and a snooze was hard to resist. Beth scrolled down her phone, selecting Jack's number.

'Hi,' he said, sounding surprisingly pleased to hear from her.

'Any luck?'

'Nothing. I've driven to Inverness Airport, kept my eyes peeled, had a look all over town and checked all the hostels in case she's checked in but none of them have heard anything.'

'What are the police saying?'

There was a long silence.

'Jack?' Beth narrowed her eyes in thought. 'You have called them, yes?'

'I'm just seeing what I can do myself first.'

She stood for a moment, looking over the acre of neatly planted land she'd worked so hard on, and the trees of Applemore estate that stretched out towards their family home beyond that. It was easy for her – with the generations of privilege she took for granted – to assume that the police would be there if something went wrong, ready to help and support her in her hour of need. She'd never thought before meeting Jack about how it might feel to have a residual undercurrent of fear and trepidation that came with everything that had passed before. No wonder he didn't find it easy to trust – he'd been betrayed by his father, not once but constantly, and then had his adolescence taken away from him as a result.

'Beth?'

'Sorry,' she said, her voice low. 'I was thinking. Okay, look, keep me posted. I'll go and have a look around the village, see if anyone has seen anything. Don't worry –' she pre-empted him, hearing him about to protest '– I won't give anything away.'

'I appreciate it. Right now, the fewer people know the better.'

She wished him luck and hung up, standing for a moment in the bright silence of the garden before turning to leave.

Jimmy the farmer had worked hard with his sons, clearing the detritus of fallen branches from the road. Heading home, exhausted and filthy after a long afternoon of putting the flower farm to rights, as they approached the clearing where Jack had abandoned his pick-up with the keys still in the ignition, Beth leaned forward, narrowing her eyes.

'Hang on,' she said, tugging on Lachlan's sleeve. She peered across her brother, trying to make out what she thought she could see in the shadowy interior of the cab.

'What's that?'

He slowed Rilla's car, following her gaze, then slammed on the brakes so they both jerked forward.

'Don't you mean *who*?' Beth shoved the door open and climbed out, turning to Lachlan and putting a warning finger to her lips, indicating for her brother to stay where he was. She crept forward, opening the door to the pick-up cautiously. Inside, sitting fast asleep in a patch of sunlight, head lolling on the passenger seat was a girl of about sixteen. Her dark hair untidy, hands folded in a childlike pose. Looking at her profile and the determined set of her jaw even in repose, there was no question whose daughter she was. Beth stood for a second, torn between waking her first to be sure, and calling Jack to put him out of his state of utter panic. Jack won. There was no way that there could be another random sixteen-year-old with the same dark, high-cheekboned look who just happened to have landed in a Wildcat Adventures branded truck.

She stepped backwards, movements cat-like and cautious, not wanting to startle her. Lachlan stood by the edge of Rilla's car, a questioning look on his face. He lifted a hand. Beth shook her head, motioning once again for her brother to stay quiet.

She tiptoed across the track, hitting Jack's number on her phone, willing him to reply. There was a pause – God, this was no time for the cell service to start playing up – and she waited for him to answer, tapping an impatient hand against her thigh.

'Beth?' Jack's tone was urgent.

'She's here.' Beth turned away to look back towards the walled garden of the flower farm in the distance, thinking how strange it was that everything looked as it always had, but she was here, dealing with a situation she couldn't ever have imagined in her wildest dreams.

'What?' There was a long pause. She could visualise Jack pushing an anxious hand through his hair, eyes narrowed in thought, working out what to do next.

'We've found her. Here, fast asleep in your truck.'

'What the hell?' She heard a long exhale of relief. 'Beth. Oh God, thank you.'

'Hang on,' she started back towards the pick-up, heart thumping against her rib cage, motioning to Lachlan to be ready. If she bolted, there wasn't really anywhere she could go, but Beth didn't want to give her the chance. 'Let me put you on to her.'

Carefully, quietly, she pulled open the passenger door. The girl opened her eyes, half-asleep for a moment, then snapping them wide with surprise when she came to and saw Beth looking in at her. Her expression changed and she went to grab the door handle, movements lighting fast.

'Hey, Anna,' said Beth, gently. 'I've got your dad on the phone here.' She handed the mobile over, watching as Anna looked at the screen for a moment, reading the name and realising that she wasn't being tricked.

'Dad?' Her shoulders dropped, and she raised a thumb to her mouth, biting the nail anxiously.

'I'm okay. I'm here, in your truck. Where are you?'

In that instant, Beth could see the little girl in the teenager. The little face softened. Beth wanted nothing more than to reach out and comfort her. She stepped away, giving them privacy, and turned back to Lachlan who was still hovering out of earshot.

'We better ring the police and let them know she's safe.' He was holding his phone, as if waiting for the nod.

Beth thought on her feet. 'Oh, Jack said he'd do that.' The situation was complex, and she knew that this wasn't the time to start trying to explain this to her brother, no matter how easy-going he was. There was plenty of time for that later, once things had settled down. They stood in silence for a couple more minutes, and then she strolled back over to the pick-up.

'I'm sorry,' Anna was saying, twisting a long strand of hair around her finger. 'I just wanted to see you.'

Beth's heart melted.

'I'll ask.' Anna said, and held out the phone. 'Dad says can he talk to you.'

Beth took the phone and flashed Anna a reassuring smile. 'Of course.'

'I'm heading back now,' Jack said. 'I was waiting for a seat on the next flight. Are you okay to keep hold of her until I get back?'

'Of course. I'll take her to mine, give her something to eat.' She looked at Anna, who was still sitting in the passenger seat, gazing out of the window, lost in thought.

'You're an angel.' Jack's tone was gruff with gratitude. 'Take my truck. I don't want her having any more opportunities to escape.'

'I don't think she's going anywhere,' Beth said, and Anna's eyes met hers. She gave a small smile and shook her head. 'I'll make sure she's safe until you get home.'

'I missed this,' Anna volunteered, after they'd been driving for a couple of minutes.

Beth, slightly surprised, turned to look at her. She'd tucked her hair behind her ears and was tracing her finger along the dashboard. 'I used to sit here every morning on the way to school when we lived in Glasgow. Dad used to take me.'

Beth looked across at her. 'You miss your dad a lot.'

Anna bit her lip and nodded. 'How come you know him? Do you work together?'

'We work next to each other,' said Beth, slowing up the truck and pulling into a passing place as a huge motorhome made its way down the single-track road. 'I have a farm next door.'

'Ooh,' Anna perked up. 'What kind of animals have you got?'

Beth smiled. 'Well, I've got two cats, but it's not a farm – I grow flowers.'

'That sounds nice.' Anna put a hand to her mouth to try and stem a huge yawn.

'You must be exhausted,' Beth said, as they pulled up outside the farmhouse. 'Come in, I'll get you something to eat. Your dad won't be long.'

She held open the door, moving out of the way so Beth could go in ahead of her, noticing that the baskets she'd planted had been flattened by the storm. All of the flower stems were squashed, as if something had steamrollered across the top of them.

Anna hovered in the hall, chewing the inside of her cheek. Beth could imagine how uncomfortable she was feeling, standing in a stranger's house, miles from home – a home where right now she felt she didn't belong. She reached over, squeezing Anna's arm, gently.

'I'm sorry, this is a bit weird for you.'

For a moment, Anna looked as if she might start to cry,

then she seemed to gather herself, raising her chin slightly and giving a small, brave smile. 'A little bit.'

'You've come a long way. I'll leave it to your dad to tell you why upping sticks and jumping on a flight from Paris isn't the best idea, but I have to admit I'm quietly quite impressed you managed to get here in one piece.'

Anna's smile picked up slightly. 'Really?'

Beth led her through to the kitchen and flicked on the kettle, scrubbing her filthy hands then rummaging in the fridge and finding some cheese to make a sandwich. 'Yes, really. But if one of my children did it I'd go completely bonkers with worry.'

'I didn't mean to stress them out.' Anna leaned against the kitchen counter and looked out of the window. The garden, post-storm, looked as if someone had picked up all the children's plastic toys and thrown them willy-nilly across the lawn. The sun shone innocently in the sky, as if to make the point that it would never create such havoc.

'Your dad said he was planning to come and see you?' Beth buttered some bread and sprinkled grated cheese on top. Without thinking, she sliced the sandwiches into quarters, putting them on a plastic plate with a Peppa Pig design.

'Thank you,' Anna said politely.

'Oh sorry,' Beth laughed, 'I didn't mean to give you a toddler plate.'

'I don't mind. Reminds me of when I was little.'

Beth wiped the chopping board and shook out the cloth, slipping past Anna to fetch a couple of mugs. She made some coffee for them both, and found some chocolate biscuits from the cupboard. She suspected that – adrenalin starting to wear off, and the enormity of what she'd done beginning to sink in – Anna was starting to flag.

'It's lovely weather. Do you want to sit outside, or would you rather just flop on the sofa?'

'Would you mind if we stayed inside?'

Beth shook her head. 'Not at all. Come on, let's go and have a sit down. I've had a busy day too.'

She shifted a pile of soft toys to one side, gesturing for Anna to sit down.

'Sorry it's a bit untidy.' Beth unwrapped a chocolate biscuit. 'Help yourself.'

'It's nice.' Anna sat on the sofa, looking around at the untidy sitting room. 'Mum's place is always spotless. I mean our house. Well, it doesn't feel like our house since we moved.' She picked up one of the teddy bears and twirled it around in her hand, settling it down on the cushion beside her. Once again Beth was reminded that Anna was still very young and her generous heart squeezed with fondness for her.

'You preferred staying with your dad at his place?'

Anna nodded.

'Even though his flat was really small it always felt like home. Mum's place is too tidy, if you know what I mean?'

'Totally.' Beth nodded. 'I mean I grew up in a house that was total chaos, but really tidy places have always freaked me out a bit. You feel like you can't relax.'

Anna sat back against the cushions of the sofa, looking relieved. 'Exactly.'

'I ran away from home, once,' said Beth, thoughtfully. She'd forgotten about it until just now when she was sorting out some food. 'I didn't manage to get from one country to another though, just from our house into the village. They found me feeding the ducks at the water's edge. I was only ten.'

'Why did you run away?'

Beth frowned. 'I was tired of being the invisible one. It felt like everyone else in the family got noticed for something, and I was – well, I felt like nobody would notice if I wasn't there.'

'I bet they did,' said Anna, curling her feet up on the sofa.

'They did. My dad took me out for pie and chips at the Applemore Hotel, and told me I was his favourite Beth. I told him he only *had* one Beth, and he said how did I know he didn't have a whole supply of them locked in a cellar somewhere.'

Anna giggled. 'Your dad sounds nice.'

'He was.'

Beth checked her phone, which had bleeped while they were speaking. 'Talking of dads, yours is nearly here. Half an hour, he says.'

Beth heard the familiar rumble of Lachlan's Land Rover engine and stood up almost before he'd pulled it to a halt outside the farmhouse.

'He's here,' she said, giving Anna a gentle squeeze on the shoulder. She'd been drooping like a wilting flower, her eyelids getting heavier and heavier, but hearing the words she shot out of the sofa and scrambled to the door, throwing herself into his arms.

'Hello AB,' he said, dwarfing his daughter, wrapping his big arms around her in a tight squeeze. He looked at Beth over the top of her head, widening his eyes, making a show of puffing out a breath of relief. 'Can you please not do that again,' he said, dropping a kiss on the top of Anna's head. 'That's quite enough adventuring for one lifetime.'

'I won't.' Anna's voice was muffled. Eventually he

released her and stood back, looking her up and down. 'Well you look like you're in one piece. That's something.'

Beth could tell he was trying to keep his tone light. She could read the depths of the unspoken stress and anxiety and see it written all over his face, which looked as if he'd aged about a decade since she'd seen him last.

'Thanks,' he said, his eyes meeting hers. Her stomach twisted then, in a brief recollection of the night they'd spent together, and she felt suddenly shy and after smiling in acknowledgement, she ducked her head and pushed her hair behind her ear, looking away. Jack had enough to deal with now. They were friends, and last night – well, it was one of those things. He probably regretted it – he certainly had enough going on in his life.

'It's fine,' said Beth, eventually. She lifted her chin slightly, and offered him a small, brave smile.

'Okay,' he said, giving Beth's arm a gentle squeeze as she stood to one side of them, 'I'd better get this girl home and out of your hair. I'm sure you've got lots to do.'

Beth tried to protest, but he had his hand on the farm-house door as he spoke, and gently propelled Anna through the doorway and out into the late evening sunshine. 'Can you give Lachlan these?' He passed her the keys for the Land Rover. 'And tell him thanks. I don't have his number, or I'd tell him myself.'

It felt oddly final. 'Of course I will,' she said, and stood back as the two of them climbed into his pick-up.

'Thanks for having me,' said Anna, politely, winding down the window.

'Any time,' Beth said, then caught Anna's eye and smiled. 'Maybe not under the same circumstances, though.'

Anna giggled. 'Maybe not.'

'Thanks again. I'll speak to you later,' said Jack, and with that he pulled away.

Beth sighed as she closed the door. Of course he couldn't do anything else but leave, but it didn't stop the nagging feeling that she'd lost something she never quite had in the first place.

CHAPTER TWENTY

'WELL.' Jack looked at his daughter, who was sitting in the passenger seat of the truck, chewing her lip. They drove down the road to Applemore village in silence. He looked across the water at the islands, the sun dropping down and casting long shadows over the purple heather-covered hills. The sea was smooth and suffused with a gold and orange glow. It was absolutely beautiful, and even more so because Jack was overwhelmed with such relief that his baby girl was here, sitting on the passenger seat, not kidnapped or harmed or goodness knows what else, having been intercepted on her journey.

'I'm sorry.' She grimaced. 'I didn't mean to stress you out.'

'No,' he said, shaking his head. 'I am. We need to talk. But first you need to speak to your mum, let her know you're safe – I mean she's heard from me, but she needs to hear it from your lips.'

Anna made a face. 'Do I have to?'

They drove into the village. Danny's truck was parked

outside the cottage. By the harbour rail opposite, a string of bunting lay tattered on the pavement, a casualty of last night's storm.

'You do.' He hit the call button and passed Anna the phone. 'I'll nip into the cottage, let Danny know what's happening.'

'No, it's not Dad, it's me.' Anna's chin wobbled as she listened to her mother's stream of invective. He wasn't going to come the heavy with his daughter when he knew that Rebecca, who never held back, was going to go at her all guns blazing.

'Two minutes.' He left Anna on the phone to her mother and headed into the cottage. Danny was standing in the kitchen in his outdoor gear, tipping water into his travel coffee mug to rinse it out.

'Another uneventful day,' he said, mildly.

Jack shook his head. 'Don't even start.'

'You okay?'

Jack nodded briefly. 'Been a bit of a day.'

'You're not joking. Look, I'm going to need to take a few days, get Anna home, sort some stuff out. Are you okay to hold the fort?'

'Course. What's the plan?'

Jack screwed up his face, thinking. 'I think I'll head back over to Inverness, book us into a hotel. Much as I'd like to keep Anna here, show her round and all that stuff, the reality is she's got school and it's an exam year. But also I don't want her to think the reward for going AWOL is an unscheduled holiday in the Highlands.'

'You don't think she'll boomerang back here?'

He shook his head. 'Not once I've explained the situation, no.'

Danny turned to look at Jack, focusing all his attention on him. 'You can't hide forever.'

'Aye,' Jack conceded. 'I know. I need to see how the land lies once he gets out of prison. I don't want to risk anything.'

'Alright. Well, anything I can do, say the word.'

Jack nodded, touched at his loyalty. It was good to have someone who had his back.

'There's one thing.'

'Go on?'

'Keep an eye on Beth? I feel bad that I'm disappearing on her after…'

'Oh aye?' Danny chuckled. 'After what exactly?'

'Nothing,' said Jack, firmly. 'Just after she rescued Anna, and got caught up in all of this. She knows, by the way.'

Danny gave a brief nod of acknowledgement. 'I'll keep an eye out.'

As they drove towards Inverness, he explained to a stunned Anna exactly why he'd made the choices he had, and why he'd encouraged Rebecca to take the job in Paris.

'It came at the perfect time.'

'Not for me it didn't,' said Anna, indignantly.

'Living with your mum, you can have everything you want.'

'I don't want everything,' she said, glaring out of the window, her shoulders turning away from him.

'I know, darling,' he said, glancing across at her. It was easy for her to say that – she'd never known the life he'd had growing up, nor would she. He saw a younger version of himself, jaw set and dark eyes focused on the road ahead, and felt another wave of relief that she'd been found safe. He'd driven back towards Applemore with his mind racing, every single terrible possibility running through his head as if on a repeated reel.

'I hate France – I hate it there. I could stay with you and go to college up here. Beth said she's got an apprentice who works on the flower farm and she's at college.'

'I thought you wanted to go to university and study biology?'

'Changed my mind.' She crossed her arms and looked out of the side window.

He decided to change tack.

'Look, you're old enough now to hear all this, but you need to realise that it's a lot to take in. Maybe it'll make sense of why things are the way they are.'

An hour later, when she'd exhausted every question she could think of, they were just arriving on the outskirts of Inverness. Anna's head was drooping, the long days of travel catching up with her, and Jack made a quick decision to pull in to one of the budget hotels which sat – anonymous and uniform – by the out-of-town shopping centre. Later, when he'd got her settled, he'd nip out to one of the fast food places and grab something for them to eat, if she woke up. He suspected she wouldn't.

The next morning, Anna having slept sixteen hours solidly, they woke early and headed to the tiny airport, parking his truck and heading inside where they sat drinking coffee and waiting for their flight to come in. Jack was on high alert, but trying to conceal it from Anna. While she sipped hot chocolate and – with the capriciousness of teenagers – told him how much she was looking forward to seeing her new friend Elodie, he scanned the airport lounge. Inverness Airport was all on one level, which made it easier

RACHAEL LUCAS

to keep an eye on the people who were coming and going, but his mouth was dry and his heart pounding. He glanced at his phone over and over, torn between texting Beth updates and feeling that maybe they should leave what happened in the past. He had enough to deal with, making sure Anna was safe – and the last thing he wanted was to drag her into the world he couldn't escape from. Anna scrolled though her phone as they sat on the runway. Jack – knowing that only now they'd passed through security and were airside could he relax – sat back, leaning against the headrest, taking a long, slow breath. He looked down at his phone as the cabin crew passed by, checking seatbelts and asking people to switch their phones to airplane mode.

Safely on board. Will text from Paris.

He sent the message to Beth, then turned off his phone.

CHAPTER TWENTY-ONE

FIVE DAYS PASSED, and Beth threw herself into work to distract herself from thinking about everything that had happened. She'd had a message from Jack to say that he'd arrived safely, but that was it – since then there had been radio silence. Logically she knew that he had enough on his plate, but she couldn't help kicking herself for being silly enough to think – or hope – that something could have come out of their night together. As the days passed, it felt less and less likely and she felt the carefully constructed barriers she'd built around her heart over the years reactivating and strengthening. No, she was better off alone, focusing on the things she was good at. She was a good mother, she was doing well with business – the paperwork she'd done that week showed her that profits were soaring and her projections for the year were unambitious, if anything.

The morning of the first pick-your-own flowers day dawned with glorious sunshine. Everyone had mucked in to make it a success – Polly brought up a couple of trestle tables with a spread of cakes and biscuits from the shop, and took a day off to man it herself. Lachlan and Rilla painted a sign and guided visitors down the track towards the flower farm, Rilla with flowers woven in her dark curls, a long summer dress hiding the beginnings of a tiny bump. Miranda was at the front gate, taking money from visitors and instructing them where to go.

'You can pick anything from the beds with the yellow flags on the corners,' she was explaining, 'but try and take some of everything, rather than wiping out an entire bed of whatever you fancy, if that makes sense?'

Beth was amused to see Dolina and her daughter Jenny nodding very seriously as they listened to Miranda's instructions. They'd turned up with their own buckets and despite the sunshine were clad in wellington boots.

'Were you expecting to be wading through mud?' Miranda gave them an amused look.

'Well it said flower *farm*,' said Dolina, stoutly, 'and farms can be muddy.'

'That they can,' said Beth, being kind, 'although not in the driest summer we've had in years.'

By lunchtime, there was a steady stream of people coming through the painted gate and into the walled garden, collecting a bucket (if they hadn't brought one of their own) and some gardening scissors, and wandering off to the marked out beds where they snipped the blooms, not minding at all – to Beth's relief – that a lot of them were still tighter in bud than she'd hoped. She wandered around, helping people choose flowers, chatting about the way she worked, and for once taking the time to soak it all in.

'Well look at this,' said a familiar voice. She turned, as the twins crashed into her legs with shrieks of excitement.

'Simon,' said Beth, amazed. He hadn't been near the

place since they'd split up nearly two years ago. He was standing in a pair of red shorts (must be Morag's doing, she thought) and a pair of very new-looking deck shoes, with a blue sweater draped around his shoulders. Morag was following behind, looking very much like an off-duty bank manager in a pair of neatly pressed cropped beige trousers and a Breton top. Beth, who couldn't even remember if she still owned an iron, automatically brushed at her linen pinafore, which was scattered with round seed heads which had stuck to it like tiny decorative pom-poms.

'Thought we'd come and see how you were doing.'

'And see if I'm making enough money that you can feel less guilty about giving up work and dropping me in it?' She half-regretted the words as soon as they came out of her mouth, but mainly thought that he bloody well deserved it.

'Actually, no.' He bent down as Edward toppled over and almost landed in a bed of goldenrod. Morag joined them. Pregnancy had softened her pale face – she looked younger, somehow. Her hair had been cut into a loose bob which skimmed the collar of her top.

'Have you told her?' She looked from Simon to Beth.

'Told me what?'

'I've had a job offer I can't refuse. Look, I know I've been a bit of an arse –'

Beth felt her eyebrows edging skywards, and looked at her ex-husband with an expression she knew he'd read instantly.

'– a lot of an arse,' he corrected himself. 'And you've put up with it. All of it.'

'The thing is,' Morag said, taking over, 'it didn't really hit me until I had the scan. And I looked at that tiny little person and thought about you with the twins, and about the fact that it wasn't fair on you to expect you to pick up the pieces, and…'

'What we're trying to say is that you don't need to stress. I'm not going to give up work. You'll still get your child maintenance.'

'I –' There was a tiny bit of Beth that wanted to tell them to stick their child maintenance where the sun didn't shine, but she caught a glimpse of Edward and Lucy, who – having spent a huge proportion of their three years playing in the garden as she worked – were now stomping around self-importantly and showing off to the children of a couple who had just arrived. '– thanks,' she said, eventually. She was trying to work out what to say next when she realised with horror that the twins were shrieking with laughter, having pulled down their little jeans and mooned the unsuspecting visitors.

'Oh my God,' Morag said, putting a horrified hand to her mouth.

Simon burst out laughing. 'Apparently, someone did it at nursery and it got such a reaction that they came home absolutely full of it.'

Beth clapped her hand to her eyes. 'They are absolute horrors.' She rushed over. 'Come on, you two,' she said, taking them by the hand. 'You can go and find some cookies with Daddy and Morag. Look, Aunty Polly is over there.'

The couple grinned. 'Don't worry,' the woman said, adjusting the bucket half-full of flowers on her hip, 'Ours have done way worse. The biting stage was the worst.'

'Don't give them ideas,' said Beth, shaking her head and laughing. She handed the children over to Simon and Morag, watching as they wandered across to say hello to Polly.

A moment later, before she'd had a moment to take in

what had happened, she realised that Gina, complete with Gregor the grey-bearded cameraman, was floating towards her, huge sunglasses making her look like a bug, arm flapping a huge wave of greeting.

'Beth, this is marvellous. Wonderful.'

'I wasn't expecting you here,' she said, as Gina kissed her hello.

'We had a bit of last-minute to do – long shots, that sort of thing. The weather is perfect, and when I realised you were open for the day, I persuaded Gregor to take a quick detour. This will look absolutely fab on camera,' she said, beaming to someone who was walking past on their way to pay for their bucket of flowers and gorgeous, tangled foliage. 'Oh, they're beautiful,' she called out, in her carrying voice.

'If we can get a few shots of the garden, that would be wonderful. Won't get in your way, I promise. Just think of the publicity.'

The afternoon rolled on. Gina and Gregor seemed in no great rush to get off, settling down with a drink and some cake in the shade of the elder tree and looking over the shots they'd taken. By three o'clock Beth had reached the point where she was having to stand guard over the beds that weren't available for picking to avoid scissor-happy customers helping themselves.

'I'm going to get off,' said Polly, giving her a kiss goodbye. 'Are those two here for the duration?' She nodded towards Gina and Gregor.

Beth shrugged. 'I have no idea.'

Polly pulled her into a hug. 'You're amazing, you know that?'

Beth recoiled slightly. 'What's that for?'

'Oh come on, I know we're all fond of being terribly

Scottish and dour and all that, but praise where it's due – you've worked bloody hard to make this place a success. I'm surprised you didn't shove a sunflower where the sun didn't shine when Simon turned up. What a bloody cheek he's got after everything.'

Beth shared the news, realising as she said it out loud that it still hadn't quite sunk in.

'Maybe now you can take a bit of a breather?' Polly rubbed her arm, affectionately. 'You've worked your backside off this year to make this place pay. If Simon's doing the decent thing, perhaps it's time for a bit of time to focus on life outside the walls of the garden?'

Beth shrugged. 'Doing what?'

'Doing who, more like,' said Polly, giggling. 'It can't have escaped your notice there's an extremely handsome Glaswegian who seems to have the hots for you.'

'Oh shush,' said Beth, feeling herself going pink. She turned away for a moment, pretending to be looking to see if anyone was coming in the gate. 'He's not here, anyway, he's in Paris.'

'He's not staying there, though, is he?'

'I guess not.'

'Well,' said Polly, shifting the bag on her shoulder, 'I'm just suggesting maybe it's time for you to have a bit of a life of your own. You deserve happiness, too.'

The last of the customers were herded out of the gate, having paid for their buckets of blooms. Beth looked down at the table, marvelling at the amount of money that Phoebe had taken. Most of the business cards she'd left out had gone, and her phone had pinged several times with notifications telling her she'd had online orders via the website. It had – she had to admit to herself – been a resounding success. All that, and Simon's news too. It had been a pretty amazing day. She checked her phone, wondering if there was any word from Jack, but there was nothing. Despite Polly's excitement, she felt a gnawing sense of worry that their night together had been a mistake, and his silence – even though she tried to tell herself he had enough on his plate while dealing with Anna – suggested he felt the same way. She'd never been the sort of person to go in for one-night stands. She grimaced and looked up to see Gina bearing down on her.

'Hello again,' she said, with a slightly cautious smile. 'We've been holding on, because I – well, as I always say, once a journalist, and all that... I've got a bit of a quandary.'

Beth shifted so that the table stood squarely between them, holding her at a distance.

'What kind of quandary?'

'We were working on the rushes when Gregor realised why Jack looked so familiar. It had been nagging at me, too. Has he talked to you about his past?'

She'd realised the other day that Fliss must've remembered his father's face from the newspapers, and that's why Jack had looked familiar to her, too. Fortunately it had clearly slipped her mind, because she hadn't heard a word about it since. Seeing Gina's questioning expression, Beth shook her head, feeling her heart thudding against her ribcage. 'No, we don't really know each other that well.'

'Interesting,' she said, with a catlike smile. 'You certainly looked very friendly when we were filming your piece. And I was chatting to some of the locals, who seemed to think you two were like this –' she crossed two fingers together.

'We work in close proximity, that's all.' Beth picked up her phone, putting it in her jeans pocket out of sight.

Knowing her luck, he'd text then and there and Gina would spot it.

'So he hasn't said anything to you about his father, or about how he got here?'

Beth shook her head.

'Interesting,' she said again. 'Well, you might ask him. And if you see him, can you let him know we'd love to have a chat? He hasn't returned my calls.'

'He's not here,' Beth began, not thinking.

'Oh?'

'Away working,' she said, trying to cover her tracks. Gina looked unconvinced.

'Well if you see him, as I say, do let him know it would be –' She paused, as if selecting the right word, '– helpful if he got in touch.'

CHAPTER TWENTY-TWO

JACK RETURNED ten days after they left Inverness, having spent some time with Anna which seemed to help settle her back into Paris and give her a sense of rootedness that she'd been missing. The flight from Glasgow to Inverness landed at midday, and desperate to see what had been happening up at the centre, he left his bag in the truck and headed up there to find the cabin empty. Sandra was in the bunkhouse, clearing out a bedroom.

'What happened here?'

'Oh some mischief with a bottle of fizzy orange,' she said, shaking her head. 'I've had to change half the sheets. This group are right terrors.'

Jack laughed. 'You mean they're exhibiting some challenging behaviour?'

'Aye,' She chuckled, and shook out a duvet cover. 'That's exactly what I meant.'

'Danny up at the river?'

'I saw them passing earlier. They're taking them tubing as the weather's so nice.'

'It's a match for Paris,' he said, looking at the cloudless sky.

'It is,' she said in her soft Highland accent. 'I hope you're appreciating this, for I can't imagine we'll have another summer like this next year. Normally it's rain and midges all the way.'

'Not so good for the garden,' he said, without thinking.

'Talking of which,' said Sandra, looking at him side-ways, 'I saw Beth was chatting to that producer woman from the television the other day. I took my granddaughter to have a wee look at the gardens when she was having her pick-your-own day, and she forgot her wee purse, so I left her in the car and nipped back up to see if I could find it on the grass. Chatting away quite the thing, they were.'

'Probably doing some last-minute stuff,' said Jack. 'I'm going to go and see if I can find Danny.'

He looked at his phone as he walked back to the truck. Gina – who'd been persistent from the off – had tried to call several times while he'd been in France, and she'd left a voicemail that morning.

'Jack, hi. Just a quickie to say that I'd love to catch up when you're back from France. Let me know when you've got time to talk.'

He frowned, looking at her number on the screen. He had warned Danny not to mention where he was going – the last thing he wanted was anyone getting wind of Anna's whereabouts. He leaned back against the door of the truck, and hit the call button.

'Jack,' she said smoothly, 'Thanks so much for getting back to me.'

'No problem.' He tried to keep his tone light, but some-thing was nagging at him and he felt a twist of apprehen-sion in his gut. 'How can I help?'

'I had a chat with Beth the other day. I'm not going to beat about the bush, Jack,' she went on. 'We're both busy, and you strike me as the sort of chap who'd rather I was direct.'

Jack gazed into the middle distance, thinking as he did that he had an irrational dislike of people who over-used his name in conversation.

'I was telling Beth that it had been nagging at me since we did the filming – I never forget a face.'

He clenched his jaw. This was it, the moment he'd feared for all these years. He'd been a fool to think that he'd get away with filming, even briefly, without someone seeing him and putting two and two together.

'So I did a bit of research, and there's an angle here that's going to make the most amazing television.'

'No.' His tone was flat and final.

'Oh, come on, you have to admit it makes for a good story. Bad boy comes good, son of the head of a criminal gang, how the centre changed your life, all of that.'

He shook his head. God, if he'd just followed his instinct. Instead he'd only agreed to the filming because – he'd hardly wanted to admit it to himself – he'd hoped it would give him a chance to spend more time with Beth. If Danny hadn't messed it up, he could have stayed in the background. Now he was in danger of blowing everything.

'I can't.'

'You're worried your father might work out where you are, now that he's out?'

'He's out?' He spoke without thinking.

'He got out at the end of last week,' said Gina, and he could picture her face from her tone. Gotcha, she was thinking.

He closed his eyes for a moment. Anna was in Paris, and at least now she knew the truth and why he'd sent her away.

'Nobody knows about my past – well, nobody besides Nathan who runs the charity, and a couple of other people.'

'Yes,' she said smoothly, 'I'm aware of that. It took some digging to get the facts, but we got there in the end.'

Nathan would never have said anything. He knew for a fact that Danny was completely loyal. There was no way on earth that Rebecca – not that she'd have found her – would have risked Anna's safety. It could only have been Beth – but he couldn't imagine it. He felt a wave of nausea roll over him. He'd been an idiot to think he could keep this lie going once his dad was released.

'Fine,' he said, hauling in a long breath. 'I'll talk to you. Once.'

'Oh, that's great news,' she said, the triumph in her voice all too evident. 'We can come up tomorrow, do a bit to camera. It's going to give it that human element people love.'

He shook his head. 'No. I'll come down to Glasgow. I don't want this connected to the centre.'

'What do you mean?'

'Glasgow, or not at all.'

Gina clearly knew when she'd been beaten. She agreed a time and a place. Jack drove, grim faced, back to the cottage. He threw his things into the back of the truck, and left a note for Danny. There was no way he could tell him by phone, and he couldn't face being in Applemore a moment longer, knowing Beth had dropped him in it, whether knowingly or not. He drove away, jaw gritted in tension, knowing what he had to do.

The next day he met Gina in the garden of the production company in the leafy West End of Glasgow. Birds sang overhead, and the sun shone down, dappling the flagstones under the cast iron table and chairs where they sat, a camera focused on him as she questioned him about his past, and he explained what the centre had done for him, and why he believed that teenagers who found themselves in trouble deserved a second chance.

'This is gold,' said Gina, as they wrapped up. 'It's going to make really good television, and it'll make people understand what a difference the centre can make. I mean look at *you*.'

Gregor shot Gina a look which seemed designed to shut her up.

'If that's everything,' he said, pushing the chair back and standing up, 'I'm going to get going.'

'Thanks, Jack,' Gina offered her hand as he made to leave. 'I enjoyed shooting you and Beth. It was fun. You two made a lovely pair, you know.'

He shook her hand but said nothing. Half of him had wanted to grill Gina about what Beth had told her, the other half – well, he didn't want to know. He'd thought long and hard about it on the drive south and realised that maybe it didn't matter what she'd said, if anything at all. The reality was there was no future for the two of them – they were from completely different worlds. And now he was about to take a step back into a world he thought he'd left behind forever.

He'd thought about it, and made some enquiries – it had been a long time, and it had meant calling in a few favours that he thought he'd never ask for, but he'd decided that the only thing he could do was bite the bullet. He got in the truck and headed from the West End of Glasgow, driving towards the river and away from the leafy, expensive looking streets and towards scruffy, ill-maintained tenements. His stomach churned with anxiety but he gritted his teeth as he pulled up to a halt on the street, parking between a battered white panel van and an ancient Nissan. He hoped the pick-up wouldn't be stolen or torched by the time he got back to it.

'That your car, mister?'

Two young lads with close cropped hair circled him on BMX bikes. They had a look he remembered well – pale, hollow cheeked, wary.

'Aye,' he said, giving them a brief nod. 'I'll give you both a couple of quid if you'll keep an eye on it. I need to see a man about a dog.'

'Alright,' said the blond lad. 'If you show us the money now.'

Jack shoved his hand in his pocket and pulled out a handful of loose change. The boys took it in then circled off down the pavement.

He headed up the stairs to the sixth floor – the lift was, predictably, out of service. The stairwell smelled faintly of disinfectant and most strongly of stale urine. It was a smell that reminded him of the tenement stairs of his childhood – a far cry, he thought, climbing steadily up the stairs, from the scent of wood polish and horse tack that Beth must have grown up with.

He rapped on the door of Flat 28b. Flakes of the peeling green paint came away as the door rattled in its frame, revealing a faded grey undercoat. He heard footsteps and then a long bout of chesty coughing before the safety chain rattled and the door was pulled back to reveal a once-familiar face.

'Hello, son.'

'Dad.'

'I thought I'd make it easier for you, seeing as you think

I'm a grass and you wanted me warned that I had to watch my back. So here I am.' He took a breath in, slowly and carefully. The one thing he couldn't do was show fear.

'I dinnae ken what you're talking about.'

Prison time hadn't been kind to his father. Back in the old days, he'd been swarthy and tall, with razor-sharp cheekbones and a frame that shouted to all the world that he wasn't to be messed with. Now he was haggard and seemed almost to have collapsed in on himself, his hair thin and grey above a face which was almost skeletal. He turned, coughing again, and beckoned for Jack to follow him into the tiny sitting room. The television was on, showing a quiz programme, and a packet of rolling tobacco sat with some cigarette papers on a cushion on the battered velour sofa.

'Have a seat.' He gestured to a brown mismatched armchair beside the television. 'And I think you and me have a wee bit of catching up to do.'

'I'm okay,' Jack said, moving to the side of the room but opting to stay standing.

The old man shrugged. 'Fair enough.' He sat down and started rolling a cigarette, pausing only while coughs racked his body.

'You need to get that cough looked at,' said Jack, surprising himself.

'Aye.' His father licked the cigarette paper. 'So to what do I owe this unexpected pleasure?'

There it was – a glimmer of the man with the patter Jack knew of old.

'I'm not here because of me. I'm here because of your grand-daughter.'

'Aye, I heard you had a bairn.'

'I should think you'd heard, given you sent me a warning note threatening her safety.'

His father shook his head. 'I have no idea what you're on about, son, but I can tell you one thing – there's been no such thing from me.'

~

'I don't understand.' Back in Applemore, when Jack arrived at dusk, Danny's voice was raw with emotion. 'You can't just walk away from everything.'

'The centre isn't about me. It's about the kids.' He shrugged. It hurt like hell to walk away but right now it was the only thing he could do.

'It's about kids like you were,' said Danny, angrily. 'Teenagers who need someone to listen and give them an opportunity to rise out of the situation they were born into.'

Jack shook his head. 'I was getaway driver for an armed robbery. Someone was killed. When that comes out it's going to make a splash of publicity, and not the right kind. Would you want your kids spending time with someone who'd done something like that?'

'You did your time,' Danny insisted. 'Why the hell can't you judge yourself as fairly as you do others?'

Jack turned away from the window, looking at the heap of bags on the floor that amounted to his worldly belongings.

He'd faced up to his fear and gone to confront his father. What he hadn't expected was that it would transpire that the threat was from an accomplice of his, who'd sent similar messages to several other members of the gang that had been involved in the robbery.

'It's under control,' his dad had said, cagily. 'The less you know, the better. It would be best if you lay low for a wee bit, if you can.'

Jack had sat down on the sagging brown armchair and dropped his head into his hands. 'I've tried to make things better and somehow I've ended up screwing them up,' he'd said, more to himself than anything.

'I think you've probably done your penance, son. Leave it with me.' His dad had clambered out of the chair, wheezing, and dropped a hand on Jack's shoulder. For a moment, he'd had a glimpse of what it might have been like to have a father.

'It's complicated.' Jack turned to look at his friend. 'I need to lie low for a bit.'

Danny made a noise of disgust. 'I think you're making a mistake.'

'I know.'

CHAPTER TWENTY-THREE

TWO MONTHS LATER

'SHH, IT'S COMING ON.'

The sun was low in the sky, bathing the village with a golden glow outside, and tourists sat drinking cold beer and looking out at the blue skies that hung over the harbour. Despite the weather, the bar of the Applemore Hotel was noisy and crammed with people holding drinks, but when Harry put a finger to his lips silence fell. A jaunty theme tune rang out.

'Move over,' said one of the old men by the bar, 'I canna see the screen with your big head in the way.'

There was a ripple of laughter and then everyone waited as the big television screen showed a long shot of waves breaking on an all too familiar beach, the sand as white and clean as any Jamaican resort.

'For the locals of the north coast of the Highlands, the tourist trail known as the North Coast 500 has proved a blessing and a curse…' the voiceover began. Joan, who had brought her new partner George over for a visit, glanced across at Beth and gave her a ghost of a wink. Everyone sat, enthralled, watching as familiar faces popped up, and towns up and down the coastal route were shown. Tourists were interviewed chatting about how much they loved the chance to visit such a beautiful part of Scotland, and locals talked about the benefits that the tourism brought, and the lack of infrastructure provided by the council, and the problems it brought. And then there was a long shot of Applemore House, the familiar turrets set against a pale blue sky, and then –

'Oh God, I feel sick,' said Beth, seeing herself on screen. Her stomach flipped in anticipation, then she was jolted back to reality by the sound of Jack's deep voice, chatting to her offscreen.

'So what made you decide to turn this overgrown garden into a flower farm?'

She'd tried hard to forget him, but it couldn't be more clear that she'd failed completely. Her heart was thumping in her chest and her fingers were curled into clammy palms. As she watched, it was painfully clear – no matter how much she might have tried to deny it – that the chemistry between them was off the scale. Their bodies naturally inclined towards each other, and as they walked through the garden, Gina had followed behind, taking in the beauty of the flowers, but also clearly aware that there was a love story happening in front of the camera. Harry, standing behind the bar, looked across at Beth and lifted an eyebrow.

'Now you can't still tell me Jack MacDonald didn't have the hots for you,' said Polly, leaning over and whispering quietly. 'Have you heard from him?'

'Shh.' Beth glared at her sister. 'And no.'

'Pity.'

Danny had come to see her the day after Jack had left, cautiously alluding to his past, clearly not wanting to give away any information that she didn't already know. She got the impression he'd decided that she was somehow to blame for his leaving.

'He's a good man, you know,' he'd said, as he left, Archie at his heels

'I know.'

Now Jack was on the screen, and somehow the room seemed to have become even quieter. He explained about his past, and how he'd first visited the Loch Lomond branch of the charity when he was only seventeen, and how it had changed his life. His voice cracked with emotion as he described how lucky he'd been to be given a chance, and to make a career out of something that made so much to him. Beth wiped away a tear. Polly patted her arm, gently.

Afterwards, when everyone had trickled out of the bar to enjoy the evening sunshine, Beth sat perched on the low stone windowsill of the Applemore Hotel, a glass of wine cupped in her hand.

'Penny for them?' Joan's voice was gentle.

Beth looked up. In all the years she'd known Joan, she'd never seen her look so happy and relaxed. Falling in love with George on the cruise had been the best thing that had ever happened to her.

'I was just thinking about Jack, and what he's been through.'

'Has he been in touch?' Joan edged herself onto the windowsill. 'Budge up a wee bit there,' she said, with a chuckle.

'He hasn't.' Too proud to message him, Beth had left it after he'd gone away, warned off by Danny who clearly felt that she'd been the catalyst for his leaving.

'Have you contacted him?'

Beth shook her head. 'I think he got the impression that

I'd given away his secret to the producer. Why would he want to have anything to do with me?'

'But you didn't?' Joan looked at her for a moment.

'Of course not. I wouldn't ever. I think when you've got that sort of stuff in your past, though, it's probably hard to trust someone.'

'I think we all have a lot of baggage,' Joan said, narrowing her eyes in thought and gazing across the little harbour. 'At the end of the day, though, you need to make a choice as to whether you're going to carry it or let it go and live your life. Look at your dad.' Joan put a hand on Beth's leg and squeezed it. 'You've worked so hard to make the flower farm a success, darling. Maybe it's time you put yourself first, and took some of the risks in life you've taken in business.' After George came out, Beth watched as Joan and her new love wandered away hand in hand, looking blissfully, peacefully happy. Joan's words echoed in her ears. Maybe it was time to be brave. Or – she stood up, waving a goodbye to Polly, who was deep in conversation with Harry – to think about it, at least. That would be a start.

A day later, on a meltingly hot afternoon where even Parisians were baking in the heat, Jack sat in the sleek designer kitchen of Rebecca's Paris flat, holding a cup of strong black coffee. Anna was sitting on the table beside him, her hair newly cut into a chic gamine style which made her look very French. Rebecca was standing by the kitchen island with her new partner, Karl, the Danish architect Anna had loathed on sight. Jack had been travelling for a month, but was glad to see that they'd reached a relatively comfortable détente.

'Ready?' Anna's finger hovered on the play button.

'Go on.'

He sat back on the uncomfortable designer chair and watched – trying to hide the ache he felt – as the beautiful scenery of the north-west coast of Scotland played out on Anna's laptop screen.

'Are you actually in this? Maybe they cut your bit out.' Anna spun her mug around on the table, impatiently.

'Give it a chance,' said Rebecca, looking at Jack. Their eyes met, fleetingly. She mouthed 'You ok?'

He gave a curt nod. Yes, he was great. He was sitting in his daughter's mother's house, watching a film about a place he loved and had lost, and any time soon he was going to be reminded of the woman he'd fallen for, and everything that had meant.

'Oh look, it's Beth,' said Anna, happily.

'Shh,' said Rebecca, then 'Oh, she *is* pretty, you're right, Anna.'

Jack sat forward, watching the screen. God, he missed her smile. And the way she made him laugh. The shot panned out, and he sat, watching himself walking alongside the woman who had filled his dreams pretty much every night since he left Applemore. He'd judged her without even hearing her side of the story – an action he'd spent his entire adult life warning people against. In that moment, he realised he'd made the biggest mistake of his life and it was too late to do anything about it.

'When are you going back to Scotland?' Karl said, strolling across the kitchen.

'I'm not.' Jack shrugged.

Anna looked at him, then at her mother, who was still watching the credits roll, chin in her hand. Noticing her daughter, she gave her a brief smile then straightened up, steepling her red-nailed fingers.

'You can't spend the rest of your life running away from the past.'

'Mum's right.' Anna folded her arms. 'You can't live half a life because you're scared something's going to happen to me. I could get hit by a bus tomorrow.'

'When did you grow up to be so smart?'

Anna gave a knowing smile. 'Good parenting. Obviously.'

'She's learned the art of flattery, at least,' said Karl.

'It's a start.' Rebecca joined them, leaning on the table and staring at Jack so intently that he looked away for a moment, tussling with his conscience.

'It's probably too late. I messed up.'

'We all make mistakes. You're always telling me that.'

'I'm going to stop talking to you if you don't stop,' he teased Anna, but he got up from the table and picked up his phone.

'If you want a lift to the airport, you just have to say.' Rebecca looked at Karl as she spoke, and Jack had a brief moment of thankfulness.

As he sat in the departure lounge the next morning, passport in hand, it struck him that despite everything, he'd been as lucky as anyone could hope to be. He had a daughter he adored, a pretty amicable relationship with her mother, a career he loved – not bad for a lad from the roughest part of Glasgow with the past he had. The only thing he'd screwed up was the chance of a relationship with Beth. At least he could go back and make peace, apologise for walking away, and maybe – in time – she'd find a way to forgive him and they could at least be friends. He'd settle for that.

~

Despite the warmth of the August sun, something had shifted in Applemore – a sense that autumn was waiting in the wings, the green of the trees changing hue from the verdant green of early summer to a darker, duller shade. The sun hung lower in the sky, bathing the hills of the distant islands with a golden glow. It felt good to be back.

'I'm not planning on treading on your toes,' he told Danny, hauling his bags out of the back of the pick-up. He'd been more than happy to drive over and collect him from the airport, leaving one of the other instructors in charge for the day. Archie, who'd spent the last two months grumpily waiting for his master to return, had spent ten minutes of the journey sulking before creeping onto Jack's lap, licking him thoroughly on the hand, and falling into the sleep of the just, snoring so loudly it had made them both roar with laughter.

'I've had more than enough of being in charge,' Danny said, putting a hand to his head in a mock-dramatic gesture. 'Believe me, pal, I'm more than happy to step back.'

'You don't have to.' Jack had thought it through long and hard – he wasn't the sort of person who was caught up with hierarchy – he simply loved the job, and if returning meant that Danny would be at the helm and he'd be second in command to his younger friend, well, so be it.

'I don't have to, but I want to. This is your place. It's no' been the same without you here.'

'Thanks mate,' Jack said, his voice thick with emotion.

'Here,' said Danny, tossing him the keys to the truck. 'You'll be needing these.'

'What for?'

'What d'you think?' Danny widened his eyes and

nodded his head in the direction of the road out of the village. 'I get the feeling there's someone you need to talk to.'

Jack squared his shoulders. 'I think you're probably right.'

CHAPTER TWENTY-FOUR

BETH HAD BEEN CUTTING dahlias all morning, and staking them in all afternoon. If she never saw another one, it would be too soon. She straightened her back with a groan, pausing for a moment to look at the long swathes of dark red flowers nodding in the slight breeze. She turned to head back to the polytunnel. Another hour, she decided, and she'd call it a night. There was so much to do. She'd had countless bookings since the first pick-your-own day, and the television programme that week had sent interest through the roof. She'd been working so hard that she'd found the perfect excuse not to reach out to Jack – not that she hadn't thought about it since her talk with Joan. But it was easier to throw herself into work where she was guaranteed a result than to make a leap into the unknown and risk her heart, which she'd kept carefully guarded for so long. For the first time, she was beginning to think that maybe she could afford to hire Miranda to work alongside her full-time.

She was scraping compost into the bucket, humming to

herself gently, when she heard the sound of someone clearing their throat. Turning, her heart leapt.

'I wanted to apologise,' said Jack, in his deep voice. He was taller, darker, and more tanned than she remembered. And definitely more handsome. She put a hand on the table to steady herself.

'When Gina came to see me, she led me to believe it was you who'd told her the truth about who I was.'

'I guessed that.' Beth had worked it out pretty much straight away, when he'd disappeared without a word. 'I thought about it a lot,' she said, and she took a step towards him. 'The thing is, I think we're alike in a lot of ways. I'd have done the same thing.'

'You would?'

She nodded, and looked down at the ground for a moment as she spoke. 'When you first turned up here in Applemore, my first thought was that I didn't want you bringing delinquents around here, wrecking my business, causing trouble. I always felt guilty for that.'

'I think it's perfectly natural. I mean, it's just human nature.' He stood in the doorway and lifted his hands in an apologetic gesture.'

Beth felt tears sting at her eyes and she looked away for a moment, blinking hard to drive them away, a sense of indignance rising. 'I wouldn't. I would never —'

'I know,' he said gently. 'Trusting someone – believing in them – it's hard. Trusting yourself is even harder.'

Beth nodded.

'Can I come in? I mean, assuming I promise not to trash the place again?' His eyes twinkled.

'I don't mind if you do.' Beth took another step towards him. 'I…' she hesitated for a second, looking up at his dark eyes and the expression on his face. 'I missed you.'

She put her hands to her cheeks, feeling them burning with heat, and looked at him, feeling terrified, and vulnerable, and hopeful, and -

'Beth,' he said, his voice low.

She couldn't catch her breath. Her heart thudded so loudly in her ears she thought it might burst. Jack stepped towards her and somehow a moment later he'd pulled her into his arms, and then he'd stepped back and his hands were cupping her face, his thumbs gently stroking her cheeks. 'I'm sorry. You have no idea how sorry. I wanted to -'

She shook her head slightly, biting her lip. Looking up at him she saw love in his dark eyes, and noticed the furrow of anxiety on his brow. A breath caught in her throat and a moment later she'd reached up, hands spread across his broad shoulders, feeling the tension in his muscles. His mouth grazed hers but then he pulled away for a second.

'You wanted to what?' As she spoke she felt his smile curling against her mouth and then his lips parted hers and he kissed her, pulling away, leaving her longing for more.

'I wanted to do that,' said Jack, thickly. 'And a lot more. I want you, Beth Fraser.'

He reached out, snapping off a dahlia of darkest, deepest red, and tucking it into her hair behind her ear in a gesture of infinite gentleness. 'I want you, difficult and complicated as it might be, with everything that might entail. I think we deserve a bit of happiness, don't you?'

Beth slid her hand down his back to where his T-shirt had ridden up, feeling the hardness of his muscle beneath the soft skin. She took a long, slow breath in, soaking in the scent of his body, and the sounds of the drowsy bees humming in the lavender outside, and the sensation of safety, and trust, and generosity, and kindness. These were hers for the taking.

'I think we do.'

EPILOGUE

OCTOBER

'You lot must be mad going to the beach in this weather,' said Gavin in his Welsh lilt, as he fastened the lid onto three cups of coffee and handed them over to Jack.

'I promised Anna we'd take her with the twins,' Jack said, tapping his payment card on the machine and pocketing the brown paper bag of chocolate brownies.

Gavin wiped the counter and tossed the dishcloth into the sink behind him. 'How long is she over for?'

'Just the French half-term holiday. Danny and Phoebe have gone to Morocco so we've got the cottage to ourselves. She's already turned the place into a bomb-site – there's make-up and hair stuff everywhere.' Jack laughed, shaking his head.

'You wouldn't have it any other way.'

'I would not.' He nodded. It was funny – all that time he'd spent obsessing over Anna having every material thing he'd missed out on growing up, and she was perfectly content sleeping on a sofa bed in the tiny, spartan little cottage with its old-fashioned furniture.

'Beth looks happy,' said Gavin, almost as an afterthought as he went to leave. 'You two make a cute couple. And believe me,' he leaned over, smacking a bent-over Tom on the behind 'I know a cute couple when I see one.'

Tom straightened up. 'Don't touch what you can't afford,' he said to Gavin, waggling his eyebrows. He turned to Jack. 'He's right, though. Beth's a sweetie, and it's so nice to see her all loved up. It'll be wedding bells before you know it.'

Jack raised an eyebrow. 'Hardly, we've only been together a few months.'

'When you know, you know,' said Gavin, looking fondly at Tom.

'That's as maybe,' Jack said, shaking his head and laughing. 'I'm in no rush, and neither is Beth. We're more than happy the way we are.'

'Well that's the main thing,' Tom said, putting an arm around Gavin's shoulders. A woman with a blue and white striped hat which looked like a tea cosy stared at them with an odd expression. Gavin leaned across, kissing his husband on the cheek. 'When you think about the stir you made when you came up here at the beginning of the year, though. It was the biggest scandal Applemore's seen in blooming ages. And we thought that was going to be it…'

'Gavin,' said Tom, shaking his head. 'What he's trying to say is that we're really bloody happy you're happy.'

'Cheers.' Jack raised his coffees in a toast, and turned to leave. 'I'll drink to that.'

Polly, who was serving the first of a queue of people on the other side of the farm shop, gave him a beaming smile and a wave as he pushed open the door with his foot. It looked like the big supermarket chain was definitely going to take over the village shop, but he suspected that it wouldn't have a huge effect on her business, plus she was full of plans to turn the remaining outbuildings into little outlets and rent them out to local artisans. It had surprised him how easily the Frasers had taken them to their heart, welcoming him in to the big, untidy house where they shared delicious dinners cooked by Lachlan and served with far too much red wine. The plus of Rilla being pregnant was that she was always free to give them a lift home. He wandered across the court-yard where scaffolding was being put up around one of the old stable blocks and nodded a hello to the workmen.

Beth was waiting in the pick-up. He handed her the coffees, and she turned to give one to Anna who was sitting behind her, wedged in beside Edward's car seat.

'I think I've been given the official Applemore Farm Shop seal of approval from the boys.'

Beth grinned. 'Funny, I got that the other day from them when I was in and they heard Anna was coming over. It's sweet, isn't it?'

'Made me laugh.' He put the truck into gear and pulled away. They bumped down the track towards the flower farm, pausing for a moment while Beth peeked in to check and see how Miranda was getting on with the preparations for an evening class they were running later in the week. Most of the flower beds were dug over for the winter now, the others scruffy with tired foliage which was left as food and shelter for wildlife.

'Everything's under control.' She jumped back into the passenger seat with a smile of relief.

'Let's go,' shouted Edward, delightedly, from the back seat.

They drove down as far as the stile that led down to the beach path, and then unloaded the twins, dressed in water-proof suits and bright red wellie boots.

'Come on,' said Anna, taking them both by the hand, 'Let's go and see if we can see any starfish.'

Edward and Lucy, who were completely enamoured, gazed up at Anna with delighted faces.

'She's so cute with them, isn't she?'

Beth took his hand as they walked behind the children. He loved watching the three of them together, cheerfully accepting of the changes they'd had in their lives. It was funny how now that they'd found each other, that love seemed to be able to expand. He'd opened up to the possibility of a future with Beth, and the idea of being jointly responsible for the twins and Anna – and being a family, something he'd never experienced – warmed his heart. They walked along in silence for a while then Beth turned to look at him, her cheeks rosy in the wind, freckles dusting her nose.

'You okay?' She lifted a hand to his face and he felt her fingers, warm despite the October chill, steal around his neck as she tipped her face up towards him in expectation of a kiss.

'It's funny, isn't it? I came to Applemore to get away from everything,' he brushed his mouth against hers then pulled away slightly to look into her eyes. 'And somehow I ended up *with* everything.'

Beth turned slightly in his arms, and together they watched the three children making their way down the track towards the beach with the sky bright blue overhead and the promise of autumn in the Highland air.

'Everything that matters,' she said, as he bent to kiss her once again.

ACKNOWLEDGMENTS

It's been lovely to return to Applemore to write The Flower Farm, especially as it meant living in summer in my head when we've been in the middle of winter here in England. I can't wait to escape back to the Highlands again and see the flowers on the machair for myself (and dip a toe in the freezing cold sea).

Thanks as always to Alice, Hayley, Josie, Keris, and Miranda for writerly moral support when juggling life, deadlines and minor pandemic issues. Huge love to the Book Camp and Word Racers gang, too, for cheering me on to the end of another book.

Special thanks to Hayley Webster, my brilliant editor, who has a way of making hard work feel like the best sort of fun, which is definitely a talent. Thanks also to Diane Meacham, my cover designer, who turns my scribbled ideas into gorgeous reality.

Thanks to Amanda Preston, my brilliant agent, and to Alison, Hannah, and everyone at LBA Books for sending my books off on their travels to be published around the world.

To Verity, Archie, Jude and Rory, who are almost all grown up now, thank you for putting up with me being vague and saying yes when I mean no, and forgetting to listen because I'm in the middle of a chapter. I love you all very much.

And to James, for the idea in the first place - thank you, darling. I love you.

Made in United States
North Haven, CT
02 August 2023